PRAISE FOR *THE STRANGE JOURNEY OF ALICE PENDELBURY*

"One of Marc Levy's best novels to date."

—Mohammed Aïssaoui, *Le Figaro*

"Another success for Marc Levy."

—*L'Express*

"Levy is always great at surprising readers with twists and turns in his stories . . . The journey is enjoyable and leads to many smiles."

—*Le Parisien*

"Once again, Marc Levy reveals his talent at telling stories."

—*Le Parisien*

"*The Strange Journey of Alice Pendelbury* is full of poetry and full of soul. In this funny and endearing novel, the author continues to weave through the themes he so enjoys—the intersection between friendship and romance, humility and courage, the true love of others and self-fulfillment."

—*Le Matin*

"A fine-tuned, well-executed intrigue, which moves at a good pace. Full of humor and humanity, it raises questions about identity, about one's story and past. A book full of poetry, about the quest for true happiness."

—*L'Union*

THE STRANGE JOURNEY OF ALICE PENDELBURY

ALSO BY MARC LEVY

THE STRANGE JOURNEY OF ALICE PENDELBURY

a novel

MARC LEVY

TRANSLATED BY CHRIS MURRAY

amazon crossing

Previously published as *L'Étrange voyage de Monsieur Daldry* by Robert Laffont in 2011 in France. Translated from French by Chris Murray. First published in English by AmazonCrossing in 2019.

Published by AmazonCrossing, Seattle

www.apub.com

Amazon, the Amazon logo, and AmazonCrossing are trademarks of Amazon.com, Inc., or its affiliates.

ISBN-13: 9781542040563
ISBN-10: 1542040566

Cover design by Kimberly Glyder

Printed in the United States of America

To Pauline

To Louis

To Georges

"Predictions are difficult to make, particularly when they concern the future."

—*Pierre Dac*

PROLOGUE

"I never believed that I had a particular destiny, or that signs in my life were guiding me toward a path I ought to take. I didn't believe in fortune-tellers or tarot cards. I just believed in simple coincidence and in the significance of chance happenings."

"Why did you come on such a long journey if you didn't believe in those things?"

"Because of a piano."

"A piano?"

"It was out of tune, like the old dance hall pianos that used to end up in army barracks, but there was something about it—or at least, something about the person playing it."

"Who was it?"

"My neighbor across the corridor. At least I think it was. I'm not entirely certain."

"You're here tonight because your neighbor was playing the piano?"

"You could put it that way. When I heard the music echoing up the staircase, I felt as though my solitude had been set to music. I wanted to escape it so badly that I agreed to go to Brighton."

"You will have to start again and tell me the story from the beginning. I think I'll understand better if you go in order."

"It's a long story."

"There's no hurry. The wind is blowing in from the sea. It's raining. I won't set sail for another two or three days. Let me make us some tea, and you can tell me everything. But you have to promise not to leave anything out. If what you say is true, if we're really going to be tied to each other for the rest of our lives, I need to know why."

He knelt before the cast-iron stove, opened the door in its belly, and blew on the coals.

The house was as modest as the rest of his life. Four walls, a single room, a simple roof. Worn plank floors, a bed, and a basin beneath an old spigot where the water ran icy cold in the winter and warm in the summer. There was only one window, but it had a majestic view of the Bosporus. From the table where Alice was sitting, she could see ships sailing through the strait, and beyond them, the European shore.

She took a sip of the tea he had served her and began telling her story.

1

Friday, December 22, 1950

A heavy winter rain drummed on the skylight above the bed. The war had ended only five years ago, and most of London's neighborhoods were still scarred from the Blitz. Fewer products were rationed now. Although it had been a few years since the war ended, it was recent enough to serve as a reminder of the days when almost everything was rationed.

Alice was spending the evening at home with her motley group of friends. Carol had been an army nurse and now worked at St Bartholomew's Hospital. The three men were aspiring jazz musicians. Sam was an excellent bassist and sold books at Harrington & Sons; Anton played the trumpet like nobody else could but worked as a carpenter; Eddy scraped by singing for coins at Victoria station and in pubs (when they would let him, that is).

It was Eddy who suggested that they should celebrate the coming of Christmas by taking a trip to Brighton the following day. The amusement park on the pier was open again, and the carnival would be at its best on the Saturday before the holiday.

They each counted up what little they had. Eddy had earned some money in a bar in Notting Hill. Anton had received a modest year-end bonus from his boss. Carol didn't have a penny, but then she never did, and her friends were used to paying for her. Sam had just sold an American woman a first edition of *The Voyage Out* and a second edition of *Mrs Dalloway*, which had been enough to make a week's wages in a single day. Alice had worked hard the entire year. She had some savings and felt she deserved to spend them. Besides, she could rationalize the expense to spend time with her friends and escape the solitude of her flat.

The wine Anton had brought was corked and tasted like vinegar, but they had all drunk enough of it to start singing. They got louder with each song, until Mr. Daldry, Alice's grouchy neighbor across the landing, came and knocked on the door. Sam was the only one brave enough to answer. He promised the noise would stop immediately, as it was time for everyone to go home anyway. Mr. Daldry accepted their apology, but not before haughtily insisting that he was trying to get some sleep. The Victorian house they lived in had no business turning into an amateur jazz club. It was already unpleasant enough to have to overhear every word of their conversations through the paper-thin walls.

Alice's friends packed up to go. They promised to meet up at Victoria station for the ten o'clock train to Brighton the next morning. Once they had left, Alice tidied up the room that, depending on the time of day, served as her workplace, dining room, and bedroom. She was just turning down the bedspread when she stood and looked indignantly toward Mr. Daldry's flat. Where did he get the nerve to break up such a lovely evening? What right did he have to interfere? She put on a shawl, and then took it off, deciding it made her look too motherly. She went and knocked on Mr. Daldry's door and waited, hands on her hips.

"Please tell me the house is on fire and you've come to save me from the flames," he said sarcastically when he finally came to the door.

"First of all, eleven is not that late on a Friday night, and second of all, I put up with your blasted scales often enough for you to tolerate a little noise on the rare occasions I have some friends over."

"Your noisy friends are here every week, and they have a regrettable habit of mixing song and drink. It affects my sleep." He raised an eyebrow to underline this last point before continuing. "And I'm not the one with the piano. Maybe it's the woman downstairs. I'm a painter, not a musician. If you only knew how quiet this house was before you arrived."

"What exactly do you paint, Mr. Daldry?"

"Urban landscapes."

"I never had you down as a painter. I imagined . . ."

"What did you imagine, Miss Pendelbury?"

"Oh, call me Alice. You ought to know my name if you really hear all my conversations."

"Now that we've been officially introduced, would you mind terribly if I went back to bed?"

Alice glared.

"What is the matter with you?" she asked.

"I beg your pardon?"

"Why do you insist on being so distant and hostile? We're neighbors. We could try to get on, or at least pretend."

"My life here used to be peaceful, Miss Pendelbury, but ever since you moved into that flat, which I myself had hoped to rent, I haven't had a moment's rest. Need I remind you how often you've come knocking on my door asking for some salt, or some flour, or a bit of margarine when you're cooking for your charming friends, or a candle when there's a blackout? Have you considered that your intrusions might bother me?"

"You wanted my flat?"

"I wanted to turn it into a studio. You're the only one in the building with a skylight, but alas, you won over the landlord with your feminine wiles. I have to make do with what little light comes through my tiny windows."

"I never met the landlord. I rented through an agent."

"Can we just leave it at that?"

"Is that why you've always been so cold? Because I took the studio you wanted?"

"Miss Pendelbury, the only coldness I feel right now is in my poor feet. If you don't mind, I'm going to go to bed before I catch something. I hope you have a good night's sleep."

Mr. Daldry shut the door in Alice's face.

"What an unpleasant man," she muttered under her breath.

"I heard that!" called Mr. Daldry from inside his flat. "Good night, Miss Pendelbury."

Alice returned to her flat, washed her face, and went to bed. Mr. Daldry was right about the cold. Winter clutched the old house in its grasp, and the feeble heating did little to raise the temperature. She took a book from the stool that served as her bedside table and read a few lines before putting it down again. She turned out the light and waited for her eyes to adjust to the dark as she watched the rain stream across the skylight.

Alice shivered and began dreaming of the forest, the wet earth, and the decomposing autumn leaves in the beech groves. She inhaled, and the smell of the forest floor filled her nostrils.

Alice had a rare gift: she was a "nose." Her sense of smell was so acute that she could distinguish and memorize the slightest odor. She spent her days alone, bent over the long wooden table in her flat, blending different essences to obtain combinations that might one day become a perfume. Every month she made the rounds of the London perfume shops, offering them her new creations. The previous spring, she had convinced a shop in Kensington to produce a scent she called "Eau d'églantine." The perfume had become relatively popular among the shop's upper-class clientele, and it brought in a little money every month. For the time being, it allowed her to live better than she had in previous years.

Alice couldn't sleep. She turned on the light, went to her table, and set to work, dipping strips of blotting paper into the little bottles and vials, spreading them in a fan under her nose, and taking notes until late into the night.

◆　◆　◆

When the alarm clock woke Alice the following morning, the sun was shining in her eyes, veiled only slightly by the morning mist. She groaned and turned over before remembering she was supposed to meet her friends at the station. In a single bound, she was out of bed and rifling through her wardrobe before taking a quick sponge bath.

On the way out of the door, Alice glanced at her watch and realized she'd never make it in time if she took the bus. She hailed a cab and told the driver to be quick.

A long queue was snaking in front of the ticket windows when she arrived at the station. She only had five minutes before the train left for Brighton. Alice ran to the platform instead.

Anton was waiting outside the first carriage.

"For heaven's sake, where have you been? Climb in," he said, helping her up into the carriage.

She joined her waiting friends in the compartment they had chosen for themselves.

"What are the chances our tickets will be checked?" she asked them, falling into a seat, completely out of breath.

"I'd give you my ticket if I had one," said Eddy.

"One in two?" guessed Carol.

Sam was more optimistic. "On a Saturday morning? I'd say more like one in three. Anyway, we'll see when we get there."

Alice rested her head against the window and closed her eyes. Brighton was an hour away, and she slept the entire trip.

At Brighton station, a railway official was checking the passengers' tickets as they left the platform. When it was Alice's turn, she pretended to search her pockets. Eddy imitated her. Anton smiled and handed each of them a ticket.

He took Alice by the waist and led her into the station's main hall.

"Don't ask me how I knew you'd be late. You're always late. And you know as well as I do that Eddy never buys a ticket. I didn't want the day to be ruined before it even began."

Alice took two shillings from her pocket and offered them to Anton, but he closed her hand around them.

"Your money's no good here," he joked. "The day's going to fly by, and I don't want to miss a moment of it."

Alice watched him amble off ahead of her and smiled as she had a brief vision of the teenage Anton she had once known. He turned back and asked if she was coming along.

They walked down Queen's Road to West Street and toward the promenade that ran along the seafront. The crowds were thick. Two long piers extended out over the waves, and the wooden buildings perched along their lengths made them look like two hulking ships. The carnival was on Palace Pier. Alice and her friends soon found themselves standing beneath the tall clock that marked its entrance. Anton paid for Eddy's and Alice's tickets again.

"You can't pay for me the entire day," she whispered to him.

"And why not, if it makes me happy?"

"Because there's no reason to."

"Do I need a reason, if it makes me happy?"

"What time is it?" asked Eddy. "I'm hungry."

A few steps away, in front of the large building that housed the Winter Garden, was a fish-and-chips stand. The smell of fried food and vinegar wafted in their direction. Eddy rubbed his stomach and took Sam over to the stand with him. Alice made a face but joined them in the end.

Everybody placed their orders, and Alice paid. She smiled at Eddy as she passed him a piece of fried fish wrapped in newspaper.

They ate their lunch by the balustrade. Anton silently watched the waves lapping at the pilings below, while Eddy and Sam went over their plans for reorganizing the world. Eddy's favorite pastime was disapproving of the government. He accused the prime minister of doing nothing to help the poor, and criticized him for not rolling up his sleeves and getting to work on the construction projects that were needed to rebuild London. The way he saw it, they just needed to hire everybody who was out of work and the problem would be solved. Sam tried to reason with him about the economy and argued that it was too difficult to find properly trained workers. When Eddy yawned with uninterest, Sam lost patience and called him a "lazy anarchist," much to Eddy's pleasure. During the war, they had served side by side in the same regiment. Their bond of friendship was unbreakable, in spite of their differing political opinions.

Alice stood to the side of the group, trying to stay upwind of the fried fish. Carol joined her, and they stood in silence, watching the shore.

Carol spoke first. "You should be more careful with Anton."

"Why? Is something wrong?" Alice asked.

"He's lovesick for you! You must be blind to have not noticed."

"But we've known each other since we were kids—"

"I'm just asking to you be careful," Carol interrupted. "If you have feelings for him, there's no need to beat around the bush. We'd all be happy to see the two of you together. You deserve each other. But if it isn't the case, you shouldn't be such a tease. You're making him suffer for nothing."

Alice turned her back to the men and faced Carol. "How am I a tease?"

"Well, for one, by pretending not to notice that I fancy him."

Carol threw the remains of her chips into the water, where two seagulls greedily wolfed them down.

Sam called over to them. "Are you just going to stand there and watch the tide come in, or are you coming with us? We're going to take a look at the games. I saw a booth where you can win a cigar if you're strong enough." He rolled up his sleeves in anticipation.

The game cost a farthing a turn. The idea was to use a sledgehammer to hit a mark on the floor that sent a little lead weight flying up a tube. If the weight struck the bell hanging seven feet above the ground, you won a cigar. A cheap cigar, it was true, but Sam thought smoking cigars the height of dignified virility. He tried eight times, two pennies' worth, and twice what he would have spent for a cigar of the same quality at the tobacconist's down the pier.

"I'll show you how it's done if you'll pay," said Eddy.

Sam handed him a coin and stood back. Eddy swung the sledgehammer with ease, the weight hit the bell, and the man running the game gave him his prize.

"This one's for me," said Eddy. "Give me another farthing and I'll win one for you."

A minute later they were lighting Eddy's prizes. Eddy was in seventh heaven, and Sam was calculating how much money he had lost. He could have bought a pack of cigarettes. Twenty Embassies for one bad cigar—it made one think.

The men exchanged knowing glances when they came to the bumper cars. Almost immediately, they were each in their own car, flooring the accelerators and smashing into one another as hard as possible. The women watched from the sidelines in amused incomprehension. At the end of the round, they dragged Carol and Alice to a shooting parlor. Anton's aim was the best, and he hit the bull's-eye until he won a little porcelain teapot for Alice.

While this was going on, Carol was absentmindedly gazing at the carousel, with its old wooden horses turning beneath the wreaths and garlands of colored lights. Anton came up behind her and took her by the arm.

Carol sighed. "I know it's a kids' thing. But would you believe me if I told you I'd never ridden on one?"

"Not even when you were little?" asked Anton.

"I grew up in the country, and the fair never stopped in our village. When I finally came to London to study, I was already too old, and then the war came and . . ."

"And now you want to go for a ride. Follow me." Anton took Carol to the ticket booth. "Your first wooden horse is my treat. Go on. Get on that one," he said, pointing to a horse with a brassy blond mane. "The others look a little skittish, and I think it's best to choose a reliable mount your first time."

"You're not coming with me?" asked Carol.

"Uh, no, not me. Just looking at them makes me dizzy. But I promise I won't take my eyes off you."

A bell rang, and Anton stepped down from the platform as the merry-go-round began to turn. Sam, Alice, and Eddy came over to watch Carol. She was the only adult in the middle of a ride full of children. By the second turn, tears were streaming down her cheeks, in spite of her efforts to brush them away.

"Nice going," said Alice to Anton, punching him in the arm.

"I don't understand. She said she wanted . . ."

"She wanted to go on the ride with you, not public humiliation."

"He said he didn't do it on purpose," said Sam, butting in.

"Why don't the two of you act like gentlemen for a change instead of just standing there?" Alice said.

While Sam and Anton were still bickering about who should rescue Carol, Eddy had already jumped on the turning carousel and made his way up through two rows of horses until he reached her.

"In need of a groom, milady?" he said, resting his hand on the horse's mane.

"Oh please, Eddy, just help me down from here."

But instead Eddy hopped in the saddle behind her, squeezed her in his arms, and leaned over to whisper in her ear.

"What's all this? Where's the strong Carol I used to know? You shouldn't forget that when I was loafing around in pubs, you were carrying stretchers under the bombs. The next time we turn past our friends, I want you laughing like a fool."

"How do you expect me to do that, Eddy?" asked Carol with a hiccup.

"Well, if you think you look silly on this nag in the middle of all these kids, just imagine me here behind you with my terrible cigar and my newsboy cap."

On the next turn, they were both chuckling as though nothing had happened.

To show he was sorry for abandoning Carol, Anton bought everyone a round of beer at the refreshment stand. While they were drinking, Alice noticed a sign announcing that Harry Groombridge and his orchestra were playing in the old theater that had been transformed into a café after the war.

"Shall we go?" she asked the others.

"What's stopping us?" said Eddy.

"We'd miss the last train, and I don't fancy the idea of sleeping on the beach this time of year," Sam said.

"Oh, I don't think so," said Carol. "When the first set is over, we'll still have half an hour to walk back to the station. It's cold, and a little dancing would warm us up. What could be merrier just before Christmas?"

The men didn't have a better idea, and Sam quickly realized that the tickets were only twopence. If they didn't go dancing, his friends would want to have dinner in a pub, which would be far more expensive.

The hall was full of people eager to hear Harry Groombridge and his men. Nearly everybody was dancing. Anton took Alice and pushed

Eddy into Carol's arms. Sam watched the two couples from an amused distance.

As Anton had predicted, the day had flown past. When the orchestra stood up and bowed, Carol made a signal to her friends that it was time to head back. They maneuvered their way through the crowd to the exit.

The lanterns swinging in the breeze of the winter night made the pier seem like an ocean liner steaming full speed ahead into an ocean it would never cross. Alice and her friends were almost off the pier when they noticed a fortune-teller smiling at them from her small caravan.

"Have you ever wondered what the future has in store for you?" asked Anton.

"Never," said Alice. "I don't believe in that kind of thing."

"At the beginning of the war, a fortune-teller told my brother he'd stay alive as long as he moved house," said Carol. "He'd forgotten all about it when he joined up, but two weeks later, his block of flats got hit by a bomb. None of the residents survived."

"Amazing," said Alice dryly.

"Nobody knew that the Blitz was coming back then," retorted Carol.

"Why don't you go and see what she says?" Anton asked Alice, visibly amused by the idea.

"Don't be silly. We have a train to catch."

"There's time. Go on, I'll pay for it."

"No, really. I don't feel like hearing a lot of nonsense."

"Leave Alice alone," said Sam. "Can't you see she's scared?"

"Listen to the three of you. I'm not scared. I just don't believe in things like tarot cards and crystal balls. Besides, why are you all so interested in my future?"

"Maybe one of them is secretly dreaming you'll end up in his bed," said Carol.

Anton and Eddy looked stunned. Carol blushed and wished she hadn't said anything.

"You could ask her if we're going to miss our train," added Sam, pretending not to have heard Carol's gaffe. "That way we can test her accuracy without having to wait too long."

"Joke all you like," said Anton, "but unlike you, I believe in these things. If you go, I'll go after you."

Alice's friends surrounded her.

"You've all gone quite mad," she said, trying to push past them before finally giving up. "But since I'm dealing with four children bent on missing their train, I'll go and listen to whatever foolishness that woman has to say, and then we'll go home. How does that sound?" She held out her hand to Anton. "Are you giving me twopence or what?"

Alice went over to the caravan. A gust of wind made her lower her head as though she had suddenly been forbidden to look the old woman in the eyes. Maybe Sam was right. The thought of having her future read bothered her more than she had expected.

The woman invited Alice to take a seat on the stool across from her. Her eyes were large, her gaze penetrating. She never stopped smiling an eerie but enchanting smile. She had no crystal ball or tarot cards, just long, age-spotted hands that she extended, taking Alice's fingers in her own. When Alice touched them, a strange, gentle feeling filled her body, a comforting sensation of well-being that she hadn't known in a very, very long time.

"I've seen you before, my girl," said the fortune-teller.

"Ever since you started watching me just now, I imagine."

"I see. You don't believe in my gifts."

"I'm a rational person," Alice replied.

"No, you're an artist, an independent and free-thinking woman. Although it's true that your fears—what you call 'being a rational person'—sometimes hold you back."

"Why is everybody calling me a coward this evening?"

"You didn't look very sure of yourself when you decided to come and see me."

The fortune-teller leaned over and peered deep into Alice's eyes. Their faces were only inches apart.

"Where have I seen those eyes before?" the old woman asked.

"In a past life?" asked Alice.

Visibly disturbed, but not by Alice's sarcasm, the fortune-teller suddenly sat up.

"Ambergris, vanilla, and leather," whispered Alice.

"I beg your pardon?"

"Your perfume. You love the East. I can read certain things about people too."

"Ah, yes. You have a gift; it's true." She paused. "But what is more, you carry a story without even realizing it."

"Don't you ever stop smiling?" asked Alice teasingly. "Is that how you lull your prey into a false sense of security?"

"I know why you came to see me," the old woman continued, ignoring Alice's question. "It's funny when you think about it."

"You heard my friends daring me to do it?"

"Well, yes, I did. But you're not an easy person to dare. Your friends have nothing to do with it."

"What, then?"

"The solitude that haunts you and keeps you awake at night."

"That doesn't sound very funny to me. Go on. Tell me something astonishing. It's not that I don't enjoy your company, but I've got a train to catch."

"No, it isn't funny. You're right . . ." Her voice had grown quiet and thoughtful. She gazed into the distance, and Alice felt like she had been abandoned.

"You were going to say something?"

"What is funny," she said, speaking normally again, "is that the most important man in your life, the one you've been looking for without even knowing it, was walking behind you just a few moments ago."

Alice couldn't resist the desire to turn around and look, but when she turned she only saw her friends waving to say it was time to go.

"Is it one of them?" Alice asked. "Eddy or Sam or Anton?"

"Listen to me, Alice. Don't just hear what you want to hear. I told you that the man who will matter the most in your life was just behind you. He's not there anymore."

"And where is my Prince Charming now?"

"Patience, my girl. You'll have to meet six other people first."

"Six? That's an awful lot."

"An amazing journey, I'd say. You'll understand one day, but it's late and I've revealed everything you need to know. And since you don't believe a word I say, the consultation is free."

"No, I'd rather pay."

"No need. We'll call our time together a chat between old friends. I'm glad I got to see you, Alice. I wasn't expecting it. You're somebody very special, or at least, your story is."

"What story?"

"We don't have time for that, and besides, you won't believe me. Go on, or your friends will blame you for making them miss the train."

They both fell silent, and then exchanged smiles before Alice returned to her friends.

"You should see the look on your face! What did she tell you?" asked Anton.

"I'll tell you later. Have you seen the time?" Alice hurried past them and toward the exit off the pier.

"She's right," said Sam. "The train leaves in twenty minutes."

They all began running. The ocean breeze mixed with a fine rain.

Eddy took Carol by the arm. "Watch out. The ground is slippery," he said, leading her in the race for the station.

The weak glow of the streetlights led the way as they headed up the road. In the distance, they could see the lights of Brighton station. They shouted to the railway official as they ran up to the platform. He held his lantern high and motioned for them to board the nearest carriage. The men helped the women up, and Anton was still on the running board when the train began to move forward. Eddy grabbed him by the shoulder and pulled him inside.

"A minute later and we would have missed it," gasped Carol.

Eddy turned to Alice. "Poor thing. You're as white as a sheet," he said.

Alice said nothing. Immersed in her thoughts, she watched Brighton disappear into the distance. She was thinking about what the woman had told her.

"So, are you going to tell us about your glorious future?" asked Anton, interrupting her reverie. "After all, we almost had to sleep out in the cold because of you."

"Because you stupidly goaded me," snapped Alice.

"Did she tell you anything crazy?" asked Carol.

"Nothing I didn't know already. Those people are just con artists. With a decent sense of observation, some intuition, and self-assurance, you can string anybody along."

"But you still haven't said what she told you," insisted Sam.

Anton intervened out of mercy. "We've had a wonderful day. Let's leave it at that. I'm sorry, Alice. We shouldn't have insisted. You didn't want to, and we were all a little too . . ."

"Silly. And I was the worst of us," apologized Alice in return, her voice softening. "But I have a much more pressing question. What are you all doing for Christmas Eve?"

Carol was going to see her family in St Mawes. Anton was having dinner with his parents in town. Eddy had promised his sister he'd spend the evening with her because his nephews were expecting Father Christmas, and his brother-in-law had already rented him a costume to wear. It was difficult to turn down because his brother-in-law had often helped Eddy out of a tight spot without ever telling Eddy's sister. Sam had been asked to lend a hand at a charity event that his boss had organized for the children in the Westminster Orphanage.

"What about you?" Anton asked Alice.

"Oh, I've been invited to a party."

"Where?" he insisted.

Carol gave him a discreet kick in the shin before taking a packet of biscuits from her handbag and passing it around, proclaiming she was hungry as a horse. She glared at Anton as he nursed his wound in outraged silence.

The train's acrid smoke swept across the platform as it pulled into Victoria station. In the streets outside, a thick smog from the city's coal-burning fireplaces gripped the neighborhood and floated in the depressed yellowy glow of the sodium streetlights.

They all took the same bus. Alice and Carol were the first to get off—they lived just a few streets apart from each other.

"If you'd like," Carol said as they were parting ways on Alice's doorstep, "I mean, if you change your mind about the party, you're welcome to spend Christmas with us in St Mawes. My mother has wanted to meet you for such a long time. I often mention you in my letters, and she's intrigued to know more about what a 'nose' does exactly."

"Oh, I'm not very good at talking about what I do," said Alice, thanking Carol for the kind offer.

She kissed her friend good night and headed upstairs. She could hear the footsteps of her neighbor Mr. Daldry on the staircase ahead of her, and waited a moment on the landing so she wouldn't run into him.

◆ ◆ ◆

It was almost as cold in her flat as it had been outside. Alice kept her coat and mittens on as she filled the kettle and put it on the gas, only to discover she was out of tea. She took a few dried rose petals from her worktable and crumbled them into the teapot before pouring the hot water over them and settling into bed. She picked up the book she had abandoned the night before. Suddenly, the room went black.

Alice put down her book, climbed up on her bed, and peered out of the skylight. The electricity had gone out in the entire neighborhood. Often such cuts lasted until morning. She got down off the bed and stumbled round the flat, patting around in the dark, trying to find a candle, but the little stub of wax by the sink reminded her there were none left.

She tried in vain to light its practically nonexistent wick, but the flame only vacillated a moment before going out.

How frustrating. Alice wanted to note down the ideas she had about the smells of the sea wind, the salt water, and the pilings eaten away by the spray. If she went to bed now, she would never fall asleep. She hesitated a moment before sighing and heading across the landing to ask her neighbor for help.

Daldry came to the door holding a candlestick. He was wearing cotton pajama bottoms and a turtleneck sweater under a navy-blue silk dressing gown. His face had a strange pallor in the glow of the candlelight.

"I've been expecting you, Miss Pendelbury."

"You've what?" she asked, startled.

"Ever since the electricity went out. I don't sleep in these clothes, as you might imagine. Here's what you came for." He handed her an unlit candle.

"I'm sorry, Mr. Daldry," she said sheepishly. "I'll be sure to buy some more and make it up to you."

"I don't expect you will, Miss Pendelbury."

"You can call me Alice, you know."

"Good night then, Alice."

Daldry closed his door, and Alice went back to her flat.

A moment later there was a knock, and Alice opened the door to find Daldry standing there with a box of matches.

"I suppose you'll be needing these too? You didn't have any matches last time, and since I'm going to bed now, I thought I'd make sure." Alice said nothing, but it was true that she had just used her last match. Daldry lit the wick of the candle he had given her. "Did I say something that offended you?" he said.

"Why do you ask?"

"You look so serious."

"I'm sure it's just the shadows, Mr. Daldry."

"If I'm to call you Alice, you also should know my Christian name. I'm Ethan."

"Very well. I'll call you Ethan," said Alice with a smile.

"Shadows or not, you look upset."

"I'm just tired from a long day."

"Then I'll leave you to sleep. Good night, Alice."

"Good night, Ethan."

2

Alice went out to do some shopping, but all the shops in her neighborhood were closed, so she took the bus to a local market.

She stopped at a grocer's stall and decided she would buy the makings of a holiday meal. She chose a fresh egg and forgot about her resolution to save money at the sight of two strips of bacon. A baker's stall just a little farther down the road was full of small but delicious-smelling cakes, so she treated herself to a fruitcake and a little pot of honey.

That evening she would have dinner in bed with a good book. A sound night's sleep and she knew she would feel ready to work again. Alice tended to feel gloomy when she hadn't got enough sleep, and she'd been spending too much time at her worktable over the past few weeks.

A bouquet of old-fashioned roses in the window of a florist's shop caught her eye. It wasn't very thrifty of her, but it was Christmas. Besides, she could let them dry and use the petals for her fragrances. She went into the shop, spent two shillings, and left with the flowers in the crook of her arm and her heart singing. Farther down the street, she came to a perfume shop. A CLOSED sign hung in the window, but when she approached to peer through the glass, she could see one of her creations on a shelf among the lines of bottles. She waved, as though waving to a friend, and headed back to the bus stop.

Back at home, she put away her shopping, put the roses in a vase, and decided to go for a walk in the park. On her way out, she ran into Mr. Daldry on the street. He also seemed to be just coming home from the market.

"Christmastime," he said, visibly embarrassed to be seen holding such a well-filled shopping basket.

"Christmastime indeed," said Alice. "Do you have guests this evening?"

"God, no. I hate that sort of thing," he whispered, aware it was blasphemous to admit as much.

"You too?"

"Don't even get me started on New Year's Eve—it's even worse. How can you decide ahead of time whether or not it's going to be a day worth celebrating? Who knows until they get up that morning whether they'll even be in the mood to have a party? I think it's phony to force oneself to be jolly just because it happens to be marked on the calendar."

"I suppose celebrations are nice for children though."

"I don't have any. All the more reason to give up playtime. And that whole business of making them believe in Father Christmas—say what you like, but I think it's rather nasty. One day you'll have to tell them the truth, so what's the use? It's so cruel. The slow ones wait for him for weeks, thinking he's on the way, only to feel betrayed when their parents confess the rotten truth. The smart ones have to hold their tongues and play along, which is just as bad. Is your family coming then?"

"No." She paused. "I don't really have one."

"A good reason not to invite them over."

Alice laughed at this, but Daldry still blushed violent purple. "I'm sorry, that was horribly clumsy of me, wasn't it?"

"No. A very sensible observation."

"I do have one. A family, I mean. A father, a mother, a brother, a sister, and a dreadful nephew."

"And you're not spending Christmas with them?"

"No. I haven't for years. We don't get along."

"Another good reason to stay home."

"I've tried for years, but every family celebration has always been a disaster. My father and I agree on nothing. He thinks it's ridiculous that I'm a painter, and I think his business is ghastly dull. We can't stand each other. Have you had breakfast?"

"How did we go from your father to breakfast?"

"I'm not sure."

"Well, since you asked, no, I haven't."

"The café on the corner serves a winning porridge. If you'll just give me a minute to put this decidedly feminine but very useful shopping basket in my flat, I'll take you there."

"I was just about to go for a walk in Regent's Park."

"On an empty stomach in this cold? Very bad idea. Let's go eat, and then we'll feed the ducks. The nice thing about ducks is that you don't have to dress up like Father Christmas to make them happy."

Alice smiled and acquiesced. "All right. Take your things upstairs and then we'll go and have some of your porridge and give the ducks Christmas dinner."

"Marvelous," said Daldry, already on his way up the stairs. "I'll just be a minute."

A few moments later he reappeared, winded from having hurried and doing his best to hide it.

At the café, they took a table next to the window, looking out on the street. Daldry ordered a tea for Alice and a coffee for himself. The waitress brought them two bowls of porridge, and Daldry asked for some bread. Instead of eating it, he slipped it into his pocket when the waitress wasn't looking, much to Alice's amusement.

"What kind of landscapes do you paint?"

"Oh, I only paint utterly useless things. I know some people go crazy over the countryside or the sea or the forest, but I just paint intersections."

"Intersections?"

"Yes, street intersections. Junctions. You can't beat the amount of life and activity at a junction. There are thousands of details. Some people are in a hurry, others are trying to find their way. There are all sorts of modes of transportation and so much movement—buses, automobiles, motorcycles, bicycles, people on foot, deliverymen with their carts. Men and women from all walks of life cross paths, bother each other, meet each other, ignore each other, run into each other, get into arguments with each other. An intersection is a fascinating place!"

"What a curious idea," said Alice, trying to imagine what one of his paintings must look like.

"Perhaps. But you have to admit, it beats a plate of fruit. What could possibly happen, apart from some mold? Yesterday, for example, I set up my easel in Trafalgar Square. It was difficult to find a vantage point where I wasn't constantly being jostled, but I've got a knack for finding the right spot. There was a woman, panicked at being caught in a sudden rain shower, and who was probably trying to find shelter for her hair, which had just been done. She started across the street without looking, and the driver of a dray had to swerve to avoid her. It gave her a terrible fright, but she was fine. The kegs of beer on the back of the cart, however, rolled off into the street. A bus coming from the other direction hit one of them, and it exploded upon impact. It was a scene straight out of *A Tale of Two Cities*, complete with a couple of old vagrants ready to lie on the ground and lap up the damages! Of course, there was an altercation between the driver of the dray and the bus conductor, not to mention the passersby who got mixed up in it. And in spite of the fact the police were in attendance, a pickpocket still managed to steal what looked like a day's earnings off the rubbernecks.

Meanwhile, the woman whose distraction caused the whole disaster just crept away in shame."

"And you painted all that?"

"No. For the time being I've just painted the intersection. I've got a lot of work ahead of me. But I can still see the entire scene, that's the important part."

"I don't think I've ever noticed so much . . ."

"I've always had a fascination with detail, for the little, almost invisible events that are always happening around us. Don't turn now, but at the table behind you there's an old woman. I want you to get up and take my seat as though it were normal."

Alice traded seats with Daldry.

"Now," he said, "look at her carefully and tell me what you see."

"A woman of a certain age eating alone. She's rather well dressed and she's wearing a hat."

"Be more observant. What else?"

"Nothing in particular. She's wiping her mouth with the napkin. Why don't you just tell me what I'm not seeing? She's going to think I'm staring."

"Well, she's wearing make-up, isn't she? Not much, but her cheeks are powdered, there's a bit of kohl around her eyes, and she's wearing lipstick."

"Yes. Well, I think so anyway."

"Look at her lips now. Are they still?"

"No, you're right," said Alice, surprised at Daldry's powers. "They're moving ever so slightly. Maybe it's a tic? Old age?"

"Not in the least! That woman is a widow. She's speaking to her dead husband. She's not eating alone—she's continuing to talk to him as though he were still sitting across from her. She's made up her face because he's still part of her life. Isn't it incredibly touching? Imagine the kind of strength it takes to constantly reinvent the presence of a loved one. And she's right to do so. Just because somebody is gone doesn't mean they don't exist anymore—with a little imagination, you're never alone. When it's time to pay, she'll push her money over to the other side of the table because it was always her husband who paid. When she gets up to leave, you'll see that she waits a few moments on the pavement before crossing because her husband was always the first to step out into the street. I'm sure that she talks to him every night before she goes to bed and every morning when she wakes up, no matter where he might be now."

"And you saw all that in just a few minutes?"

Daldry smiled knowingly, and as he did so, an old drunk staggered into the café. He went over to the woman and made a sign that it was time to go. She paid her bill and followed her husband out of the door, no doubt to Wimbledon for the greyhound racing. Daldry, his back to the scene, saw nothing.

"You're right," said Alice. "She did exactly what you said she would. She pushed the money across the table, got up, and left. I saw her thank an invisible man for holding the door for her as she went out."

Daldry beamed with satisfaction and continued to eat with relish. "Great stuff, isn't it? The porridge, I mean."

"Do you believe in fortune-tellers?"

"I beg your pardon?"

"Do you believe that it's possible to predict the future?"

"That's a complicated question," he said, signaling to the waitress for a second serving. "Imagine how boring that would be if the future was already written! What about our own free will? I think that fortune-tellers are just extremely intuitive people. But apart from the real charlatans, the sincere ones have a certain talent. Maybe they just manage to see what people are aspiring to, the things that they will try to do one day, sooner or later. Why not? Take my father, for example. He's got perfect eyesight but sees nothing. My mother, on the other hand, has terrible vision, yet she sees things that my father would be incapable of noticing. She knew ever since I was a child that I would become a painter. But she also imagined that my paintings would be hanging in the greatest museums, and I haven't sold a thing in five years, so what can I say? I'm a sorry excuse for an artist. But I'm just going on about myself without really answering your question. What makes you ask?"

"Something strange happened to me yesterday, the sort of thing I would never have paid any attention to before. Yet, ever since, I haven't been able to stop thinking about it—to the point that I'm beginning to feel obsessed."

"That's rather vague. Why don't you tell me what happened yesterday, and I'll tell you what I think?"

Alice leaned in and told Daldry about her day in Brighton and her encounter with the fortune-teller. Daldry listened without interrupting. Once she reached the end of the fortune-teller's strange predictions, Daldry turned to ask the waitress for the bill. He suggested they go outside and get some fresh air.

As they walked back to the house, he asked with false consternation, "So, if I understand you correctly, you have to meet six other people before you'll meet this important man?"

Alice corrected him. "'The man who will matter most in my life.'"

"Nearly the same thing, I suppose. And you didn't ask any questions about who that man might be or where he might be found?"

"No. She just told me that he had walked behind me while we were talking."

"And she spoke of a journey?"

"Yes, I think so, but it's all so absurd. I'm terribly silly for telling you such a ridiculous story."

"A ridiculous story, as you call it, which seems to have kept you awake for a good part of the night."

"Do I look that tired?"

"Your pacing made the floor creak."

"I'm sorry if I bothered you."

"Well, I can only think of one solution for us to get a normal night's sleep. I'm afraid the ducks' Christmas will have to wait until tomorrow."

"What are you talking about?" asked Alice as they reached the house.

"Go upstairs and put on something warmer and I'll meet you back here in a few minutes."

"What an odd day," Alice said to herself on her way up the stairs. Christmas Eve wasn't at all panning out as she had imagined. First breakfast with her crabby neighbor, a man she could barely stand but who now didn't seem so bad, and then her unexpected confidences . . . Why had she gone on for so long about something she herself found absurd and insignificant?

She opened her wardrobe and had a terrible time finding a jumper and a scarf that went together. She hesitated between a navy-blue cardigan that showed off her figure and a heavier wool coat.

She looked in the mirror, fixed her hair, and decided to forgo make-up. She was, after all, just going on this walk out of courtesy.

When she returned to the street in front of the house, Daldry was nowhere to be seen. Perhaps he had changed his mind. He was an odd man.

A car honked its horn, and she turned to see a midnight-blue Austin 10 pull up to the curb. Daldry got out to open the passenger door for Alice.

"You have a car?" she asked, surprised.

"I stole it."

Alice's eyes grew wide.

"Of course I have a car. Do you take me for a thief?"

"Well, excuse my astonishment, but you are now officially the only person I know who owns a car."

"I bought it used. It's no Rolls, as you'll note once you've experienced the suspension, but it gets me from point A to point B quite effectively. I always put her somewhere in my intersections. It's a sort of ritual. She's in all of my paintings."

"You'll have to show me your paintings one of these days," Alice said, getting in.

Daldry muttered something unintelligible under his breath as he closed the door. He got in the driver's side, and with the gears making a grinding sound, the car lurched into motion.

"I don't mean to pry, but might I know where we're going?"

"To Brighton, of course."

"Brighton? What on earth for?"

"To go visit that fortune-teller and ask her a few of the questions you ought to have asked her yesterday."

"But that's crazy!"

"We'll be there in an hour and a half, two hours if there's ice on the roads. I don't see anything crazy about it. We'll be home by dusk, and if by any chance we get held up, the chrome things you see on either side of the bonnet are headlights. Nothing perilous is lying in wait for us."

"This is all very generous of you, Mr. Daldry, but would you be so kind as to stop poking fun at me?"

"I promise to make an effort, Miss Pendelbury, but please don't expect the impossible."

They left London by way of Lambeth and drove to Croydon, where Daldry asked Alice to take the road map out of the glove box and find Brighton Road, somewhere to the south. Alice told him to turn right before telling him to turn around because she had been holding the map upside down. After a few more wrong turns, a passerby put them on the correct route.

At Redhill, Daldry stopped to fill the tank and check the tire pressure. Alice preferred to stay in the relative warmth of the car with the map open on her lap.

After Crawley, Daldry had to drive more slowly. The countryside was white with snow, and the windscreen began to fog up. A few times the Austin skidded on sharp turns in the road. An hour later, they were so cold that it became impossible keep up a conversation. Daldry had turned the heat up as far as it would go, but the little heater was powerless against the icy wind that blew under the bonnet and into the car. They stopped at an inn called the Eight Bells and warmed themselves up at a table near the fireplace. After one last cup of boiling hot tea, they set off again.

Nearly four hours after they had left London, Daldry announced that Brighton wasn't much farther. When they finally got there, the carnival was already beginning to close for the evening and the long pier was nearly deserted. The last few merrymakers were heading home to celebrate Christmas.

"All right then," said Daldry as he got out of the car. "Where is this fortune-teller I've heard so much about?"

"I doubt she waited for us," said Alice, blowing on her hands and stamping her feet in an attempt to warm up.

"Don't be pessimistic. Come along."

They went to the pier ticket window. It was closed.

"Perfect," he said. "Free entrance."

When they saw the caravan, Alice was overcome by a wave of anxiety. She hesitated. Daldry could sense her unease.

"That fortune-teller is just a human being, a woman like you and me. Well, like you, I should say. There's no reason for you to be worried. We're going to do what it takes to break the spell."

"You're poking fun again."

"I was just trying to make you smile. Why don't you go and hear what the old bat has to say, and we'll laugh about it on the way home. By the time we're back in London, you'll be so tired you'll sleep like a baby no matter what she says. Go on, be brave. I'll wait for you here; I won't move an inch."

"Thank you. And I'm sorry for acting like a child."

"Yes, well . . . get on with it. It would be better if we didn't have to drive home in the pitch-black—I should have mentioned that only one headlight is properly functioning."

Alice approached the caravan. Its shutters were pulled shut, but a light was on inside. She knocked on the door. The fortune-teller seemed astonished to see her again.

"What are you doing here? Is something wrong?"

Alice shook her head.

"You don't look well. You're pale," continued the old woman.

"I'm a bit cold."

"Well, come in and warm yourself by the stove," she said.

Alice stepped into the little room and noticed the now-familiar vanilla-note perfume. It was stronger near the stove. She sat on a little bench, and the fortune-teller came and sat at her side, taking Alice's hands in hers.

"So you came back to see me."

"I happened to be passing by, and I saw the light."

"Well, welcome back."

"Who are you?" asked Alice.

"Oh, just a fortune-teller, but the locals have respect for me, you know. Some people even come a long way for me to tell them about their future. But yesterday I could see in your eyes that you thought I was nothing but a crazy old woman. I suppose if you're back it's because you've changed your mind. What do you want to know?"

"The man who walked behind me while we were talking yesterday. Why do I have to meet six other people before I'll meet him again?"

"I'm sorry, my darling, but I don't have answers to everything. I just told you what came to me. I can't just make things up. I never do. I don't like lies."

"Neither do I," said Alice.

"But you didn't just happen to be passing by my caravan just now, did you?"

31

Alice admitted as much with a shake of her head.

"Yesterday, you knew my name. I never told you my name," Alice said.

"And you? How are you able to name the ingredients of a perfume?"

"I don't know—it's a gift. I'm a nose."

"And I'm a fortune-teller. We're both talented women in our own domains."

"I came back because somebody pushed me to do so. It's true that what you said yesterday has been bothering me. I didn't sleep a wink last night because of it."

"I understand. I might have felt the same in your position."

"Tell me the truth. Did you really see all of the things you told me yesterday?"

"The truth? God help us. The truth isn't engraved in stone, you know. Your future depends on your choices, on your will. It belongs to you."

"So your predictions are just stories?"

"They're possibilities, not certainties. You decide."

"Decide what?"

"Everything. Whether or not to ask me to reveal what I see. But knowledge has its consequences."

"Well, first of all, I'd like to know if you're sincere."

"Did I ask to be paid yesterday or today? You're the one who came back. But you seem so worried, so tormented, that it's probably better if we leave it there. Go home, Alice. If it reassures you, know that nothing grave menaces your future."

Alice studied the fortune-teller in silence. She wasn't intimidated anymore. To the contrary, her company had become agreeable, her gravelly voice soothing. Alice hadn't come all this way to leave without knowing something more, and the idea of defying the old woman didn't appeal to her. She straightened her back and held out her hands.

"You're right. Tell me what you see. It's up to me to decide what I want to believe or not."

"Are you certain?"

"Every Sunday, my mother dragged me to Mass. In the winter, it was dreadfully cold in the church. I spent hours on end praying to a god that I never saw and who never spared any of us, so I think that I can spend a few minutes listening to what you have to say."

"I'm sorry your parents didn't make it through the war."

"How did you know that?"

"Hush now. You came here to listen, and all you've done is talk." She turned Alice's palms upward. "You have two lives in you, Alice. The one you know, and another one. One that has been waiting for you for a very long time. They have nothing in common, apart from you. The man I spoke about yesterday is to be found somewhere along the path to that other, unknown life, but he will be forever lost to you unless you go on a long journey. A journey that will lead you to discover that nothing you believe in is real."

"But that doesn't make any sense," Alice protested.

"Perhaps. After all, I'm just a fortune-teller at a carnival."

"A journey where?"

"To the place you come from, my darling. To your past."

"Well, I just came from London, and I intend to return there this evening."

"I'm talking about the land you were born in."

"Which is also London. I was born in Holborn."

"No, you weren't," said the fortune-teller with a smile.

"I know where my mother gave birth to me, for heaven's sake!"

"You weren't born in England. You come from farther afield. There's no need to be a fortune-teller to see that. Your features betray your true origins."

"I'm sorry to tell you, but my ancestors are from the Midlands and the North. Birmingham on my mother's side, and Yorkshire on my father's side."

"No. Both of them were from farther east," whispered the woman. "They came from an empire that no longer exists, from a very old country, a land thousands of miles from here. The blood that flows in your veins has its source between the Black Sea and the Caspian. Look in the mirror and see for yourself!"

"You're just making things up."

"I don't mean to repeat myself, Alice, but if you're going to undertake this journey, there are certain things you are going to have to accept. From the way you're reacting, I'd say you're still not ready. Let's leave it at that for now."

"Oh, no you don't—I'm not going to spend another sleepless night. I'm not going back to London until I'm sure that you're a charlatan." The fortune-teller's face dropped. "Pardon me, I'm sorry. That's not really what I think. I don't mean to be disrespectful."

The old woman let go of Alice's hands and rose to her feet. "Go home and forget everything I've told you. I'm the one who should be sorry. The truth is that I'm nothing but a rambling old hag who amuses herself at the price of others' dignity. I tried so hard to predict your future that I got caught up in my own tricks. Go on and live your life free from worry. You're a beautiful woman. There's no need to be a fortune-teller to see that you'll meet a man to your liking no matter what happens."

She went to open the door, but Alice stayed put.

"You were more believable before. Let's play the game. After all, nothing is preventing us from thinking of this as a game. Suppose I were to take your predictions seriously. Where would I begin?"

"You're starting to wear me out, my darling. Like I said, I never predicted anything. I just say whatever happens to come into my head, so there's no use in you wasting your time. Don't you have anything better to do on Christmas Eve?"

"You don't have to debase yourself. I promise I'll leave when you answer my question."

The fortune-teller looked at a timeworn little Byzantine icon hanging above the door of her small caravan and fondly touched the saint's face before turning back to Alice.

"You'll meet somebody to guide you to the next step in Istanbul. But remember, if you follow the trail to its end, the world you live in today won't remain. Now leave me. I'm exhausted."

She opened the door and the cold winter air swept into the room. Alice pulled her coat around her and reached for her purse, but again the fortune-teller refused her money. Alice wound her scarf around her neck and said goodbye.

The pier was deserted and the lights that hung along the length of the dock swung in the wind, emitting a strange clinking melody. The Austin's single headlight blinked at her from the street.

Daldry had taken refuge from the cold inside his car.

"I was starting to worry. I thought perhaps I should come and get you, but it's so blasted cold out there."

"I'm afraid we're going to have to drive in the dark," said Alice.

"You were in there for a while," he said as he started the engine.

"It didn't feel like very long."

"Well, it did to me. I hope it was worth it."

Alice picked up the road map and unfolded it across her lap. Daldry put his foot on the accelerator and the back end of the car skidded a bit on the ice.

"Funny way to spend Christmas Eve," said Alice in guise of an apology.

"A lot better than sitting bored to death next to the radio at home. If the roads aren't too icy, we'll have time for dinner when we get back. Midnight's still a long way off."

"So is London, I'm afraid," said Alice with a sigh.

"How much longer are you going to keep me in suspense? Did she tell you the rest of the story? Are you going to be able to sleep through the night?"

"Not exactly."

Daldry opened his window a crack. "Mind if I smoke?"

"Not if you offer me one."

"You smoke?"

"No," admitted Alice. "But tonight, why not?"

Daldry took a pack of Embassies from his coat pocket.

"Hold the wheel," he told Alice. "You know how to drive?"

"No more than I know how to smoke," she said, leaning over to grip the wheel while Daldry slipped two cigarettes between his lips.

"Well, try to keep us on the road."

He lit both cigarettes and corrected Alice's steering with his free hand before passing her one.

"So we came all this way for nothing. You seem worse than you did this morning."

"I think I put too much faith in that woman's predictions. I'm just tired, I suppose. She was even crazier than I remembered."

The first drag on her cigarette sent Alice into a coughing fit. Daldry plucked it from her fingers and threw it out of the window.

"Go on then, sleep. I'll wake you up when we get there."

Alice leaned back and felt her eyelids grow heavy. Daldry watched her for a moment before turning his concentration back to the road.

Daldry pulled up in front of the house and turned off the engine. He wondered how he ought to wake Alice. If he said something, she would jump, but putting his hand on her shoulder would be unseemly. He could clear his throat, but would she even notice? She had slept all the way home, in spite of the roaring motor and squeaky suspension.

"We're going to freeze to death if we spend the night out here," Alice whispered, opening an eye.

When they were upstairs, Daldry and Alice stood a moment in the hallway, not knowing what to say next. Alice took the lead.

"It's only eleven o'clock."

"You're right," said Daldry. "Just a little past eleven."

"What did you get at the market this morning?" asked Alice.

"Oh, some ham, some piccalilli, red beans, and a piece of Cheshire."

"Well, I have an egg, bacon, fruitcake, and honey."

"A regular feast. I'm dying of hunger," said Daldry.

"Let me invite you to dinner. You took me out to breakfast and I must have cost you a fortune in petrol. I haven't even thanked you."

"With pleasure. I'm free every night this week."

"I meant tonight, Ethan."

"I'm also free tonight."

"I had my doubts."

"It would be silly for each of us to celebrate Christmas alone on either side of a wall."

"I'll make us an omelet."

"Wonderful. I'll just hang up my coat and be right over."

Alice lit the gas ring and melted some butter in a frying pan. While she waited for it to heat up, she pushed her trunk into the middle of the room, covered it with a tablecloth, and set two places, putting two large cushions on the floor on either side.

Daldry knocked and came into the room wearing a flannel suit and holding his shopping basket.

"I thought I'd bring along a little something I bought at the market this morning. It will be perfect with dinner." He revealed a bottle of wine, which he immediately opened with the corkscrew he took from his pocket. "It's Christmas, after all. We can't just drink water."

Over the course of dinner, Daldry told Alice stories from his childhood. He talked about the difficult relationship he had with his family, evoking the hardship his mother endured from having married a wealthy man who shared neither her tastes nor her vision of the world, let alone her delicate wit. He talked about his dull but ambitious brother, who had done all he could to drive Daldry away from his parents in hopes of becoming the sole inheritor of their father's business. Daldry continually asked Alice if he was boring her, but she reassured him that, to the contrary, she found his family portrait sad but fascinating.

"And you?" he finally asked. "What was your childhood like?"

"Oh, very happy really. I was an only child. I always wanted a brother or sister, but in the end, I suppose I benefitted from having my parents' full attention."

"What did your father do?"

"He was a pharmacist. He used to experiment with medicinal plants in his free time. He ordered seeds and cuttings from all over the world. My mother helped him in the shop. They met at university. We didn't live in the lap of luxury, but we were comfortable. My parents loved each other. It was a happy home."

"You were lucky."

"Yes, I realize that. But at the same time, maybe growing up surrounded by so much love leaves one with unrealistic expectations."

Alice took their plates to the sink, and Daldry cleared the glasses. He stopped in front of her worktable and contemplated the rows of little vials and bottles, the small earthenware pots full of thin strips of paper.

"The absolutes are on the right. They're derived from concretes or resinoids. In the middle are the accords I'm working on right now."

"You're a chemist, like your father?"

"No, I'm what they call a 'nose.' I try to create new compositions, new fragrances. Absolutes are essential oils, and concretes are obtained by extracting perfume from natural vegetal sources like rose, jasmine, or lilac blossom. That table is known as an organ. Perfume makers and musicians share a lot of vocabulary—we talk in terms of notes and their accords, which are comparable to musical chords . . . I'm sorry, this is all terribly boring."

"Not at all. It sounds like an interesting trade. Have you already invented perfumes? I mean, perfumes that I could buy in a shop? Maybe something I know?"

"Yes. I manage to sell them sometimes," said Alice with amusement. "Most of my fragrances are relatively unknown for now, but you can find them in a few shops in London."

"It must be wonderful to see your work on the shelf. Just think—a man might have charmed a woman thanks to the cologne he was wearing, one you created."

Alice laughed. "I'm sorry to crush your fantasy, but I've only ever created perfumes for women. But I might make a men's cologne—it's an idea. Maybe I'll try for a peppery note, something woodsy and masculine, cedar or vetiver . . . I'll think about it." She cut two slices of fruitcake. "Let's have dessert, and then I'll let you go. I've had a wonderful evening, but I'm afraid I'm exhausted."

"So am I," said Daldry with a yawn. "I'm completely drained from concentrating on the road in the dark. You know, it snowed quite a bit while you were sleeping."

"Well, thanks for staying awake and keeping us on the road."

"I'm the one who should be thanking you. I haven't eaten fruitcake in years."

"And thank you for taking me to Brighton. It was very kind of you."

Daldry looked up longingly at the skylight. "It must be so bright in here during the day."

"It is. I'll invite you for tea sometime, so you can see for yourself."

With his fruitcake finished, Daldry stood. Alice walked him to the door.

"I'm glad I don't have too far to go," he said from the hallway.

"True, you don't."

"Merry Christmas, Alice."

"Merry Christmas, Daldry."

3

Alice sat up in bed but couldn't see outside. Snow had blanketed the city in the night, and a fine layer of it had covered the skylight, dimming the room. She stood on the bed and lifted the pane.

As the snow fell away, a draft of icy air rushed in, making her close it as quickly as she could.

With her eyes still fogged with sleep, she teetered over to the gas ring and put the kettle on. Daldry had generously left his box of matches behind, and she smiled as she thought of the evening they had spent together. She didn't feel like working today. It was Christmas, and since she didn't have any family to visit, she decided she would go for a walk in Hyde Park.

She bundled up against the cold and tiptoed out of her flat. The old house was completely silent. Daldry was probably still asleep. Outside, the street was an immaculate white. It enchanted her to see the city transformed and to think how even the plainest houses had a certain beauty when cloaked in snow.

A bus was coming in her direction, so she ran to the stop and climbed aboard, buying her ticket from the conductor before settling onto the bench seat at the back.

Half an hour later, she walked into Hyde Park through Queen's Gate, taking the diagonal footpath toward Kensington Palace. She stopped when she came to Round Pond. The ducks glided toward her across the inky-black water, hoping to be fed. On the other side of the pond, a man sitting on a bench waved in her direction. He stood and waved harder. It was Daldry. When he took some bread from his pocket and began tossing pieces of it into the water, the ducks shot off in his direction. Alice walked along the edge of the pond to meet him.

"What a surprise to see you here. Did you follow me?" Alice said.

"I was here first. How on earth could I have followed you?"

"What are you doing here?"

"I went out to get some fresh air and I found the bread in my pockets, so I decided I might as well give the ducks Christmas while I was at it. What are you doing here?"

"Oh, it's just a place I like."

Daldry broke a heel of stale bread in half and gave part of it to Alice.

"So our seaside escapade was all for naught."

Alice crouched to feed the ducks and said nothing.

"I only mention it because I heard you pacing around. You didn't sleep, did you?"

"I fell asleep, but I had a nightmare in the middle of the night."

They had given away all of the bread. Daldry helped Alice up.

"Why don't you tell me what that woman said?"

Alice recounted the fortune-teller's predictions as they strolled down the deserted, snow-covered footpaths of Hyde Park. She even mentioned the moment when the woman had insisted that she wasn't a fortune-teller at all.

"What a strange shift in attitude. But why did you stay after she admitted she was a fraud?" "Because it was precisely at that moment that I began to believe her. You may find it hard to credit, but I'm a rational person. I'm sure that if my best friend told me even a quarter of the things that woman said, I would never let her hear the end of it."

"What bothers you so much about what she said?"

"What doesn't bother me? Everything she told me is utterly shocking! Try to imagine yourself in my position."

"And she said you should go to Istanbul?"

"Yes . . . Perhaps you can drive me in your Austin."

"I'm afraid that Turkey is probably beyond our range of attack."

They crossed paths with a couple coming from the other direction. Daldry waited for them to pass before he continued.

"I know what bothers you about this whole story. It's that she promised you that the man of your dreams would be waiting for you at the end of your journey."

"What bothers me," Alice corrected him, "is that she seems so certain I was born over there."

"But your birth certificate affirms the contrary."

"I distinctly remember walking past the Holborn Hospital when I was ten, and I can still hear my mother telling me it was the place she gave birth to me."

"So then just forget about all this nonsense. I shouldn't have taken you to Brighton. I thought I was doing you a favor, but I see I've blown the whole thing completely out of proportion."

"I just need to get back to work. I've never been very good at being idle."

"What's stopping you?"

"Well, I'm afraid I caught a slight cold yesterday. It's nothing serious, but in my line of work, a stuffy nose is debilitating."

"You'll have to bide your time. But if you've got a cold, you'd do well to stay warm. My car is parked on Prince's Gate. I'll take you home."

The Austin refused to start. Daldry asked Alice to take the wheel while he pushed. She was to release the clutch once the car had a bit of momentum.

"It's simple," he reassured her. "First the left foot, then a little with the right foot when the engine starts, and then both feet on the pedals to the left. And don't forget to steer."

"I thought you said this was simple!" said Alice, dismayed.

Daldry pushed and the car rolled forward more easily than he had expected, making him fall flat on his face. Alice couldn't help but laugh as she watched him disappear from sight in the rearview mirror. In the merriment of the moment, she got the idea to turn the key in the ignition. The engine coughed to life. This made her laugh even harder.

"Are you sure your father wasn't a mechanic?" asked Daldry, brushing himself off as he got in the car on the passenger side.

"I'm sorry. I know it's not funny. I can't help it," she said, stifling a giggle.

"Well then, go on," grumbled Daldry. "Since this bloody car seems to have taken a liking to you, let's see what happens when you accelerate."

"You do realize I've never driven before," said Alice cheerfully.

"A first time for everything," said Daldry, straight-faced. "Push the pedal on the left, put her in gear, and gently release the accelerator a bit."

The tires slid across the icy road, but Alice put them back on course with astonishing dexterity. It was nearly noon on Christmas Day and the streets were deserted. She heeded Daldry's instructions with care and, apart from braking too hard and stalling twice, she managed to drive them home without major incident.

"What a marvelous sensation," she said once they had arrived. "I love driving."

"You can have a second lesson later in the week, if you like."

"That would be wonderful, thank you."

Alice and Daldry said good afternoon in the corridor. Inside her flat, Alice spread her coat across the foot of the bed and climbed under the covers for a nap.

◆ ◆ ◆

Fine dust floated in the air, stirred up by a warm wind. At the end of a narrow dirt road, a long flight of steps led down to the city below.

Alice walked barefoot and looked around. The brightly colored shop-fronts on either side of the street were closed.

A voice called from the distance. At the top of the stairs, a woman signaled for her to hurry. Something dangerous was behind them. Alice ran toward the woman, but as she did so, the woman fled and disappeared.

She could hear the sounds of a mob behind her. There were cries and screams. Alice hurried to the steps. The woman was waiting for her at the bottom, but she forbade Alice to follow. She told Alice she loved her and said goodbye.

As the woman's figure disappeared into the distance, Alice could sense her image taking root in the depths of her heart.

Alice tried to follow, but the stairs cracked and fell apart beneath her feet. The sound of the crowd behind her became deafening. She lifted her head. A fiery red sun burned her skin. She felt damp; there was salt on her lips, earth in her hair. Clouds of dust filled the air, making it difficult to breathe.

Just a few feet away she could hear insistent wails, moaning, murmured words she couldn't understand. Her throat felt tight—she was suffocating.

Somebody's hand suddenly gripped her by the arm and pulled her up just before the earth gave way beneath her feet.

Alice screamed, fought as best she could, but the hand that held her was too strong. She felt as though she might lose consciousness. She knew it was useless to resist. The sky above had grown vast and red.

Alice opened her eyes and was blinded by the bright winter sunlight. She shivered. Her forehead burned with fever. She patted around for the glass of water on the stool beside her bed, but she was overcome by a racking cough on the first sip. She was too weak to move, but she knew she had to get up and find another blanket to keep the cold from chilling her to her core. In vain, she tried to prop herself up before falling back into her fevered dreams.

◆ ◆ ◆

She heard somebody whispering her name—a familiar and soothing voice.

She hid in a cupboard, curled up on herself, and buried her head between her knees. A hand covered her mouth, forbidding her to speak. She wanted to cry, but the person holding her begged her to remain silent.

Somebody was pounding at the door. The sound grew louder. Now they were kicking the door. Somebody entered the room. There was a sound of footsteps. In the shelter of the tiny cupboard, Alice stopped breathing.

◆ ◆ ◆

"Alice! Wake up!"

Daldry leaned over the bed and put his hand on her forehead. She had a fever. He helped her sit up, propping a pillow behind her back, and left to call a doctor. He returned a few moments later.

"I'm afraid you must have something worse than a cold. The doctor will be here soon. Keep resting. I'll be here if you need anything."

Daldry sat at the foot of the bed and waited. The doctor arrived in less than an hour. He examined Alice, taking her pulse and carefully listening to her breathing and her heart.

"She's in a pretty bad state. It's probably the flu. She should stay warm and try to sweat it out. Make sure she drinks plenty of fluids," he told Daldry. "A bit of honey in warm water or herbal tea, small sips, but as often as possible." He gave Daldry a packet of aspirin. "This ought to bring down the fever. If her condition hasn't improved by tomorrow, bring her to the hospital."

Daldry thanked the doctor for coming at Christmas. He went to his flat and brought back two heavy blankets, which he spread over Alice. He pushed the armchair next to her worktable into the middle of the room and settled down for the night.

"I wonder now if I didn't prefer it when you and your noisy friends kept me up at night—at least I was in my own bed," he grumbled to the slumbering Alice.

◆ ◆ ◆

The noises coming from the room outside subsided. Alice pushed open the cupboard door. There was a stifling atmosphere of silence and absence. The furniture was knocked over, the bed unmade. A broken picture frame lay on the ground. Alice carefully removed the shards of broken glass and put the picture back in its place on the bedside table. It was an Indian-ink drawing of two faces smiling up at her. The window was open, and a breeze blew in from outside, rustling the curtains. Alice went to look out of the window, but the sill was too high. She had to climb onto a stool to see down into the street. She hoisted herself up and parted the curtains—the light was so bright she had to squint.

A man on the pavement looked up and smiled at her. His face was kind and gentle. Her love for the man was boundless. She had always loved him, had always known him. She wanted to jump down to him, for him to take her in his arms. She wanted to call his name and keep him from going, but she couldn't speak. She waved. The man waved his cap in return, and smiled again before disappearing.

◆ ◆ ◆

Alice opened her eyes. Daldry had propped her up and was holding a glass of water to her lips, telling her to drink slowly.

"I saw him," she murmured. "He was there."

"The doctor already came," said Daldry. "On Christmas Day, no less. A very dedicated man."

"No, not a doctor."

"Well, he certainly seemed like one to me."

"I saw the man that's waiting for me."

"We'll talk about it when you're feeling better. Get some rest now. I think the fever might be starting to break."

"He's much more handsome than I imagined."

"I don't doubt it for a second. Maybe if I catch the flu, I'll have a vision of Esther Williams. She was positively ravishing in *Take Me Out to the Ball Game*."

"Yes," whispered Alice from her delirium. "He'll take me to the ball."

"And while you're doing that, I'll just take a little nap."

"I have to find him. I have to go there." Her eyelids drooped.

"You might want to wait a few days. I'm not sure you'd make a good impression in your current state."

Alice was asleep. Daldry sighed and returned to the armchair. It was four in the morning. His back was aching from having slept in the chair, and there was a crick in his neck, but the aspirin seemed to be working, and Alice's fever was beginning to subside. He turned out the light and tried to sleep.

A deafening snore woke Alice from her sleep. Her arms and legs ached, but the chills were gone, and she felt relaxed and warm. She turned her head to see Daldry sprawled across the armchair, an afghan at his feet. Alice watched his right eyebrow rise and fall with each breath. Suddenly, she realized he had spent the night watching over her, and she felt terribly guilty. She wrapped herself up in a blanket and did her best to prepare herself some tea without waking Daldry. His snoring grew so loud that it finally woke him. He shifted position and slid out of the armchair and onto the floor.

"What are you doing out of bed?" he asked with a yawn.

"Making tea," said Alice, pouring two cups.

Daldry sat up and rubbed the small of his back.

"Get back in bed this instant."

"I'm feeling much better. Really."

"You remind me of my sister, and that's not a compliment. Don't be stubborn and careless. You've barely got your strength back and you're already traipsing about barefoot in a drafty flat. Get back into bed. I'll take care of the tea. That is, if I can make my arms work. I think my whole right side has fallen asleep."

"You shouldn't have gone to so much trouble," said Alice, finally obeying. She sat in bed and gladly received the tray Daldry placed on her lap.

"Are you hungry?" he asked.

"No. I don't feel like eating."

"Well, you should eat something anyway. Feed a fever, they say."

He went across the corridor to his flat and came back with a biscuit tin.

"Is that real shortbread?" she asked, peering at its contents. "I haven't had shortbread in ages."

"As real as can be. Homemade," he said, proudly dipping one in his cup of tea.

"Well, they look delicious."

"Did I mention I made them myself?"

"Amazing. Really."

"There I have to draw the line. What could possibly be amazing about shortbread?"

"Certain flavors can take you back to your childhood. My mother used to make shortbread on Sunday, and during the week I'd eat it with hot chocolate when I was done with my schoolwork. I didn't think much of it then; I just let it form a sludge in the bottom of my cup. Mother pretended not to notice. During the war, when we were waiting in the air-raid shelters for the sirens to stop, I remember thinking about that shortbread. Dreaming of childhood treats with the bombs going off all around us . . ."

"I don't think I ever shared something that intimate with my mother," said Daldry. "And I doubt my biscuits can live up to such fond memories, but I hope you like them anyway."

"May I have another?"

"Speaking of dreams, you had quite a series of nightmares last night."

"I know. I still remember some of them. I was walking barefoot down a dirt road. It felt like something from another age, but also strangely familiar."

"There's no logic to the impression of time in dreams."

"No. It was a place I felt I knew."

"Probably just old memories. Everything gets mixed up in nightmares."

"Well, it was terrifying. I was more at ease during the Blitz."

"Was the war in part of the dream?"

"No. I was far away from London. I was being hunted; something wanted to harm me. Then a man appeared, and my fear vanished. I felt like nothing could hurt me."

"Who was it?"

"A man standing in the street. He smiled at me and waved goodbye, and then he was gone."

"You speak of it as if it really happened."

Alice sighed.

"You should get some rest, Daldry. You look exhausted."

"You're the invalid, not me. But I will admit, your armchair is not a particularly comfortable place to sleep."

There was a knock at the door. Daldry opened it to find Carol in the hallway holding a large wicker basket.

"What are you doing here? Don't tell me that Alice disturbs you when she's all alone." Carol came into the room and was surprised to find Alice lying in bed.

"Your friend has a bad case of the flu," explained Daldry, smoothing the wrinkles out of his coat, visibly ill at ease under Carol's inquisitive gaze.

"Well, I arrived just in the nick of time, then. I'm a nurse. Alice is in good hands now." She showed Daldry to the door. "There now, Alice needs to get her rest. I'll take good care of her."

"Ethan?" called Alice from her bed. Daldry craned his neck, trying to see around the insistent Carol. "Thank you for everything."

Daldry forced a smile and retired to his flat.

The door closed, and Carol went over to the bed, put her hand on Alice's forehead, felt her neck, and told her to stick out her tongue.

"You've still got a bit of a fever. I brought you all sorts of wonderful things from the country. Fresh eggs, milk, jam, and even some fruitcake that Mother made yesterday. How do you feel?"

"A bit overwhelmed ever since you came through the door."

"Thank you for everything, Ethan darling," simpered Carol teasingly as she filled the hot-water bottle. "Your relationship has certainly taken a turn for the better since my last visit. Is there something you want to tell me?"

"That you're nosy and your insinuations are completely off the mark."

"I wasn't insinuating, I was observing."

"He's my neighbor."

"He was also your neighbor last week. But back then things were decidedly more formal. You weren't on a first-name basis; it was still Miss Pendelbury and Mr. Killjoy. What broke the ice?"

Alice refused to talk. Carol looked at her pointedly, one hand on her hip, the other holding the kettle suspended in midair. She raised her eyebrows.

Alice finally gave up. "We just went back to Brighton together."

"That was your mysterious Christmas invitation? What an idiot I was. And I thought you'd just made something up to throw the boys off your trail. I kept kicking myself for letting you stay behind in London alone instead of insisting you come along with me to see my parents. And the whole time Miss P was out on a seaside romp with the boy next door." Carol paused. "Has it ever crossed your mind to buy some real furniture?" Suddenly, her eyes lit up. "Wait a minute! Don't tell me that when he barged in last time it was just an act to get rid of us and spend the rest of the evening together!"

"Carol!" hissed Alice, pointing toward Daldry's flat. "Stop talking and sit down. You're more exhausting than the flu."

"Oh, you don't have the flu; you've just got a bad cold," said Carol, fuming.

"I hadn't planned on going back to Brighton. It was an unexpected and generous offer on his behalf. And you can stop smirking—there's nothing between Daldry and me apart from a civil, reciprocal appreciation for each other. Besides, he's not really my type."

"Why did you go back to Brighton?"

"I'm too tired to go into it now."

"I'm touched to see you so affected by my care and empathy."

"Oh, give me a slice of that fruitcake and hush," Alice said, just before sneezing.

"See? Nothing but a cold."

"And just when I was about to get back to work," said Alice, pushing herself back up. "I'm going crazy from sitting around doing nothing."

"Get used to it. Your seaside joyride is going to cost you at least a week without the use of your nose. Now, go on. Tell me why you went back."

Carol listened intently as Alice told her about the second trip to Brighton. When she was done, Carol let out a long whistle, looking just as upset as Alice. "I would have been terrified too. No wonder you fell ill as soon as you got home."

"Very funny."

"Come on. It's ridiculous twaddle. What on earth is 'nothing you believe is real' supposed to mean? In any case, it was very kind of Daldry to drive you such a distance, though I know plenty of other men who would have gone even farther to take you for a ride, if only they had a car. Life really isn't fair. Here I am with so much love to give, and you're the one surrounded on all sides by panting suitors."

"Suitors? I'm alone all day long, and it's not any better at night."

"Do I have to remind you about Anton? If you're alone, it's your own fault. You're an idealist who doesn't know how to take advantage of opportunities when they present themselves. But maybe you're right to be that way." A note of sadness had crept into her voice. "I should be going. I'm going to be late for my shift. I don't want to be in the way if your neighbor comes back."

"Oh stop. I told you, there's nothing between us."

"I know, not your type, and besides, Prince Charming is waiting for you in a distant land . . . You should take a holiday and find him. If I had some money, I'd gladly come along for the ride. A trip with just us girls would be such fun. It's warm in Turkey, and I hear the men have beautiful golden skin."

Alice fell back into her pillow. Carol pulled up the covers from the foot of the bed to tuck her in.

"Sleep well, love," she whispered. "I know I'm a jealous wench, but you're my best friend and I love you like my sister. I'll come back when I get off duty tomorrow. You're going to feel better soon."

Carol put on her coat and left. She ran into Daldry in the corridor as he was heading out to do his shopping. They went downstairs together.

"She'll be better soon," she told him once they were in the street.

"Wonderful news."

"It was very kind of you to have taken care of her like that."

"It was the least I could do," he said. "As a good neighbor."

"Goodbye, Mr. Daldry."

"Yes, well, I'd just like to say, even though it's none of your business . . . she's not at all my type of woman either. Not in the least!"

He stormed off without saying goodbye.

4

It was a week that felt as if it would never end. Alice didn't have a fever anymore, but she could barely taste her food, let alone smell anything. Daldry hadn't returned to visit, and although Alice had gone and knocked on his door several times, his flat remained silent.

Carol came to visit Alice between shifts, bringing her groceries and newspapers she took from the hospital waiting room. Once she even slept over, too exhausted to walk the three blocks to her flat in the cold. In the middle of the night, Carol had shaken Alice to wake her from the nightmares that returned almost every time she fell asleep.

On Saturday, just as Alice was thinking about getting back to work again, she heard footsteps on the landing. She pushed back her chair and hurried to the door. Daldry held a small suitcase and was about to go into his flat.

"Hello, Alice," he said without turning around. He unlocked his door and hesitated. "I'm sorry I didn't have time to see you before I left. I had to go away for a few days." He kept his back turned.

"There's no need to apologize. I was just worried when I didn't hear you moving around."

"I should have left a note." He rested his head against the door.

"What's wrong?" asked Alice.

Daldry turned. He was pale and hadn't shaved in days. There were dark circles under his eyes that were red and swollen from crying.

"Oh dear, what happened?"

"My father finally died on Monday. The funeral was three days ago."

"Come over. I'll make you some tea."

Daldry abandoned his suitcase in the hall and followed Alice into her flat, collapsing into the armchair with a groan. He gazed distantly at the skylight. Alice made the tea and handed him a cup. She pulled up the stool and sat across from him, respecting his silence. A long time passed and neither of them moved. Daldry finally sighed and got up.

"Thank you," he said. "That was just what I needed. I'm going to go home, take a bath, and go to bed."

"Before you go to bed, come back for dinner. I'll make an omelet."

"I'm not very hungry."

"Well, you'll eat anyway. You have to eat," said Alice firmly.

Daldry returned a short while later, wearing a turtleneck sweater and a pair of flannel trousers. He still looked haggard and hadn't shaved.

"I'm sorry about my appearance," he said, "but I left my razor at my parents' house and it's a bit late to go out and buy a new one."

"The beard is becoming on you," said Alice, welcoming him inside.

They ate seated on either side of the trunk. Alice had brought down some of the gin she kept cold by leaving it on the roof next to the skylight. Daldry wasn't hungry, but he needed no coaxing to drink. He forced himself to eat a bit of omelet for form's sake.

"I had promised myself," he said, interrupting a long silence, "to talk to him man-to-man, to explain why I had chosen to be a painter. I never judged him for his choices—I jolly well could have . . . but I wanted to tell him that he ought to show me the same respect."

"I'm sure he admired you, even if he never showed it."

"You didn't know him," said Daldry, sighing again.

"Still, no matter what you may think, you were his son."

"I suffered from his distant character for forty years. I'd got used to it. But strangely, now that he's not there anymore, the pain is even sharper."

"I know what you mean," said Alice quietly.

"Last night I went into his office. My mother found me going through the drawers of his secretary's desk. She thought I was looking for his will, but I told her that I couldn't care less about my inheritance. I just wanted to find something, maybe a note or a letter, that he might have left for me. Mum just put her hand on my shoulder and said, 'My poor darling. He didn't leave anything like that.' I didn't cry when they lowered his coffin into the ground. I haven't cried since the summer I was ten and I had to have stitches in my knee after falling out of a tree. But this morning, when the house I grew up in was shrinking in the rearview mirror, I couldn't hold back the tears. I had to pull over. I felt such a fool, sitting in my car and weeping."

"You've just lost your father. It's normal."

"You know, it's strange; I think that if I had become a pianist, he would have taken a certain pride in me. He might have come to hear me play. Painting never interested him. He didn't consider it a real job. At best, it was a pastime. But at least his death gave me the occasion to see my family all in one place again."

"You should paint his portrait and hang it in an important place in your family's home—in his old office, maybe. I'm sure he'd be touched, wherever he is now."

Daldry burst into laughter.

"What a ghoulish idea. I'm not so cruel as to do such a thing to my poor mother. But enough of this sniveling, I've kept you long enough for one night. The omelet was delicious, and the gin, of which I'm afraid I drank a bit too much, was much appreciated. Now that you're over the flu, one of these days I'll give you another driving lesson."

"I'd like that," said Alice.

Daldry said good night and turned to leave. For a man who normally carried himself with pride, he seemed slumped and hesitant. He changed his mind and turned around to take the bottle of gin before leaving for good. Alice was exhausted and went to bed as soon as Daldry was gone. She fell asleep almost immediately.

◆ ◆ ◆

"Come with me," a voice whispered. "We have to leave."

A door opened into the night. There was no light in the street outside and the houses' shutters were closed and latched. A woman took her by the hand. They crept down the street together as quietly as possible, staying in the shadows cast by the moonlight. They carried lightly packed bags. Alice had a little black suitcase with a few things in it. When they came to the top of the long flight of steps, they could see the entire city spread out before them. In the distance, flames licked the sky, staining it a violent crimson. "The entire neighborhood is on fire," said a voice. "They've gone mad! But you'll be safe over there. They'll protect us. I'm sure of it. Come along. Follow me, my love."

Alice had never been so afraid. Her bare feet were sore. It had been impossible to find shoes in the chaos that reigned over the city. An old man emerged from a coach-house door that opened onto the street. He signaled for them to turn back, gesturing toward a barricade farther down the street where a group of armed young men stood in wait.

The woman hesitated a moment. She carried a baby wound up in a scarf against her breast and stroked its head to keep it quiet. Their course through the night continued in the opposite direction.

A narrow path led to the top of an embankment. They passed a silent fountain—there was something reassuring about the stillness of the water in its basin. To their right there was an opening in the long fortified wall. The woman seemed to know the place, and Alice followed her. They crossed an abandoned garden. The tall grass stood still in the windless night, and thistles pricked Alice's legs as though they were trying to hold her back. She opened her mouth to complain but knew she must keep silent.

In the depths of a sleepy orchard, they came upon a ruined church. They crossed the rubble of the crumbling apse. The pews lay overturned, charred from a fire. Alice lifted her head and saw the remnants of centuries-old mosaics on the vaulted ceiling overhead. The faded face of Christ, or perhaps an apostle, seemed to watch over her. A door opened, and Alice passed into the second apse. In the center of the room stood a tomb covered in porcelain tiles, immense and monolithic. They went past the tomb and into an ante-chamber, where the bitter smell of charred stone mingled with the familiar scents of thyme and caraway—herbs that grew in the empty field behind her house. Even though they were mixed with the acrid smoke, she managed to make out their familiar smells.

The burnt church was now nothing but a distant memory. The woman took her through a gate, and they ran down another narrow street. Alice was exhausted, and her legs began to give way. The hand holding hers let go, abandoning her. She sat down on the paving stones. The woman continued without turning back.

Rain began to fall. Alice called for help, but the rain was too heavy. Soon the woman's outline disappeared in the distance. Alice sat alone in the street, chilled and wet. She cried out, the long, bellowing cry of a wounded animal.

Hail ricocheted off the skylight. Gasping for breath, Alice sat up in bed, searching for the switch on the lamp beside her bed. With the light on, she looked around the room, taking in the familiar objects one by one.

She pounded the mattress with her fists in frustration, furious to have fallen victim to the same exhausting nightmare that kept return-ing night after night. She got up and went to her worktable, opened the window that looked out onto the rear of the house, and took a deep breath of the cold night air. The lights were on in Daldry's flat. His invisible presence was strangely reassuring. In the morning, she would ask Carol for advice. There must be some remedy to calm her sleep. Alice just wanted to make it through the night—one long, gentle night, free from the horror of being pursued like an animal through unfamiliar streets.

Alice spent the following days hard at work. Every evening she put off going to bed, fighting the urge to sleep and battling the fear that took hold of her as darkness fell. And every night she had the same dreams that ended with her crouched on the pavement and soaked by the rain.

She went to see Carol at lunchtime. After asking for her at the hospital reception desk, she waited a good thirty minutes in the lobby among the gurneys and stretchers, watching the ambulancemen unload patients from their vehicles, which arrived with jangling bells. A woman begged the nurses on duty to take care of her sick child. A raving old man wandered among the benches where the other patients waited their turn. A pale young fellow smiled at Alice. The arch of his left eyebrow had been cut open, and a thick trickle of blood flowed down his cheek. Another man, of about fifty, held his side, racked by what seemed like dreadful pain. Sitting in the middle of so much suffering, Alice felt guilty realizing that her nights might be full of horror, but poor Carol's days weren't much better. Just as she was thinking about this, Carol appeared, pushing a gurney whose wheels squeaked as they rolled across the linoleum.

"What are you doing here?" she asked, surprised to see Alice. "Are you sick again?"

"No, I just came to take you to lunch."

"What a nice surprise. Let me park this one here and I'll be right back," she said, nodding to her patient. "They could have at least told me you were here. Have you been waiting long?"

Carol pushed the gurney over to a colleague, and left briefly to get her coat and scarf. She hurried back to Alice and led her out of the hospital.

"Come on," Carol said. "There's a café around the corner that's not too terrible. Practically the Ritz compared to our cafeteria."

"What about your patients?"

"This place is always full of people. If I'm going to be able to do anything about it, I have to eat from time to time. Let's go."

The café was packed with customers waiting for a seat when they arrived. Carol smiled and caught the attention of the owner, who nodded to a free table at the back of the room from his position behind the counter.

"Who do you have to bribe to get service like that?" asked Alice as she settled into the chair.

Carol chuckled. "I lanced a boil on his backside last summer. He's been eating out of my hand ever since."

"I never realized . . ."

"What a glamorous life I lead?" teased Carol.

"How hard your work is."

"Oh, I like what I do, even if it isn't easy every day. I used to bandage up my dolls when I was a little girl. I remember it worried my mother. Anyway, what brings you to this part of town? I don't suppose you came to the hospital in search of inspiration for one of your perfumes."

"I just came to have lunch with you. Do I need another reason?"

"You know, a good nurse doesn't just dress her patients' wounds. She can also tell when something isn't right in their heads."

"But I'm not one of your patients, Carol."

"You certainly looked like one when I found you in the lobby. You can tell me if something is wrong."

"Is there a menu?"

"Forget the menu," said Carol. "I don't have much time, so we'll just have the special."

A waiter brought them two plates of mutton stew.

"I know it doesn't look like much, but you'll see, it's not half bad."

Carol tucked in, while Alice picked skeptically at her plate.

"You might have more of an appetite if you got what's bothering you off of your chest," said Carol, talking with her mouth full. Alice poked at a piece of potato with her fork and made a face. "Fine. I'm probably just being stubborn and presumptuous, but a little while from now when you're taking the bus home, you'll think what an idiot you were for having wasted half of the day without even having tasted this stew. Especially since you're the one that's footing the bill. Come on, tell me what's bothering you. You know the silent treatment drives me mad."

Alice finally told her about the recurrent nightmare that had been plaguing her sleep, and the unhappiness that weighed upon her waking hours.

"Let me tell you a story," said Carol. "I was on duty the night of the first Blitz bombing. The wounded were pouring in. Most of them were burn victims coming in on foot, as best they could. Some of our staff had deserted the hospital to take shelter, but most of us had stayed at our posts. I was there out of cowardice, not courage; I was too scared to go out into the streets, and petrified at the idea of burning to death in a firestorm. After about an hour, the number of patients coming in dropped off, and the head doctor on duty, Doctor Turner—who, by the way, is so handsome he could turn the head of a nun—gathered us together to tell us that if nobody was coming in, it was because they were caught under the rubble and that we ought to go out and search for them. We were dumbstruck. He told us that none of us were obligated to go, but that those who weren't afraid should take the stretchers and head into the streets. There were lives to be saved out there."

"Did you go?"

"Don't make fun of me, but no. I went and hid in the broom closet for two hours. I just curled up and closed my eyes. I wanted to disappear, so I convinced myself that I was back in my bedroom in St Mawes."

"You shouldn't be ashamed. I wouldn't have been any more courageous than you."

"Yes, you would have, I'm sure of it. Anyway, when I went back to work, I was ashamed but alive. I crept around, avoiding Doctor Turner for days, but as luck would have it, I was eventually assigned to assist with an amputation he was performing. And as though that weren't humiliating enough, we happened to be in the scrub room at the same time. While we were getting ready, I confessed how I had hid on the day of the first bombing. I thought I was making a complete fool of myself."

"How did he react?"

"He asked me to help him with his gloves and told me it was only human to be afraid. He told me how he was often afraid before going into surgery."

Carol pushed her empty plate across the table and started eating Alice's untouched stew.

"But he told me that as soon as he went into the operating theatre, he left his fears behind him. I tried to sleep with him not long after that, but the fool was married and faithful to his wife. Anyway, three days later there was another raid. That time I went out into the streets with a group of doctors and nurses. I picked through the rubble, as close to the flames as I am to you now. At one point that night, I was so scared I actually pissed myself." She paused to swallow. "But enough about me. You haven't been the same since our trip to Brighton. Something is bothering you, I can tell. The flames are burning, you may not see them, but they're ruining your nights. Stop hiding in that broom closet and face your fears. I was terrified those nights that I was searching for the wounded, but doing something was so much better than staying huddled up inside my own prison."

"But what can I possibly do? I don't know the cause."

"Your solitude will be the end of you! You dream of a perfect love story, but you're too afraid to let yourself go. The idea of being dependent or even attached to somebody throws you into a panic. Do I have to remind you about Anton? I don't know whether that old woman was a charlatan or the real thing, but she told you that the man of your dreams is waiting for you. So go to Turkey for God's sake! You've got savings. Borrow some money if you have to. Take that trip and go find out for yourself whether he's waiting for you or not. Even if you don't run into him, you'll be free because you won't have anything left to regret."

"How am I supposed to get to Turkey?"

"I'm a nurse, love, not a travel agent. Speaking of which, I'd best be going. I won't charge you for the psychotherapy, but I'll let you pick up the bill."

Carol got up, slipped into her coat, and kissed Alice before leaving. Alice got up and ran after her, catching her on the pavement outside.

"Do you really mean what you just said about going to Istanbul?"

"Would I have admitted to pissing myself if I didn't? Get back inside. Do you want to catch a cold again? I can't take care of you full time."

Alice went back to the table and sat where Carol had been sitting. She ordered a coffee and a plate of mutton stew.

Traffic was dense, and Alice's bus was moving at a crawl on her ride home. Horse carts, motorcycles with sidecars, delivery trucks, and motorcars all seemed to be trying to cross the junction at the same time. Daldry would have loved it, she thought. The bus pulled to a halt, and Alice's gaze fell upon a tiny shop wedged between a grocer's and the closed shutters of an antique dealer. The sign above the door read THOS. COOK & SON LTD. She fell into daydreaming for a moment before the bus lurched forward again.

Alice got off at the next stop and walked back up the street and entered the travel agency. A stand near the entrance was covered with colorful brochures advertising holidays in exotic places, such as France, Spain, Switzerland, Italy, Egypt, and Greece. The assistant stepped from behind the counter to greet her.

"Planning to travel, madam?"

"Not really. I'm just looking."

"If you're thinking about a honeymoon, I'd recommend Venice. It's magnificent in the spring. Otherwise, there's Spain: Madrid, Seville, the Mediterranean coast. More and more of our customers are going to Spain, and they always come back thrilled."

"Oh, I'm not getting married," said Alice politely.

"Nothing forbids a person from traveling alone these days. Everybody needs to take a little break now and again. For a woman, I'd advise Switzerland. Geneva and its lake are very peaceful and utterly charming."

"Do you have anything on Turkey?" asked Alice timidly.

"Istanbul. Excellent choice. I myself have dreamed of going there one day. Hagia Sophia, the Bosporus . . . Let me see, I have the information here somewhere. Things are a bit out of order." He rummaged through the drawers of a tall cabinet. "Here it is. This is a relatively complete little booklet. I also have a guide I can loan you if you're interested, but you'll have to promise to bring it back."

"Oh, the brochure will be just fine," said Alice, thanking him.

"Here, I'll give you an extra one," he said. He saw her to the door and told her to come back whenever she felt like it. Alice said goodbye and went to catch the next bus.

A wet snow began to fall. One of the bus's windows was jammed open, and an icy wind blew through. Alice took the brochures out of her handbag and flipped through them, hoping the sight of sunny foreign landscapes and blue skies might warm her up a bit.

When she finally got home, she had to stand in the hall and sift through the contents of her handbag before she found her keys. An hour later, Daldry came home and found one of the brochures lying where it had fallen. He picked it up and smiled.

◆ ◆ ◆

There was a knock at the door. Alice opened it to find Daldry holding a bottle of wine in one hand and two glasses in the other.

"May I?" he asked.

"Make yourself at home," said Alice, standing aside to let him in.

Daldry sat down in front of the trunk and poured two generous glasses of wine. He handed one to Alice and they toasted.

"Are we celebrating something in particular?" Alice asked her neighbor.

"In a sense," he said. "I just sold a painting for fifty thousand quid."

Alice's eyes grew wide. She put down her glass. "I had no idea your work was so valuable. Will I ever get to see some of it, or is just looking even out of my price range?"

"One day, perhaps," said Daldry, refilling his glass.

"Well, you certainly have generous collectors."

"That's not a very flattering way to talk about my work." He paused. "I haven't sold anything at all. The fifty thousand pounds came from my father. I just got back from the reading of the will. The whole family was there this afternoon. I had no idea I meant so much to him. I expected much less, to be frank." There was a note of sadness in his voice. "The absurd part is that I haven't the faintest idea what to do with such a mountain of money . . . Maybe I'll buy your flat," he teased. "I could set up my easel under that skylight that I've dreamed of for so many years. Perhaps the light would allow me to finally paint something that would appeal to somebody."

"It's not for sale, and I'm just renting. Besides, where would I live if you were to buy my flat?"

"Or I could travel!" said Daldry.

"If that's what you want, why not? The world must be full of inspiring intersections just waiting to be painted."

"Why not the Bosporus?"

Alice looked at Daldry with suspicion.

"What?" he said, feigning innocence, before taking the brochure that had fallen from Alice's handbag and putting it on the trunk. "I found this in the hall, and I doubt it belongs to the woman downstairs. It would be difficult to find a more sedentary creature. She only goes out to do her Saturday shopping."

"Well, I think we've had enough to drink. I haven't inherited any money, I don't have any travel plans, and if there's any hope of me continuing to pay the rent, I have some work I ought to get back to."

"I thought that one of your fragrances brought in a little money every month."

"A little, but that won't go on forever. Fashions change and I have to create something new, which was what I was trying to do before you came over."

"What about the man of your dreams? He's waiting for you! Have you forgotten about him?" Daldry pointed at the brochure.

"Yes," said Alice sharply.

"Well, then what made you scream like that at three in the morning? You scared me so badly I almost fell out of bed."

"I stubbed my toe on this trunk on the way to bed. I worked late and wasn't looking where I was going."

"You're a terrible liar, but I can see that I'm in your way. I'll take my leave." He got up as though he were about to go and then turned. "Do you know the story of Adrienne Bolland?"

"I don't know anybody by the name of Adrienne," said Alice, growing exasperated.

"She was the first woman to attempt flying over the Andes. In an aeroplane she piloted by herself, of course."

"That was very brave of her."

Much to Alice's despair, Daldry settled back into the armchair and poured himself another glass of wine.

"The reason I bring her up has more to do with an extraordinary thing that took place a few months before her flight."

"I sense I'm about to hear about it in great detail."

"Exactly."

Alice rolled her eyes, but she could tell that Daldry needed company that evening. He had been so kind to her when she was sick, it was the least she could do to show a little patience and listen to what he felt he needed to tell her.

"Adrienne went to Argentina in 1920 as a representative of the French aeroplane manufacturer Caudron. She was supposed to meet potential clients and show them the planes. She only had forty hours of flying experience, but her boss, Caudron himself, drummed up a lot of publicity and turned her visit into a big event. He even spread the rumor that she was going to attempt to cross the Andes. She told him before she left that there was no way she would risk such a dangerous flight in the two smaller planes she was taking with her, but that she would consider it if he sent her a more powerful plane capable of flying at higher altitudes. So Caudron promised he would send the bigger plane. The evening she arrived in Argentina, a horde of journalists was waiting for her boat. There was a big celebration, and the next morning, she woke up to read the headline "Adrienne Bolland to Cross the Cordillera." The very idea threw her mechanic into a panic.

"She sent a telegram to Caudron, who confirmed that it was impossible to send her the larger, more powerful plane he had promised. The French community of Buenos Aires tried to convince her to abandon the plans, telling her it was pure folly to think a woman could attempt and survive such a dangerous solo flight. Some even accused her of being a madwoman, who wanted to mar the reputation of the French nation. But she had made up her mind to go ahead with the flight, and after delivering an official announcement, she shut herself up in her hotel room and refused to communicate with the outside world. She needed all of her concentration to prepare for a flight that was starting to seem like a needlessly complicated suicide attempt.

"Not long afterwards, while her plane was being transported by rail to Mendoza, where she had decided to take off, somebody knocked on the door of her hotel room. Furious at being interrupted, Adrienne opened the door, ready to send the intruder packing. She found herself face-to-face with a shy young Brazilian woman who told Adrienne that she had a gift for seeing the future and had something very important to tell her. Adrienne reluctantly agreed to listen because she knew that such things were taken very seriously in that part of South America. The locals often consulted soothsayers to help them make important decisions. For many citizens of Buenos Aires thirty years ago, undertaking such a risky flight without consulting an oracle would have been as unheard of as going off to war without getting blessed by a priest in other cultures. I don't know if Adrienne believed in such things, but she knew that for the locals on her team the soothsayer's predictions would be of utmost importance, and she needed their support. She told the girl she would give her the time it took to smoke a cigarette and then lit up. The young woman told Adrienne that she would survive her dangerous journey on a single condition."

"Which was?" Alice had started to take an interest in Daldry's story.

"I'm getting to it! She told Adrienne that at one point on her journey, she would fly over a valley where she would see a lake the shape and color of an opened oyster—an enormous oyster stranded high in the mountains—a sight that would be hard to miss. To the left of this stretch of frozen water, clouds would cover the sky, but to the right, the sky would be clear and blue. A pilot with any sense would fly to the right, but the fortune-teller warned Adrienne that if she allowed herself to take the easy way out, she would pay for it with her life: she would run into a chain of high peaks that would be impossible to cross. When she found herself above the lake, it was essential that she fly into the clouds, no matter how dark they seemed. Of course, Adrienne thought this a very stupid idea. What pilot in her right mind would just put down her head and fly blind? The canvas wings of her plane couldn't resist turbulent weather and would surely break in stormy conditions. She asked the young woman if she knew the area from having lived in the mountains, but the fortune-teller told her she had never been to the place and left without speaking another word.

"Adrienne left for Mendoza. In the time it took to travel over six hundred miles by train, she had completely forgotten about her fleeting encounter with the fortune-teller. She had other things to worry about. And besides, how could a girl like the fortune-teller know that aeroplanes have maximum altitudes, and that her plane would barely make it across the mountains as it was?"

Daldry paused and looked as his watch.

"I didn't notice the time pass. I'm sorry, Alice—I'm abusing your hospitality again."

He started to get up, but Alice pushed him back into his seat.

"Well, if you insist," he said, happy to have drawn her in. "You wouldn't happen to have any more of that excellent gin you served me the other night, would you?"

"You took the bottle with you."

"Nasty habit. It was the only one?"

Alice climbed onto the bed and took a second bottle of gin from off the roof. She filled Daldry's glass.

"Now, where was I?" he said, taking a considerable swig without grimacing. "Once she got to Mendoza, Adrienne and her mechanic, Duperrier, made their way to Los Tamarindos, where her plane was waiting. It was an inauspicious start: she was due to take off on the first of April and she had forgotten her navigation map. She took off anyway, flying in a northwesterly direction, her plane struggling to gain altitude, and the imposing, snowcapped peaks of the Andes rising up like a wall before her.

"Much later, as she was flying over a narrow valley, she noticed a lake the shape and color of an oyster passing beneath the wings of her plane. She could already feel the frostbite setting into her fingers from inside the improvised gloves she had made of newspapers lined with butter. She was underdressed and frozen to the bone in flight gear unsuited to such a high altitude. Overcome with fear, she kept her eyes glued to the horizon. To the right the valley opened up, and to the left it seemed blocked. She had to make up her mind that very moment. Something inside her pushed her to believe the fortune-teller that had come to her hotel room in Buenos Aires, and she flew into the dark clouds, climbing in altitude and trying to maintain her course. A few minutes later, the sky cleared, and she found herself face-to-face with a break in the mountains, a pass topped by a crucifix planted at over thirteen thousand feet. To make it over the pass, she forced the plane to climb even higher, past its supposed limit, but it accepted the challenge.

"Adrienne had been in the air for over three hours when she saw a river flowing beneath her in the same direction as she was flying. Soon, she saw a plain in the distance and then a large city. It was Santiago de Chile, with its aerodrome and the brass band waiting to welcome her. She had succeeded! With her fingers stiff and her face bloody from the cold, barely able to see beyond her cheeks, which were swollen from the high altitude, she landed her plane without damage and managed to pull it up in front of the three flags that had been planted in the unlikely event of her arrival: French, Argentine, and Chilean. Everybody claimed that it was a miracle. Adrienne and her talented mechanic, Duperrier, had pulled it off."

"Why are you telling me this story, Daldry?"

"My mouth is dry from so much talking!"

She topped up his glass of gin and watched him sip it as though it were water.

"Isn't it obvious? Because you also happened to run into a fortune-teller, one who told you you'd find in Turkey the things you can't find in London, that you would need to meet six people along the way. I think I'm the first of those six people. I feel as though I have a responsibility to join you on your mission. Let me be your Duperrier. Maybe I'm the talented mechanic who can help you cross the Cordillera." Daldry was drunk and emotional. "At least let me take you to the second person who will take you to the third . . . if that's how it works. Let me be your friend. Give me the chance to do something useful for once in my life, now that I have the means to do so."

"That's incredibly kind of you," said Alice, overwhelmed by Daldry's passion. "But I'm not a test pilot, and I'm certainly no Adrienne Bollard."

"Bolland. But you have nightmares like she did, ambition like she did, and you're willing to undertake a voyage that seems crazy from the outset."

"I couldn't possibly."

"But you could at least consider it."

"I couldn't. It's completely beyond my means, and I'd never be able to repay you."

"What do you know? You'd be spiteful not to take me on as your mechanic. Maybe you'll discover new essential oils in Turkey and be inspired to create a revolutionary perfume, an enormous success—I could be your investor, your business partner. Of course, I'll let you decide on the percentage that you'll deign to grant me for having humbly contributed to your glory. And to make things fair, if I happen to paint an intersection in Istanbul that ends up in a museum, I'll also make sure you get a fair share of the value it adds to my paintings in the gallery market."

"You're drunk, Daldry. Nothing you're saying makes any sense, and yet you've almost managed to convince me."

"That's the spirit! Don't stay shut up in your flat dreading the night like a coward. Take on the world! Let's go on this trip to Turkey together. I'll organize everything. We can leave London in a week. I'll let you sleep on it and we'll talk about it again tomorrow."

Daldry got up, took Alice by the arm, and clutched her tightly to him.

"Good night," he said, pulling back with embarrassment as he realized how carried away he'd got.

Alice saw him to the door. Daldry staggered a bit. They waved good night to each other and each of them closed their doors.

5

Alice's bad dreams continued like clockwork, and she woke up exhausted. With a blanket wrapped around her shoulders, she got up to make herself breakfast before settling into the armchair Daldry had occupied the previous evening. She glanced at the brochure with the Hagia Sophia on the cover that he had left behind on the trunk.

When she opened it, she could practically smell the Ottoman roses, orange blossoms, and jasmine. She imagined the mazelike passages of the Grand Bazaar, bargaining in the spice market, and breathing in the delicate odors of saffron, rosemary, and cinnamon. She felt her senses sharpen as she daydreamed before dropping the brochure with a sigh. Her tea suddenly seemed bland in comparison. She got dressed and went to knock on Daldry's door. He answered in his pajamas and dressing gown, stifling a yawn.

"You're more of a morning person, aren't you?" He rubbed his eyes.

"It's seven o'clock."

"As I was saying. Why don't you come back in two hours?" He closed the door.

Alice knocked again.

"What is it now?"

"Ten percent."

"Of what?"

"On my profit, if I find an idea for a new perfume in Turkey."

Daldry stared at her blankly.

"Twenty!" he said, pulling shut the door.

Alice pulled it open again. "Fifteen."

"You drive a hard bargain."

"Take it or leave it."

"What about my paintings?"

"Oh, I don't know. Whatever you like."

"You're being cruel again."

"Well then, the same thing, fifteen percent on the sale of all the paintings you paint in Turkey, or upon your return, if they're inspired by the trip."

"Such business acumen."

"Stop trying to flatter me and go back to bed. Come see me when you're awake and we'll talk seriously. I still haven't said yes. And shave."

"I thought you said my beard was becoming," said Daldry, visibly hurt.

"Well then let it grow, but make up your mind. You look unkempt with all that stubble, and if we're going to be business partners, you have to be presentable."

Daldry rubbed his chin.

"To grow or not to grow?"

"And they say that women can't make up their minds," Alice muttered, and went back to her flat.

Daldry came to see her at noon. He was wearing a suit, his hair was carefully combed, and he smelled of eau de cologne, but he hadn't shaved. Before Alice had a chance to speak, he said he was going to think about the beard until the day of their departure. He suggested they go to the pub to negotiate on neutral territory, but once they were outside, he led her to his car.

"Aren't we going to lunch?"

"Yes, but let's go to a real restaurant."

"Why didn't you say so to begin with?"

"To make it a surprise. Besides, you probably would have quibbled, and I just feel like eating a decent steak."

He opened the door and invited her to take the wheel.

"I don't know if it's a good idea," said Alice. "The last time I drove, the streets were completely empty."

"I promised you a second lesson, didn't I? I always keep my promises. Besides, we might have to do some driving in Turkey, and I don't want to be the only one behind the wheel. Go on. But wait for me to get in before you start the engine."

Daldry walked around the back of the Austin. Alice paid close attention to his instructions, but she braked in the middle of every turn until she was sure there was no oncoming traffic.

"At this rate we're going to be overtaken by the people on the pavement. I invited you to lunch, not dinner."

"You can drive yourself if you want. I'm doing my best."

"By all means, continue doing your best, but also remember to keep accelerating through the corners."

Eventually they arrived, and Daldry told Alice to pull over. A uniformed valet hurried over to the passenger side before confusedly hurrying back to the driver's side when he saw that Alice was behind the wheel.

"Where on earth have you brought me?" asked Alice, uneasy to be the object of so much unexpected and obsequious attention.

"To a restaurant," said Daldry with a touch of exasperation.

Once they were inside, Alice admired the elegant dining room. The walls were decorated with carved wood paneling and the tables were perfectly aligned, covered in fine white linen and set with a greater variety of knives, forks, and spoons than Alice had ever seen in her life. The maître d'hôtel led them to a cozy mirrored alcove and pulled back the table to allow Alice to sit on the banquette, from which she had a commanding view of the room. As soon as he had left, the headwaiter presented them with the menus. Before the sommelier had the time to offer any advice, Daldry immediately ordered a 1929 Château Margaux.

"What's wrong now?" Daldry asked once the sommelier had left. "You look furious."

"That's because I am furious!" hissed Alice under her breath, not wanting to be overheard by their neighbors.

"I don't understand. I take you to one of London's finest restaurants and order wine of the rarest delicacy, a mythical vintage—"

"Look at me! You're in a suit and a perfectly laundered shirt. I look like a schoolgirl waiting to be taken down the street for a bottle of pop. You might have had the courtesy to tell me about your plans, so I could have at least put on some make-up. All the people here must think—"

"That you're a ravishing woman and that I'm lucky you agreed to have lunch with me. What man in his right mind would waste time judging your clothes when your eyes alone could captivate anyone? Please stop worrying, and try to enjoy what we're about to be served."

Alice looked skeptical, but when she tasted the wine she was impressed. It had a silky texture—she had never tasted wine like this.

"You weren't flirting just now, were you, Daldry?"

Her comment caught him off guard, and he choked.

"By offering to accompany you on a search for the man of your life? A curious technique for courting, don't you think? If we're going to be business associates, we ought to be honest with one another. We both know we're not each other's type. That's the very reason I was able to make you this business proposition without the slightest ulterior motive. Well, almost . . ."

"Almost?"

"I asked you to lunch because there's one last detail in the terms of our association I'd like to go over with you."

"I thought we had come to an agreement over the percentages."

"Yes, but there's a final favor I'd like to ask."

"I'm listening."

Daldry refilled Alice's glass and invited her to drink.

"If the fortune-teller's predictions hold true, I'm the first of the six people that will lead you to the man of your future. Like I promised, I'll take you to the second person. Once we've found him, as I'm sure we will, my mission is complete."

"What are you getting at?"

Daldry *tsked*. "You always have to get a word in edgewise, don't you? Once my part of the mission is finished, I'll return to London and leave you to continue on your own. I certainly have no intention of hanging around and being the third wheel when you finally meet him. I do possess a certain amount of tact, after all. But, of course, your journey is financed until it reaches its end, according to the terms of our agreement."

"And I'll pay you back to the last penny, if I have to work until the end of my days to do so."

"I'm not talking about money."

"Then what?" Alice's heartbeat quickened.

"Well . . . While you're gone, however long that may be, I'd like your permission to work under the skylight in your flat. You won't be there or have any use for it, and I promise to keep the place up, which, between you and me, won't do it any harm."

"You wouldn't happen to be taking me thousands of miles from home and abandoning me in a distant land just to paint under my skylight, would you?"

"You may have beautiful eyes, my dear, but they hide a twisted mind."

"Fine, but only once we've met this supposed second person, and only on the condition that they give me good reason to pursue the hunt."

"Naturally!" Daldry lifted his glass. "Let's make a toast to it."

"We'll toast on the train," said Alice. "I'm leaving myself an escape route. This has all been very rushed."

"Speaking of which, I'm going to see to our tickets and accommodation this afternoon." Daldry put down his glass and smiled at Alice. "You look happy," he told her, "and it's most becoming on you."

"It's the wine," she said. "But thank you."

"It wasn't intended as a compliment."

"And that's not why I was thanking you. You're being very generous. I promise that once we're in Istanbul, I'll work day and night to create a perfume that will make you a proud investor. I won't let you down."

"Don't be silly. I'm as happy as you are to leave gray old London for a while. In a few days we'll be under the sun, and when I see myself in the mirror behind you, I realize it will do me some good."

Alice turned and looked in the mirror. Daldry's eyes met hers and she made a face. The idea of traveling such a distance made her head spin, but for once in her life she opened up and let herself enjoy the giddy, drunken happiness without holding back. Still looking at Daldry in the mirror, she asked him how she should break the news of her decision to go on a trip to her friends. He told her the answer was in her question. She just had to tell them she had made up her mind and that she was content in her decision. If they were really her friends, they would understand and support her for having done so.

They both decided to forego dessert. Alice suggested that they take a walk. As they strolled through the fashionable neighborhood around the restaurant, Alice couldn't keep her mind off of Carol, Eddy, Sam, and especially Anton. How would they react? She came up with the idea of inviting them to her house for dinner. Once they were softened up after a few drinks, she would tell them about her plans.

They passed a phone box, and she asked Daldry to wait for her a moment.

After making four calls, Alice felt as though she had taken the first steps on a long journey. She had made up her mind and she knew she wouldn't back out. She joined Daldry, who was waiting for her leaning against a lamppost and smoking a cigarette. She took him by the hand and spun him around in an improvised dance.

"Let's leave as soon as possible. I want to get away from the winter, from London, from my dreary routine. I wish we were leaving today. We'll get lost in the bazaar, smell the spices, cross the Bosporus . . . You can sketch the junction between Europe and Asia; what better crossroads could you hope for? I'm not afraid anymore! I can't tell you how happy it makes me, Daldry."

"Even though I suspect you might be a bit drunk, I'm thrilled to hear it. And I'm not just saying that to butter you up. Let me find you a taxi home and I'll go to the travel agency. You have a passport, don't you?"

Alice's face dropped.

"Don't worry, neither do I. But a close friend of my father's works in the Foreign Office. Where there's a will, there's a way. But we'll have to go get our pictures taken, so I suppose the travel agent can wait. I'll drive this time."

Alice and Daldry drove to a photographer's shop. Alice spent so much time fixing her hair that Daldry had to remind her that the only people who would open her passport and see her picture would be border control officers. They probably wouldn't notice a few stray hairs. Alice finished what she was doing and finally took a seat on the photographer's stool.

Daldry was fascinated by the photographer's new camera. Once the photo was taken, he pulled the card of film from the camera and removed a protective sheet of foil. A few minutes later, four identical images of Alice appeared on the photographic paper. When it was Daldry's turn to take his seat on the stool, he held his breath and smiled like a simpleton.

With their precious photos in hand, they went to the passport office at St James's. Daldry explained the pressing nature of their travels to the bureaucrat behind the counter and spoke of vague but important business interests that hung in the balance. He didn't hesitate to reel off the names of various high-placed officials in the Foreign Office hierarchy. Alice was aghast at what seemed to her to be so much blatant lying. The man behind the counter said he would do what he could, and Daldry thanked him before ushering Alice out the door ahead of him.

"Nothing gets in your way, does it?" she said, once they were in the hall outside.

"You nearly did. If he had looked at your face while I was pleading our cause, I doubt whether he'd have given our papers a second look."

"Well, pardon me for smirking, but I thought it a bit rich to claim that the hobbled English economy would never rise from its knees if we weren't in Istanbul within days."

"That poor paper-pusher's days are probably so dull that he was thrilled to be part of an important mission. We livened up his day."

"Well, you've got a lot of nerve."

"I couldn't agree with you more."

On the way out of the building, Daldry playfully saluted to the guard on duty before opening the door of his Austin for Alice.

Daldry drove Alice home before going to the travel agent. She sat at her worktable and tried to concentrate, but she found it impossible to put any ideas on paper. She was supposed to meet her friends at the pub that evening, and the hours dragged on. She uncorked a vial of rose oil, and her thoughts strayed to imaginary oriental gardens. She could hear the sound of a piano from somewhere in the building, but when she went to the door to better locate its source, the music stopped, and the old Victorian house returned to its usual silence.

Alice entered the pub and her friends were already there, engaged in an animated conversation. Anton saw her come in the door. She smoothed her hair as she came over to them. Eddy and Sam hardly paid her any attention, but Anton rose and offered her a chair before turning back to the topic at hand, a fiery discussion about Attlee's record as prime minister. Eddy wanted Churchill back, but Sam, a staunch Attlee man, predicted the end of the middle class if the old war leader returned to power.

Alice was itching to jump in, but Carol gave her a knowing look and leaned over to ask what had happened while the debate raged on.

"What are you talking about?" asked Alice.

"You," said Carol.

"Nothing that I can think of."

"You're lying. Something has changed. I can see it in your eyes."

"Nonsense."

"I haven't seen you this radiant in a long time," Carol insisted. "Have you met somebody?"

Alice laughed louder than she had meant to, and the men went silent.

"She's right," said Anton, who had obviously been keeping an ear on their conversation. "Something about you has changed."

"You're all being silly. Why doesn't somebody get us something to drink instead of reflecting upon the supposed sparkle in my eye? I'm dying of thirst."

The men went to the bar to get another round for the five of them, and Carol took advantage of the moment to continue her interrogation.

"Go on, you can tell me."

"I haven't met anybody, but if you must know, I might be meeting somebody in the near future."

"I don't follow."

"I decided to listen to the advice of the fortune-teller. The one you made me consult."

Carol became excited and took Alice's hands in hers. "You're really going? You're going to Turkey?"

Alice nodded, before gesturing to indicate that the men were already on their way back. Carol leapt up and ordered them to stay at the bar until she and Alice were done with their conversation.

They went speechless, then docilely obeyed.

"When do you leave?" asked Carol, clearly more excited than even Alice herself.

"I'm not sure yet, but I don't think it will be more than a few weeks from now."

"So soon?"

"Well, we have to wait for our passports, and we just applied for them this afternoon."

"We? You're going with someone else?"

Alice blushed and revealed that she had struck a deal with Daldry.

"Are you sure he isn't doing all of this just to seduce you?"

"Daldry? Good heavens, no. I even asked him as much, quite openly."

"You had the guts?"

"I didn't think about it, it just came up. It's not very clever to court a girl by taking her to meet another man, is it?"

"True. So he's only interested in investing in your perfumes? That's putting a lot of faith in your talent."

"More than you would, it seems. I honestly don't know what motivates him, whether it's the desire to spend his unwanted inheritance, to go on a trip to Turkey, or maybe just the opportunity to paint in my flat while I'm gone. It seems he's been dreaming about it for ages and I promised him he could. He'll be back long before I will, probably."

"You'll be gone for that long?" asked Carol, visibly upset at the idea.

"I don't know."

"Listen, Alice, I don't mean to be a killjoy, particularly since I'm the one who encouraged you to go through with this in the first place, but now that everything is becoming so concrete, I must admit, it seems rather impulsive to travel so far just because a fortune-teller promised you there might be a lover at the end of the journey."

"I'm not that desperate. You know I've been pacing up and down in my little studio like a caged beast. It's been months since I've created something original, or even had a good idea. I feel so stifled and smothered by life in London. I want to go somewhere new, get some fresh air, discover a new landscape with new odors . . ."

"Promise me you'll write."

"Of course. Do you think I'd miss such a great opportunity to make you jealous?"

"Well, you're the one leaving me alone with three men," retorted Carol.

"Who's to say that I won't occupy their minds from a distance? Absence makes the heart grow fonder."

"I've never heard such a ridiculous thing in all my life. When did you say you were leaving?"

Alice brought up her idea to organize a dinner at her flat the following evening in order to break the news to the men, but Carol told her there was no need to go to so much trouble. After all, it wasn't like she was engaged to anybody. She didn't have to ask for permission.

"Permission for what?" asked Anton, taking a seat at the table.

"To consult the secret archives," said Carol, without even knowing where the words had come from.

"Archives?"

Sam and Eddy joined them. With everybody at the table, Alice decided to just go for it and announced she was going to Turkey.

For a moment, nobody said anything. Carol rapped her fingers on the table.

"She didn't tell you she has cancer, she said she is going on a trip. You're allowed to breathe."

"How long have you known about this?" Anton asked Carol.

"She told me just now. I'm sorry I didn't send a telegram."

"Will you be gone long?" Anton asked Alice.

"She doesn't know," said Carol.

"Is it safe to travel so far alone?" asked Sam.

"She's going with her neighbor from across the hall. The grouch that interrupted our party before Christmas," said Carol.

"You're going to Turkey with *him*? Are you seeing each other?" asked Anton.

"Of course not," replied Carol. "They're just associates. It's a business trip. Alice is going to Istanbul to look for inspiration for new perfumes. If you want to contribute toward her travel costs, I'm sure it isn't too late to invest and become a shareholder. If the idea tempts you, gentlemen, please don't hesitate! Who knows, perhaps a few years from now you'll be sitting on the board of Pendelbury and Associates."

"I have a question," said Eddy, who had remained silent up until then. "I know Alice will probably be at the head of an international perfume-and-cosmetics conglomerate before long, but until then, are we allowed to talk to her directly, or is all communication to be channeled through you?"

Alice smiled. "It's really just a business trip. And since you're all my friends, instead of leaving you to come up with a thousand reasons for me to stay, I'd rather just invite you all to my place on Friday for a little goodbye party."

"You're leaving so soon?" asked Anton.

"The date isn't settled yet," said Carol, "but—"

Alice interjected. "We're leaving as soon as we get our passports. I just didn't want to make it a dramatic farewell."

The evening's energy had fizzled out. The men didn't feel much like staying out or celebrating.

They all said goodbye on the pavement outside the pub, and Anton took Alice aside.

"What are you looking for over there that you can't find here?"

"I'll tell you when I come back."

"If you come back."

"I'm taking this trip for myself, for my career. I need this. Don't you understand?"

"No, I don't. But I suppose I'll have time to reflect on it while you're gone. Take care of yourself. And only write to me if you really want to. You're under no obligation."

He turned his back on her and slunk away, head hanging low, hands shoved in his coat pockets.

Back in her flat, Alice didn't turn on the light. She took off her clothes and slipped under the covers naked, looking up at the crescent-shape moon that shone through the skylight. Almost like the one on the Turkish flag, she thought.

On Friday, at the end of the afternoon, Daldry knocked on Alice's door and came into her flat victoriously brandishing their passports.

"Everything's in order. We're ready to go!"

"So soon?" asked Alice.

"With the Turkish visas to boot. Didn't I tell you I knew people in high places? I picked them up this morning before settling our plans at the travel agency. Be ready to leave at eight o'clock on Monday morning."

He put her passport on her worktable and left as suddenly as he had arrived.

Alice flipped through the pages of her first passport and daydreamed for a moment before putting it in her suitcase.

That evening, Alice's friends tried to put on a good show, but their hearts weren't in it. Anton hadn't even showed up, and ever since Alice had told them she was leaving, the energy of the group had changed. It wasn't even midnight when Eddy, Sam, and Carol decided to go home.

They all hugged and said their goodbyes over and over again. Alice promised to write often and to bring back lots of souvenirs from the bazaar. On her way out, a tearful Carol swore she would take care of the men like they were her brothers and would try to talk some reason into the petulant Anton.

Alice stood on the landing as they left and waited until the stairwell went silent. She felt a lump in her throat as she turned back to her empty flat.

6

At eight o'clock on Monday morning, suitcase in hand, Alice took one last look around the flat before closing the door. Her heart raced with excitement as she went down the stairs.

Daldry was already waiting in a taxi.

The driver took her suitcase and put it on the seat next to him. Alice climbed in and settled next to Daldry on the wide back seat. They said hello, and Daldry asked the driver to take them to Harmondsworth.

"Not to the station?" asked Alice.

"No, not to the station," said Daldry enigmatically.

"But why Harmondsworth?"

"Because that's where the aerodrome is. I wanted to surprise you. We're flying. We'll get to Istanbul much faster that way."

"What do you mean, 'We're flying'?" asked Alice in shock.

"Flying. In an aeroplane. I see it's your first time as well. Two hundred miles an hour, twenty-two thousand feet in the air. Isn't it marvelous?"

Their taxi left the city for the surrounding countryside. Alice watched the pastureland roll past and began to wonder if she wouldn't rather travel on solid ground, even if it did mean the trip would take a little longer. Daldry, however, was clearly looking forward to his first ride in a plane.

"We stop to refuel in Paris, then again in Vienna, where we spend the night, and tomorrow evening we'll be in Istanbul, just two days of travel instead of a long week."

"I didn't know we were in such a hurry."

"Don't tell me you're scared to ride in an aeroplane."

"I suppose I don't know yet."

London's new airport was still under construction. Three cement runways were already in service, and a battalion of earthmoving machines was busy at work tracing the outlines for three others. The fledgling airlines had set up shop in tents and corrugated-metal sheds that served as their terminals. The first permanent building was still under construction at the center of the aerodrome. When it was finished, the London airport might finally look more civilian and less military, but for now, the planes of the Royal Air Force and the commercial airlines were lined up next to one another on the tarmac.

Their taxi pulled up to the enclosure. Daldry took the suitcases and pointed Alice toward the Air France tent. They presented their papers at the registration counter, and the ticketing agent welcomed them with polite deference before calling a porter to take their bags. The agent gave Daldry the two tickets they would need to board the plane.

"Your flight should leave on schedule," he said. "And we'll start calling the passengers soon. Won't you please follow the porter to have your passports stamped by the authorities?"

Once their papers were in order, Daldry and Alice waited on a bench and watched the runway.

Every time a plane took off, the tremendous noise interrupted their conversation.

"I think I am a little afraid after all," admitted Alice in the interval between two roars.

"I've been told it isn't as noisy inside the cabin. Believe me, these machines are far more reliable than ordinary motorcars. I'm sure that once we're in the air you'll be perfectly relaxed. Did you know that they even serve us a meal while we're in the air?"

"And we land in France first?"

"Outside Paris, but just for the time it takes to change planes. It's a pity we won't have time to see the city."

An Air France employee came to collect Daldry and Alice. Soon the other passengers joined their group and they were escorted onto the tarmac. Alice saw the immense, gleaming plane looming above her. A long flight of stairs led to a hatch in the rear of the cabin, where a stewardess, wearing a most becoming uniform, welcomed the passengers. Her smile reassured Alice, who imagined how incredible it would be to have her job as she walked down the central aisle of the DC-4's cabin.

The interior was far roomier than Alice had imagined. She took a seat in an armchair as comfortable as the one at home, apart from the seat belt, which the stewardess showed her how to attach if ever there was a problem.

Alice began to worry again. "What sort of problem?" she asked.

"Oh, I don't know," said the stewardess, smiling a convincing and reassuring smile. "We've never had one. There's really no need to worry, madam. Everything is going to be just fine. I take this flight every day, and I'm still not tired of it."

The cabin door closed, and the pilot came to greet each of the passengers before returning to the front of the plane, where his copilot was ticking off items on a checklist. The engines rumbled to life, and a wreath of flames licked the wings as the propellers spun in a deafening racket. Soon the blades were just an invisible blur.

Alice braced herself against the back of her seat and gripped the armrests. The cabin vibrated slightly. The ground crew removed the blocks from the wheels. Alice was seated in the second row and missed nothing of the radio exchanges from the open cockpit. The pilots communicated with the control tower, assisted by a radio mechanic with a heavy French accent.

She turned to Daldry. "I don't understand how the people he's talking to can possibly understand him."

"The important thing is that he's good at what he does. He doesn't have to be an expert in foreign languages. Sit back and enjoy the view. Think of poor Adrienne Bolland. We're flying in much better conditions."

"I should hope so," said Alice, tightening her grip.

The DC-4 aligned with the runway in preparation for takeoff. The sound of the engines got louder, and the cabin vibrated even harder. When the pilot released the brakes, the plane picked up speed.

Alice pressed her face against the window and watched the tents and sheds of the makeshift airport roll past. Suddenly, she was struck by a new sensation. The wheels had lifted off the ground, and the plane rocked slightly as it gained altitude. The runway dwindled from view beneath them before disappearing and giving way to the English countryside. As the plane continued to climb, the farmhouses that appeared in the distance below grew smaller and smaller.

"It's absolutely magical," said Alice. "Do you think that we'll fly through the clouds?"

"Well, I certainly hope they won't stop us," said Daldry, unfolding his newspaper.

Before long, they were flying over the English Channel. Alice was so elated that she tried to count the crests of the waves that rose like tiny, regular folds on the fabric of the vast blue expanse.

The pilot announced that they would soon be able to see the coast of France.

The flight took just under two hours. As the plane approached Paris, Alice could barely contain herself when she made out the Eiffel Tower in the distance.

The layover at Orly Airport was brief. An Air France employee escorted Alice, Daldry, and the other passengers continuing on to

Vienna across the tarmac to a second plane. Alice was so fixated on the next takeoff that she didn't listen to a word Daldry was saying.

The Air France flight from Paris to Vienna was more turbulent. The jolts that lifted them out of their seats amused Alice, but Daldry was a little less at ease. Still, he managed to eat a hearty meal, after which he lit a cigarette and offered one to Alice, who politely refused. She turned back to the fashion magazine in which she was currently absorbed that illustrated the latest collections of the Parisian couturiers. Never in her life had she imagined she would experience something like this, and she swore that she had never been happier. Daldry was glad to hear this, but suggested that she conserve her energy. He had plans for them in Vienna that evening.

Austria was covered in an expanse of white snow that stretched all the way to the horizon. Daldry had fallen asleep after lunch and woke up only when the DC-4 was making its descent into Vienna.

"Please tell me I didn't snore," he said as he woke up.

"The engines nearly covered the noise," said Alice.

The wheels touched down and the plane rolled to a stop in front of a hangar, from which the airport personnel wheeled a flight of stairs for the passengers to disembark.

A taxi had been reserved to take them to the city center. Daldry told the driver they were going to the Sacher Hotel. As they neared the Heldenplatz, the truck in front of them hit a patch of ice, swerved, and flipped over, blocking the street. The taxi driver braked, narrowly avoiding the overturned truck. It was over in the blink of an eye. Passersby hurried to assist the driver, who was pulled out of the cab of the truck uninjured, but the accident had blocked traffic in both directions. Daldry anxiously glanced at his watch. As the minutes ticked past, he started to mutter impatiently under his breath. Alice didn't know what to think.

"We almost got killed, and you're worried about the time?" she asked.

Daldry ignored her and asked the driver to find a way to get them out of what was now a traffic jam. The driver didn't speak English and shrugged, gesturing helplessly at the chaos that surrounded them.

"We're going to be late," Daldry muttered with disgust.

"What on earth for?" asked Alice. It was beginning to dawn on her that Daldry had once again made plans without bothering to inform her.

"You'll see when it's time. That is, if we don't end up prisoners in this taxi for the rest of the night."

Alice opened the door and got out of the taxi without speaking a word.

"Come on, don't pout," he said, leaning his head out of the window.

"You've got quite the nerve, to make plans, complain when they go wrong, and never even bother to tell me what they are. Or even ask if I want to be part of them."

"I can't tell you. That's all there is to it."

"Well, I'll get back in when you feel that you can."

"Alice, stop acting like a child. You're going to catch a cold again. It's certainly not worth making a complicated situation even worse."

"What situation are you talking about?" Alice now stood with her hands planted accusingly on her hips.

"The one we're in. Stuck in traffic when we ought to already be at the hotel getting changed."

"Do we have a ball to attend?"

"Not quite," said Daldry. "But I won't say anything more. Now get in. I have a feeling we might start moving again."

"I have a much better view from out here, and I can assure you that we're going nowhere. We're staying at the Sacher Hotel, is that right?"

"Yes. Why?"

"Because I can see it from where I'm standing. I would say it's a five-minute walk."

Marc Levy

For once, Daldry was at a loss for words. The cab ride had been paid for by the airline, so he took their suitcases from the trunk and hurried down the icy sidewalk toward their hotel. Alice tried to keep up as best she could.

"We're going to break our necks," said Alice, grabbing Daldry by the sleeve. "What in God's name is the hurry?"

"If I told you, it wouldn't be a surprise. Come on, we're almost there."

The doorman greeted them and took their luggage.

Alice admired the heavy crystal chandelier hanging high above the reception area. Daldry had reserved two rooms and received the keys from the man behind the front desk once he had filled in the hotel register. Daldry looked at the clock above the counter and his face dropped.

"There we are. It's too late."

"If you say so," said Alice.

"But maybe they won't notice anything if we keep our coats on."

Daldry led her out of the hotel and they ran across the street. Before them was a magnificent Renaissance Revival opera house, its cornices flanked by two massive equestrian bronzes that reared as though ready to gallop off into the heavens. Men in tuxedos and women in evening gowns were hurrying up the steps. Daldry took Alice by the arm and they joined the elegant crowd.

"Don't tell me that we're going to the opera," Alice whispered in Daldry's ear.

"We are. I had the idea and the travel agency in London took care of getting us the tickets. They ought to be waiting under our names at the counter. A night in Vienna wouldn't be complete without an evening at the opera."

"But not in the dress that I've been wearing since this morning. It's all wrinkled from traveling. I look like a homeless woman compared to everyone else."

"Why do you think I was losing my mind when we were stuck in that taxi? Evening wear is required here. Just follow me and stay

94

buttoned up. We'll take off our coats when the house lights go down. And don't answer back! I'd do anything for Mozart."

Alice was so delighted to be going to the opera for the first time in her life that she heeded Daldry's orders without batting an eye. They wove their way through the crowd of operagoers, trying to avoid the vigilant eyes of the doorman, ushers, and program vendors who roamed the vast lobby. The woman behind the ticket counter adjusted her glasses when Daldry told her his name. She paused before taking a long wooden ruler and sliding it down a list in the register that was open before her.

"Mr. and Mrs. Ethan Daldry, from London," she said with a thick Austrian accent as she handed him their tickets.

A bell began to ring, announcing that the opera would begin soon. Alice would have liked to linger and admire the opulent surroundings, the grand staircase, the chandeliers and gilded decorations, but Daldry didn't let her dawdle. He pulled her along, trying to keep both of them well hidden inside the crowd flowing toward the ticket-takers. When their turn came, Daldry held his breath. The ticket-taker asked them to check their coats in the cloakroom, but Daldry pretended not to understand. Behind them, the other operagoers started to grow impatient, and the ticket-taker rolled his eyes, ripped their tickets, and let them pass. Before entering the hall, the usherette who came to seat them took one look at Alice's coat and told her to check it in. Alice blushed and Daldry pretended to be offended, but the usher had him figured out. She stood her ground and asked him in flawless English to please comply by the rules. The dress code was strict. Evening wear only.

"Since you speak English, miss, perhaps we can come to an agreement. Our plane just landed a short while ago and an unfortunate accident on your city's icy roads made us late. We simply didn't have time to change."

"That's 'madam' to you," corrected the usherette, "and whatever your reasons may be, men must be in black tie, and women must wear a long evening gown."

"What on earth does it matter? We're not the ones on stage."

"I'm sorry, sir, I didn't make the rules, but it is my job to see that they are followed. Now, if you don' t mind, I have other people to seat. Kindly return to the ticket counter and your seats will be reimbursed."

"Come now." Daldry had lost his patience. "Every rule has an exception, and your silly requirements must surely have theirs. We're only here in Vienna for one evening, and I'm simply asking you to look the other way and let us enjoy ourselves."

The usherette fixed Daldry with such a withering gaze.

Alice begged him not to make a scene. "Come on," she said. "It's all right. It was a marvelous idea, a wonderful surprise, but it's just not happening tonight. Let's go and have dinner. We're both exhausted, and we probably wouldn't have been able to stay awake for an entire opera anyway." Daldry shot one last look of disgust at the usherette, ripped up their tickets, and stormed off, leading Alice down the stairs, through the lobby, and out onto the street.

"What a load of rubbish. It's music, not a fashion show."

"It's a question of tradition. We have to respect that," Alice said, trying to reason with him.

"The tradition is a load of rubbish."

Alice tried to calm him down. "You know, when you're angry, I can imagine how you must have looked when you were a little boy. I bet you threw dreadful temper tantrums."

"I was a very peaceful and easygoing child."

"I don't believe you for a minute."

As they began to look for a restaurant, they walked around the opera house and soon found themselves in the street that ran behind it.

"That ridiculous woman made us miss *Don Giovanni*. I'll never forgive her. And after the travel agent went to so much trouble to get us those tickets."

Alice watched a stagehand leave the theater's nondescript stage door. It had not entirely closed behind him.

"How far are you willing to go for your precious Don Giovanni?"

"Didn't I say I would do anything for Mozart?"

"Well, let's go then."

She opened the service door that had been left ajar. They stepped inside and tiptoed down a hallway that was bathed in a faint red glow.

"Where are you taking me?" asked Daldry.

"I haven't the slightest idea," said Alice under her breath. "But I think we're going in the right direction."

They followed the sound of the music until they came to an ironwork staircase that spiraled up to a catwalk suspended in the air high above them.

"What if somebody finds us?" he asked.

"We'll tell them we got lost looking for the toilets. Now stop asking questions and come on."

They climbed the stairs, and as they got higher, the singers' voices seemed to become clearer. When they finally came to the catwalk, they could see that it was suspended from the ceiling by a series of steel cables.

"Isn't this dangerous?" he asked her.

"Probably. We're very high up. But look down there—isn't it incredible?"

They crept out to the middle of the catwalk. Daldry mustered the courage to look down and realized that he was directly over the stage. They could see the top of Don Giovanni's hat. It was impossible to tell what the scenery looked like to the audience, but Alice and Daldry still had exceptional seats at one of the world's finest opera houses.

Alice sat down and leaned over the railing, swinging her feet to the beat of the music. Daldry sat next to her, transfixed by the drama unfolding on the stage below.

They stayed like that until Zerlina's scream of distress stirred Daldry from his state of near hypnosis. He whispered to Alice that the first act would soon be over.

Alice rose to her feet in silence. "It's probably better if we slip out before intermission," she said. "We don't want the stagehands to find us when the lights go up."

It was difficult for Daldry to tear himself away, but they crept back down the stairs as quietly as possible. They crossed paths with an electrician, but he paid them no attention. Soon they were slipping out of the stage door and back onto the street.

"What a night!" shouted Daldry ecstatically once they were out in the cool night air. "I'd love to go back and tell that bitch of an usherette how great the first act was."

"Listen to you!"

Daldry ignored Alice's disapproval and announced he was hungry. Their little escapade had sharpened his appetite. He eyed a tavern across the street before looking at Alice and realizing she was worn out.

"How does a quick dinner back at the hotel sound?"

He didn't have to ask twice.

When they finished their meal, they agreed to meet in the lobby at nine the following morning, said good night, and retired to their rooms, which were across the corridor from each other. It was as though they were back home in London.

Alice sat at the little desk, found some stationery, and started a letter to Carol. She described the day's events and wrote about the feeling of leaving England behind, ending with the night at the opera. She finished, read the letter to herself, then folded it in half and threw it in the wastepaper basket.

Alice and Daldry met the following morning and took a taxi back to the airport, which was visible in the distance long before they arrived.

"I can already see our plane," said Daldry. "The forecast is good, so we ought to leave on time."

He tried to make small talk to fill the silence that had reigned since they left the hotel.

Alice didn't say a word for the rest of the trip. As soon as the plane took off, her eyelids drooped and she dozed off. A patch of turbulence jostled her head onto Daldry's shoulder, and he froze, not knowing how to react. When the stewardess passed, he turned down his meal tray so as not to wake Alice. Deep in sleep, she gradually relaxed, slumping across Daldry with one of her hands on his chest. She seemed to call out to somebody in her sleep, but nothing she said was intelligible. Her body pressed up against his. Daldry coughed nervously, but nothing woke her. About an hour before they were scheduled to land, she opened her eyes and Daldry immediately closed his, pretending to have dozed off as well. She was mortified to realize that she had more or less been sleeping in Daldry's arms and prayed he wouldn't wake up, righting herself as delicately as she could.

As soon as she was sitting up, Daldry simulated a yawn and shook his left arm. It had fallen asleep under Alice's weight. He asked for the time.

"I think we're arriving soon."

"It feels like we just left," lied Daldry as he tried to massage some life back into his left hand.

"Oh, look," cried Alice, her face glued to the window. "So much water."

"I suppose it must be the Black Sea, although from here I can only see your hair."

Alice leaned back to share the view.

They soon landed. As she stepped out of the plane, Alice thought of her friends back in London. She had only been gone for two days, yet it felt like weeks. She realized how far away she was from her flat and felt a pinch in her heart as she came to the bottom of the stairs and set foot on Turkish soil.

Daldry collected their bags. At passport control, the Turkish official asked them about the reason for their visit. Daldry told the officer they were in Istanbul to find Alice's future husband.

"Your fiancé is Turkish?" he asked, taking a second glance at Alice's passport.

"To tell the truth, we're not entirely sure yet," Alice admitted. "He may be, but the only thing we're relatively certain of is that he lives in Turkey."

The officer looked suspicious.

"You come to Turkey to marry a man you don't know?" he asked Alice directly. Before she could reply, Daldry confirmed that this was indeed the case.

"You don't have good husbands in England?"

"Yes, probably," said Daldry. "But none that are good enough for Miss Pendelbury."

"And you, sir? Have you also come to find a wife in our country?"

"Heavens, no. I'm just her chaperone."

"Please wait here." Daldry's explanation had perplexed the officer, who went to a glassed-in office behind his counter to discuss the situation with his supervisor.

"Did you really have to tell that ridiculous story?" hissed Alice under her breath.

"What do you expect me to say? That's the reason for our trip, isn't it? I hate lying to the authorities."

"It didn't bother you when we needed our passports."

"Well, at home, yes, but here we're in foreign territory. I'm expected to behave like a gentleman."

"Your joking around is going to get us in trouble. I can just feel it."

"Don't be silly. It always pays to tell the truth. You'll see."

From where they stood, they could see the supervisor shrug and hand their passports back to the officer, who came back to see them.

"Everything is in order," he said. "Have a pleasant stay in Turkey, and all our best wishes for your happy marriage. May God see that you marry an honest man."

Alice forced a polite smile and put her freshly stamped passport back in her bag.

"I hate to be the one to say, 'I told you so,' but . . ." Daldry said as they walked out of the airport.

"I still say you could have just told him that we were on holiday."

"I don't think they would have liked that. We have different surnames on our passports."

"You're impossible, Daldry," said Alice as she climbed into yet another taxi.

"What do you think he looks like?" Daldry asked as he got in next to her.

"Who?"

"The mysterious man we've come all this way to meet."

"Don't be ridiculous. I came here to make a new perfume."

"And now you're in a bad mood."

"I'm in a perfectly good mood, I just don't appreciate being passed off as some sort of mail-order bride."

"Well, at least my story distracted him from your monstrous passport photo."

Alice jabbed him with her elbow and turned away to look out of the window.

"And you say I'm a grump," he teased. "You must have been a pretty difficult child yourself."

"Perhaps, but at least I have the good manners to admit as much."

The journey through the sprawling outskirts of Istanbul distracted them from their banter. As they neared the Golden Horn, they gazed down the narrow streets, where the wooden houses rose in colorful, staggered levels. Streetcars and taxis did battle in the main avenue, and the city teemed with activity.

"It's strange," said Alice, "but even though we're far from London, this all somehow feels very familiar."

"It's probably just my company."

Their cabdriver pulled up to the curb on a broad avenue. They were in front of the Pera Palas Hotel, a grand, Western-style stone edifice that dominated Meşrutiyet Street in the Tepebaşi neighborhood. They were in the heart of the European quarter. Six domes lined with glass tiles formed the ceiling of the grand lobby. The hotel's decor was an eclectic mix of English wood paneling and Byzantine mosaics.

"Agatha Christie was a frequent guest here," Daldry told Alice.

"First the Sacher and now this? We could have stayed in a small family-run hotel, you know."

"The exchange rate is in our favor," retorted Daldry. "And I'm afraid if I'm going to waste my inheritance in a reasonable amount of time, it means I have to take drastic measures."

"I stand corrected," said Alice. "I think that your temper has probably only got worse with age."

"Revenge is a dish best served cold, and believe me, I intend to present my childhood with a heaping platter of it. But enough about me, let's go and get changed. Shall we meet in the bar in an hour?"

About an hour later, Daldry wandered into the hotel bar and met a Turkish guide named Can, who was sitting alone on one of the four barstools, his gaze idly wandering over the empty room. He looked to be about thirty, perhaps a year or two older. He was well dressed in a pair of dark trousers and a white silk shirt worn under a waistcoat and an elegantly cut jacket. His eyes were a sandy-gold color that glinted from behind the round lenses of his wire-framed glasses.

Daldry took a seat on the stool next to him and ordered a raki. Can smiled at him and asked in surprisingly good English if he'd had a pleasant journey.

"Yes, it was quick and comfortable, thank you."

"Welcome to Istanbul."

"How did you know that I was English and that I had just arrived?"

"Because you dress like an Englishman and because you weren't here yesterday," said Can.

"It's a beautiful hotel."

"I don't live here. My home is on Beyoğlu hill. But I often come here in the evening."

"For business or for pleasure?" asked Daldry.

"How about you? What brings you to Istanbul?"

"I'm not quite sure yet. It's a long story. Let's say I'm here for research."

"I'm sure you will find whatever you are seeking. Our city has many richnesses: leather, rubber, cotton, wool, silk, oils, fisheries. Perhaps if you tell me what you are seeking, I can touch you with the local merchants."

Daldry did his best to keep a straight face.

"Oh, that's not why I'm here. I don't know the first thing about running a business. I'm a painter."

"You are an artist?" asked Can, clearly excited by the idea.

"I don't know if I'd go that far. Let's just say I can use a paintbrush."

"What do you paint?"

"Oh, crossroads, mostly." Can looked perplexed, so Daldry explained himself further. "Intersections, if you prefer."

"No, I don't prefer. But I can show you our amazing crossroads in Istanbul, if it pleases you. I know crossroads for people, carts, trams, automobiles, *dolmu* . . . Whatever you are seeking."

"Yes, well, why not? But I'm not really here for that either."

"Well then?"

"Well then, like I said, it's a long story. What about you? What do you do for a living?"

"I am a guide and translator. The best in Istanbul. When I turn my back, the bartender will say no, but this is because he makes a little business saying that. He is getting baksheesh from the other guides. With me, no bribe. I have a standard. In Istanbul it is impossible if you are a tourist or in business affairs with no guide. And, like I tell you, I am—"

"The best in Istanbul. I haven't forgotten."

"Yes, my repetition precedes me," said Can, brimming with pride.

"Well, I may be in need of your services."

"You should choose carefully. Finding a good guide is very important in Istanbul. I don't want you regretting this. I have only satisfied customers."

"Why would I choose somebody else?"

"Because later this bartender will be saying very bad things on my back, and maybe you will want to believe in him. But you have not told me what you are researching."

Daldry saw Alice come out of the lift and walk across the lobby toward the bar.

"We'll talk about it tomorrow," said Daldry as he stood. "You're right. I need to think carefully about this. Meet me here tomorrow at breakfast. Let's say eight o'clock. No—eight's a little early with the time change. Let's say nine. And if you don't mind, let's meet somewhere else. Perhaps in a café."

Can noticed that Daldry spoke with increasing speed as Alice approached, and he smiled knowingly. "I have had many foreign clients in my past. There is a tearoom, very nice, very pleasurable, Rue Istiklal, number 461. Tell the taxi driver 'Markiz.' It is a big classic. Everybody knows it. I will wait for you there."

"Perfect. I'm sorry but I have to leave now. See you tomorrow." He hurried over to meet Alice as she came into the bar.

Can stayed planted on the barstool and watched Daldry take Alice into the hotel dining room.

"I thought you might prefer to eat here this evening. You seemed a bit worn out after our trip," said Daldry as they took their seats.

"Oh, not really," said Alice. "I slept on the plane, and it's only two hours later here than in London. I just can't believe it's already dark outside."

"The sudden change in time is one of the exhausting things about traveling in aeroplanes, I've been told. I understand if you feel like sleeping in tomorrow morning."

"That's kind of you, but the evening hasn't even begun. I probably won't need to."

The headwaiter brought them the menu. It featured woodcock and local seafood from the Bosporus. Alice didn't like game and decided upon a fish called a lüfer, but Daldry insisted that they try the local langoustines, which he had heard were exceptional. The waiter enthusiastically agreed.

"To whom were you speaking just now?"

"The waiter?" asked Daldry, reading the wine menu with unusual concentration.

"No, I meant the man at the bar. When I came down, the two of you seemed to be having a conversation."

"Him? Some tourist guide who drums up clientele by hanging around here. He told me he was the best in Istanbul, but his English is rather odd."

"Do we even need a guide?"

"It might be useful for the first few days. It could save us some hassles down the line. A good guide would know where to find the plants or essential oils you're looking for and might be able to take us to lesser-known areas in the countryside as well."

"You haven't hired him already, have you?"

"We hardly spoke to one another . . ."

"Daldry, the lift is made of glass, I could see the two of you before I'd even arrived on the ground floor."

"He was trying to convince me to hire him and I was listening to his pitch. But if you don't like him I can always ask the concierge to find us somebody else."

"I just don't want to waste your money on something we don't need. I'm sure that if we go about things systematically we'll be fine on our own. We should just try to find a *Baedeker's*. We may get lost from time to time, but at least we won't be forced to make conversation with a perfect stranger."

The langoustines were everything the waiter had promised they would be. Daldry was now toying with the idea of ordering a second dessert.

"Carol would be green with envy if she saw me in this gorgeous dining room," said Alice as she sipped her first Turkish coffee. "To a certain extent, it's thanks to her that I've come all this way. She was the one who insisted that I talk to that fortune-teller."

"To Carol, then," said Daldry, improvising a toast.

"To Carol."

They clinked glasses.

"And to your mystery man," said Daldry, lifting his glass a second time.

"To the perfume that will make you a rich man," countered Alice, taking a second sip of her wine.

Daldry glanced at the couple seated at the table next to theirs. The woman wore a stunning black evening gown. Daldry thought she looked a bit like Alice.

"Who knows, maybe you have some distant relatives in the region."

"What on earth are you talking about?"

"Weren't we talking about the fortune-teller? She told you that your family was from Turkey, didn't she?"

"Would you drop that? That part of her story made no sense. My parents were both English and my grandparents were as well."

"Sometimes there are a few forgotten branches on the old family tree. Most of my family is from Kent, but I have a Greek uncle and a distant cousin from Venice."

"Well, there's nothing more plain and British than my family. Apart from Aunt Daisy, who lives on the exotic Isle of Wight."

"To be fair, you did say that Istanbul felt familiar to you when we arrived earlier today."

"It was my subconscious taking over. Ever since we first started talking about this trip, I've been poring over the brochure and imagining what Istanbul would be like."

"I looked at the brochure a fair amount myself and I can't say that the photographs of the Hagia Sophia and the Bosporus reminded me much of the neighborhoods we were driving through on our way from the airport."

"Oh, please. Do you really think I look like a Turk?" asked Alice, trying not to laugh.

"Well, you are rather dark for an Englishwoman."

"You just say that because you're as pale as they come. You're positively anemic."

"That's a nice way to talk to a hypochondriac. Keep it up and I'll pass out right here in the restaurant."

"Come on. Let's go for a walk. A constitutional would do us some good. You ate like a pig."

"What are you talking about? I ordered the lightest dessert on the menu."

They walked for several minutes down the broad avenue that ran past their hotel. It was completely dark, apart from the streetlamps casting their feeble glow on the paving stones and the solitary cyclopean beams of the streetcars raking through the blackness.

"Tomorrow I'll go to the British Consulate to see about getting us an appointment."

"What on earth for?"

"To find out if you have family in Turkey, or whether your parents ever came here."

"I imagine my mother would have told me about a trip to Turkey. In fact, she always complained about having traveled so little. She said she would have liked to visit foreign countries, and I think she really meant it. She never got any farther than the South of France. She and my father went there on a romantic getaway before I was born, and she always talked about walking along the Mediterranean as though it were the most incredible experience of her life."

"That doesn't help much."

"Daldry, I can assure you that the whole Turkish-family story is a dead end. I'm sure I would have been told about even the most distant Turkish relatives, if I had any."

They had wandered down a side street that was even more dimly lit than the main avenue. Alice looked up at one of the old wooden houses. The fragile framework of the second floor jutted out over the street and looked as though it might come crashing down at any moment.

"What a pity these old Ottoman houses aren't better kept up," said Daldry. "This street must have been superb a hundred years ago, and now it's all falling apart. They're like ghosts of their former selves."

Through the shadows, Daldry could make out the anguish that crept across Alice's face as she looked up at the charred remains of a house that had been gutted in a fire.

"Is something the matter? You look as though you've just had a vision of the Blessed Virgin."

"I've already seen this house. I know this place," said Alice. Her voice was hushed.

"Are you sure?"

"Maybe it wasn't here exactly, but I dreamt about a house very much like it. In my nightmares . . . They always finished with me in a little street that ended with a flight of steps leading down to the city."

"I'd be happy to go farther to see if there aren't some stairs, but I think we'd better wait until tomorrow. I can barely see my hand in front of my face, and I have no idea whether it's safe to be wandering around in this alley in the middle of the night."

"There was always the sound of footsteps," Alice continued, still remembering her dreams. "People chasing us."

"Us? Who were you with?"

"I don't know. I only remember holding hands. But whoever it was pulled me along." She shuddered thinking of it. "Yes, let's get out of here. I don't like this place."

Daldry took Alice by the arm and led her to the nearest avenue. He hailed a passing tram and helped Alice to climb aboard. They sat on an empty bench, and Alice snapped out of her haunting vision. The other passengers talked amongst themselves. A dignified old man in a dark suit read his newspaper, and three young men at the back sang together. The conductor put the tram back into gear and they rolled forward. During the ride, Alice said nothing, only stared at the conductor's back through the violet-tinted pane of glass that separated his compartment from the passengers. Soon the Pera Palas came into view. Daldry placed his hand on Alice's shoulder and inadvertently startled her.

"This is our stop."

Alice followed Daldry across the avenue and into the hotel. He accompanied her back to her room. She thanked him for dinner and apologized for her behavior. She couldn't explain what had come over her.

"It can't be very pleasant to have the sensation of reentering a nightmare, especially when you know you're awake," said Daldry, trying to be understanding. "I know you feel strongly about it, but I'm going to try to set up an appointment at the consulate tomorrow."

He wished her good night and disappeared into his room.

◆ ◆ ◆

Alice sat on the edge of her bed and let her body fall backward. She looked at the ceiling for a long while and then sat up and walked over to the window. A few people were still outside, hurrying to return home for the night, and they seemed to pull the darkness in their wake. The evening mist had given way to a cold rain, and the paving stones of Istiklal glistened in the night. Alice pulled the curtains and sat at the desk, where she began writing a letter.

Dear Anton,
Yesterday evening I wrote to Carol from Vienna, but I was thinking about you. I threw the letter away when I was done. I doubt I'll mail this one either, but I still feel the need to talk to you.

Here I am in Istanbul, in a luxurious hotel. It's the sort of place that you and I have only dreamed about. You'd love this little mahogany writing desk. Remember when we were kids and we used to fantasize about the exotic strangers staying at the Savoy?

I ought to be overjoyed to be here, but I already miss London, and I miss you as well. As long as I can remember, you have been my best friend, even though I know we've both had moments of uncertainty about the nature of our friendship.

Oh, Anton . . . I don't know what I'm doing here, and I don't really know why I left home. When we took the second plane in Vienna, I hesitated a moment, because I knew it was taking me even farther away from my regular life.

But ever since we arrived, I've felt tense—the strange, unshakable feeling that I've been here before, that I know the streets and recognize the sounds of the city, even certain smells, like that of the tram I rode in this evening. If only you were here, I could try to explain myself better, and I'm sure that just talking to you would make me feel better. But you're far away, and something inside of me is glad of it. Carol has you all to herself now. She's crazy about you, and you don't even notice. Open your eyes! She's a wonderful person, and even though I'm sure the sight of the two of you together would drive me crazy with jealousy . . . Well, I know what you're thinking, that I have everything mixed up and I don't know what I want. That's just how I am.

I miss my parents. It's so lonely not having them anymore, and I haven't managed to patch over the hole that they left behind when they died. I'll write to you again tomorrow, or maybe at the end of the week. I'll tell you about my day, and maybe I'll even end up sending the letters. Maybe you'll write back to me.

Thinking of you, from a room whose windows overlook the Bosporus (which I'll finally see in the daylight tomorrow).

Take care,
Alice

Alice folded up the letter and put it in the drawer of the writing desk. Then she turned out the light, undressed, and slipped between the sheets.

A steady hand lifted her from the ground. She could make out the faint odor of jasmine in the skirt into which she pressed her face. She was unable to hold back the tears that flowed down her cheeks. She wanted to stifle her sobs, but she was too afraid to take control of them.

A streetcar's headlight sprang from the darkness, and she was pulled into the protective shadow of a stable door. She watched the streetcar roll toward another neighborhood. The screech of its wheels faded into the night and silence returned.

"We can't stay here," the voice told her.

She hurried, stumbling over the uneven cobblestones. At one point she tripped, but the hand leading her onward pulled her to her feet.

"Run, Alice. Come on, be brave. Don't turn back."

She wanted to stop and catch her breath. In the distance she could see a crowd of men and women being led away.

"Not that way. We have to find another route."

Exhausted, they turned back, retracing their footsteps. The street ended at an immense stretch of water. The moonlight glittered on its agitated surface.

"Don't get too close, you might fall in. We're almost there. A little farther and we can rest."

Alice ran along the water's edge. The horizon grew dark and a heavy rain began pelting down.

Alice woke up with a guttural shout, the sound of a little girl racked with unspeakable terror. She sat up in panic and groped for the light switch. It was a long time before her heart stopped racing. She slipped on her dressing gown and parted the curtains to look outside. A storm was raging, soaking the roofs of Istanbul in a heavy downpour. The last streetcar of the evening rattled down Tepebaşi Avenue. She closed the curtains. Her mind was made up. Tomorrow she would tell Daldry that she wanted to go back to London.

7

Daldry quietly closed the door and headed down the corridor, tiptoe-ing past Alice's room as he went. He took the elevator to the lobby, put on his coat, and asked the porter to hail a taxi. The guide was right. Daldry had only to utter the word "Markiz" and the driver knew where he wanted to go. Traffic was dense, but it wasn't far, and the trip took ten minutes. Can was waiting at a table inside, reading the previous day's newspaper.

"I thought you were standing me up," he said, standing to shake Daldry's hand. "Are you hungry?"

"I'm famished. I left the hotel without eating breakfast."

Can ordered, and the waiter brought Daldry a number of saucer-sized plates full of cucumber slices, hard-boiled eggs seasoned with paprika, olives, kaşar, feta cheese, and chopped green pepper.

"Would it be possible to get a cup of tea and some toast?" asked Daldry as he warily eyed the Turkish breakfast that now covered most of the table.

"May I conclude this means we're engaged?"

"Can, there's something I'd like to ask you—please don't take it the wrong way. I assume your knowledge of Istanbul is less . . . irregular than your mastery of the English language?"

"I'm the best for both. Why?"

Daldry sighed. "Fine. Let's see if we can come to an agreement."

Can took a pack of cigarettes from his jacket pocket and offered one to Daldry.

"Never on an empty stomach," he said.

"What are you looking for, with exactitude, here in Istanbul?" asked Can, striking a match.

"A husband."

Can had to stifle a cough before taking his first drag.

"Not for me, idiot, for a woman. We've made a deal."

"What kind of deal?"

"It's a sort of property venture."

Can's eyes lit up.

"If you want to buy a house or an apartment, I can coordinate you very easily. Tell me your budget, and I can present you grand and interesting offers. It is a good idea to invest yourself here. The Turkish economy is going through a difficulty, but Istanbul will soon be back to its former grandness. This is an exceptional city, magnanimous. Its cartographic situation is one of a kind, and the population has talents in all specialties."

"You're very kind, but the property I want is back in London. I'm looking to buy my neighbor's flat."

"Then why are you not running this affair in England? This seems like a better idea for buying an English apartment."

"In this case, no. Otherwise I wouldn't have come all this way. The flat I want is currently occupied by a woman who will probably continue living in it, unless something in her life changes . . ."

Daldry told Can about how he and Alice had come to Istanbul. Can listened attentively, interrupting only to ask Daldry to repeat the fortune-teller's predictions.

"It seemed to me the best opportunity to put some distance between her and her flat. Now we have to find a way to keep her here."

"You don't believe in fortune-telling?" asked Can.

"I'm too educated to give such things any credence," said Daldry. "To be honest, I don't think I've ever even asked myself the question. But at a pinch, why not? I like the idea of giving destiny a nudge in the right direction."

"You are making much ado about nothing. Excuse me for saying this, but you only have to offer an astronomically correct bribe and the young lady will not refuse to leave. Everything has a price. I know this."

"I know it's hard to believe, but money isn't very important to her. She's not a particularly covetous person. Neither am I, to be quite honest."

"You are not trying to make a profit with this apartment?"

"Not at all. This isn't a question of money. Like I told you, I'm a painter. The flat she lives in has a magnificent skylight and the light is incomparable. I want to turn it into my studio."

"There are no other apartments like this in a big city like London? I know many here in Istanbul. There are even some overlooking an intersection on the street."

"Well, it's the only flat like it in the house that I currently live in. My house, my street, my neighborhood, you understand? I don't want to move."

"I don't understand. You are making business in London. Why do you come all the way to Istanbul to engage me?"

"So that you find me an honest, intelligent single man capable of seducing the woman I've told you about. If she falls in love, she may very well stay here and, according to our agreement, as long as she's here, I can use her flat as my studio. You see? It's not so complicated, really. I just want to keep her over here."

"By which you mean to say it is very complicated."

"Do you think it would be possible to get a cup of tea, some toast, and some scrambled eggs, or do I have to fly back to London for a proper breakfast?"

Can got up and talked to the waiter.

"This is the last free service I am favoring you. Your victim is the woman who was in your entourage when you left the bar last night?"

"Already blowing things out of proportion! She's hardly my victim. I'm doing her a great service."

"By manipulating her life and sending her into the harm of a man you pay me that I must find? If that is your estimate of honesty, I will be constrained to raise my price and ask for a payment in the front. There will be costs to find such a rare pearl."

"What kind of costs?"

"Costs. Tell me, what is attracting this woman?"

"Good question. If you mean to ask what sort of man she prefers, I'm afraid I still don't know. I suppose I could try to find out. In the meantime, so as not to waste any time, just concentrate on finding somebody who seems to be the complete opposite of myself. But let's get down to brass tacks and talk about what you need from me."

"I am not needing brass tacks."

"I was talking about your pay."

Can sized Daldry up and took a pencil from his jacket pocket. He ripped a corner from the paper tablecloth, scribbled a figure on it, and slid it across the table to Daldry. He glanced at it and pushed it back to Can.

"You're dreaming."

"What you ask is bigger than normal services."

"Let's not exaggerate."

"You say money is no matter for you, but you deal like a carpet seller."

Daldry picked up the scrap of paper and considered it a second time. Muttering under his breath, he slipped it back in his pocket and extended his hand to Can.

"Fine. But I'll only pay your fees if you get results."

"Deal is deal," said Can, shaking Daldry's hand. "I will find you a very nice man. But we have to wait for the right time. If I am understanding you, we must make other meetings before the prediction is granted."

The waiter brought Daldry his long-awaited breakfast.

"This is more like it," he said, greedily eying the scrambled eggs. "You're hired. I'll introduce you to the young lady in question as our guide and interpreter later today."

"That is the title of my person," said Can with a broad smile. He got up to leave and said goodbye. On his way out, he turned around and came back to the table, where Daldry was wolfing down breakfast.

"Maybe you are paying me for nothing. Maybe the woman does have strong fortune-telling powers and you are making a mistake in contesting them."

"What makes you say that?"

"Because I am a man who practices honesty. Maybe I am just number two of the six people the woman talked about. Maybe destiny decided our paths to cross."

Can turned and left. Daldry watched him cross the street and board a tram. He thought about what Can had said before pushing away his plate and paying the bill.

Daldry decided to return to the hotel on foot. When he arrived, Alice was waiting for him in the bar, reading a magazine.

"Where have you been?" she asked when she looked up and saw him. "I called your room and you didn't pick up. The man at the front desk finally told me you had gone out. You might have left me a note. I was beginning to worry."

"That's touching—I just went for a walk. I felt like getting some fresh air and I didn't want to wake you."

"I hardly slept at all last night. Go on and order something. I want to talk to you."

"Perfect. I'm thirsty and I also have something I want to tell you."

"You first," said Alice.

"No. You first. Oh, very well; me first. I thought about what you said last night, and I decided to go ahead and hire the guide, as you suggested."

"I suggested the exact opposite," said Alice.

"That's strange, I must have misunderstood. Well, it doesn't matter now. The main thing is that we'll save a lot of time with his help. There isn't much point in going out into the countryside to search for flowers now because it isn't the right season. But a guide could take you to meet the best perfume makers in the city. Perhaps discovering the work of others will help inspire you."

Alice suddenly felt indebted to Daldry for having gone to so much trouble on her behalf.

"Well, since you put it that way, yes, I suppose hiring a guide is a good idea."

"I'm thrilled to hear you say so. I'll ask the concierge to set up an appointment with him for early this afternoon. And you? You wanted to tell me something?"

"Oh, nothing important, now that I think about it," said Alice.

"Is it your bed? My mattress is much too soft. It makes me feel like I'm sinking into a slab of warm butter. We can ask to change rooms."

"No, the bed is fine."

"The nightmares again?"

Alice decided to lie. "No, it's not that either, luckily. I think it's just the disorientation of being in a foreign country. I'm sure I'll get used to it soon."

"You ought to try to get some rest if you didn't sleep. If all goes well, we'll begin our search this afternoon, and you'll need your energy."

Alice had another idea in mind. She asked Daldry if, in the time before their guide came to the hotel, they might return to the street into which they had wandered the previous night.

"I don't know if we'll be able to find it, but we can always try."

Alice, however, remembered the route perfectly. Once they had left the hotel, she led the way without a moment's hesitation.

"Here we are," she said, pointing at the imposing konak that marked the end of the side street. Its second floor jutted out precariously overhead.

Something about the place spurred Daldry to tell Alice a story. "When I was a child," he said, "I used to look up at houses and dream about what was going on behind their walls. I don't know why, but the lives of other people fascinated me much more back then. I used to wonder if they were like mine, and I would try to imagine what the other children my age did every day, playing and living in the houses that were the center of their lives. If I looked up at the same houses at night, I'd see the windows lit from inside and imagine dinners, parties . . . I can't help but wonder why this old house is in such a sorry state today. I wonder who lived here and why they deserted it."

"I did the same thing when I was young," said Alice. "There was a couple in the building across the street from where we lived that I used to watch from my bedroom window. The husband always got home around six in the evening, when I was supposed to be doing my homework. He would walk into the living room, take off his coat and hat, and collapse into an armchair. His wife would bring him a drink and take his coat and his hat. He would open his newspaper, and usually he was still reading it when I was called for supper. When I returned to my room after dinner, the curtains across the street were always drawn. I remember hating the man for taking the drink from his wife without saying anything.

"One day, when I was walking in the street with my mother, I saw him walking toward us. The closer he got, the harder my heart pounded. He even slowed down and greeted us as he passed. He smiled at me, and I was sure he was thinking, 'So you're the cheeky little girl that spies on me from her bedroom window every evening. Don't think

I'm not onto you!' I was sure he was about to say something in front of my mother, so I pretended not to see him and pulled my mother's hand to hurry her along. She lectured me for being impolite. I asked her if she knew the man, and she pointed out that he ran the grocer's shop on the corner, a shop I walked past every day. The girl behind the counter was his daughter, said my mother, and she had taken care of him ever since his wife had died. You can imagine how confusing it was. And I thought I was the queen of the spies!"

"Imagination and reality are often incompatible," observed Daldry as they continued down the narrow street. "For a long time, I was convinced that the parlor maid that worked for our family had a soft spot for me. You can imagine my surprise when I found out she was in love with my older sister. My sister wrote poems to her. They were madly in love, it turns out, and they managed to hide it for a long time. The maid only pretended to dote on me to distract my mother from the truth."

"Your sister loves other women?"

"Yes, and although most people aren't comfortable with the idea, I long ago decided that it was better than loving nobody at all. But enough storytelling. Shall we see if we can find your steps?"

Alice led the way. The old wooden houses loomed threateningly, like sentinels guarding against intruders. They reached the end of the street, but found no flight of steps. Alice said that none of it reminded her of her nightmare anymore.

"I'm sorry. This was a waste of time."

"Not at all. This little stroll has put me in a good mood and worked up my appetite. I noticed a little café along the way that seemed much more authentic than the hotel dining room. You don't have anything against branching out and eating in more local sorts of places, do you?"

"Quite the contrary." Alice took Daldry's arm and they turned back.

The café was thronged with customers, and a thick haze of cigarette smoke made it almost impossible to see the back of the room. Daldry and Alice wove through the crowd of regulars, and he managed to find them a little table. Over the course of their meal they told each other more stories about their childhoods. Daldry had grown up the middle child between his brother and sister, and his family had always been well-off, whereas Alice was an only child and came from a more modest background. Both of them remembered their childhood as a lonely time, but they saw their past solitude as having nothing to do with the love they had received, and more to do with their natural state of mind. They both loved rainy days but hated the winter. They had both daydreamed in school, met their first loves in summertime, and suffered their first heartbreaks at the beginning of autumn. Daldry had always more or less hated his father, whereas Alice had idolized hers. Now, in January 1951, Alice encouraged Daldry to try his first Turkish coffee, and Daldry was inspecting the bottom of his cup.

"It's a custom here to read the future in coffee grounds. I wonder what yours would tell us," he said.

"We could consult an expert and see if their predictions correspond with those of the woman in Brighton." Alice was in a pensive mood.

Daldry glanced at his watch. "Perhaps another time. We had better get back to the hotel if we don't want to be late for our meeting with the guide."

Can was waiting for them in the lobby when they arrived. Daldry made the introductions.

"You are, madam, even more admirable from near than from afar," said Can, bowing deeply and blushing as he kissed her hand.

"I suppose that's better than the contrary," she said.

"It certainly is," said Daldry. He was visibly irritated by Can's directness.

"Excuse me, please, madam," said Can. "I did not mean to annoy you. It is just that you are, inevitably, more ravishing in the daylight."

"We get the idea," said Daldry.

"Of course, Your Excellency." Can stumbled over his words.

Alice interjected, doing her best to smooth things over. "Daldry tells me that you're the best guide in Istanbul."

"That is exactly true," said Can. "And I am at your entire disposition."

"And also the best interpreter?"

"Also," said Can, his face flushing scarlet for the second time.

Alice couldn't help but giggle.

"Well, I can tell we won't be bored in your company. You seem very nice. Let's take a seat in the bar and we'll tell you about what brings us to Istanbul."

After listening to Alice tell him about her plans, Can told her how he could help. "I can take you to meet the perfume makers of Istanbul. They are not many, but they are perfectly excellent in their domain. If you stay in Istanbul until the beginning of spring, I can also take you to the countryside, where we have extraordinarily splendid rosebushes. The hill country welcomes fig trees, lindens, jasmine . . ."

"I doubt we'll stay that long," said Alice.

"Don't say that. Who knows what the future will give you?" said Can.

Daldry gave him a discreet kick in the shin under the table, and Can turned and glared at him. "I need the afternoon to prepare these introductions," continued Can. "I will execute a few telephone calls and I can come for you on this very spot tomorrow morning."

"I'm thrilled to hear it. Thank you so much," Alice said, shaking Can's hand.

Alice felt like a little girl waiting to open her presents on Christmas morning. The very idea of meeting her fellow perfume makers and studying how they worked in Turkey had made her forget about wanting to leave.

Can rose to his feet, and Daldry accompanied him into the lobby, leaving Alice in the bar to finish her tea.

"My tariffs have just had an augmentation!"

"What on earth for? We agreed on your price."

"That was before receiving your footy fury upon my leg. Because of you, I will have a limp tomorrow, which will make me late."

"Don't be ridiculous. I barely touched you. And if I did anything at all, it was to shut you up before you made a blunder."

Can looked hurt.

"Fine," said Daldry. "I'm sorry. I apologize if I hurt you, but at the time it seemed necessary. But you must admit you were handling the whole thing very clumsily."

"I will not augment my tariff, but only because your friend is of a very great ravishment, which makes my work pleasanter."

"What on earth do you mean by that?"

"That in one day I could easily find a hundred men who would happily beguile her."

Can said goodbye and left through the revolving door. Daldry returned to the bar, where Alice was waiting.

"What did the two of you talk about just now?"

"Nothing important. His remuneration."

"I expect you to keep a careful account of your expenses, Daldry. The hotel, our meals, the guide, and the cost of our travel of course. I'm going to reimburse—"

"Every shilling. I remember, you've repeated it often enough. But I'm afraid that when we dine or drink together, you're my guest. It's one thing for us to be business partners, but it's another thing for me to conduct myself like a gentleman, and I refuse to stop doing so now. Speaking of which, how about a drink to celebrate?"

"To celebrate what?"

"Oh, I don't know. Do you always have to have a reason? I'm thirsty. Let's celebrate the fact that we finally hired our guide."

"It's a bit early in the day for me. I think I'll go and lie down. I didn't sleep very well last night, you know."

Alice left Daldry in the bar. He watched her take the lift up to her room and ordered a double Scotch.

◆ ◆ ◆

A small rowing boat rocked on the water at the edge of a dock. Alice climbed aboard and sat at one end. A man untied the rope from the piling and pushed off. The dock disappeared into the distance. Alice tried to understand why the world was the way it was, why the tops of the tall pine trees seemed to close on the black of the night like a final curtain falling upon her past.

The current was strong, and the boat pitched dangerously when it crossed the wakes of larger ships that churned up the water as they passed. Alice braced herself, pushing her feet against the planks on the bottom of the boat. She couldn't reach to hold on to the gunwales. The smuggler sat in front of her, with his back turned to her, but every time the little boat plunged or reared, she felt a reassuring presence holding her and calming her.

A wind blew up from the north and scattered the clouds. The moonlight seemed to emerge from the depths of the water.

The man steered the boat to the shore, jumped out into the shallow water, and pulled it up onto the bank.

Alice climbed a hill planted with cypress trees and continued down the other side into a shadowy valley. She walked along a dirt path in the cool autumn night. The descent was steep and sometimes she had to hold on to the bushes around her, but she kept her eyes on a little light twinkling in the distance.

She followed the vine-covered walls of a ruined fortress, or perhaps a former palace.

The scent of cedar mingled with that of the wild broom, and a fainter trace of jasmine. Alice wanted to remember this succession of odors. The light in the distance grew closer and brighter. It was an oil lamp hanging from a chain. It lit a wooden door that opened to reveal a garden planted with linden and fig trees. Alice was hungry and felt tempted to steal one of the ripe fruits. She wanted to taste its red, pulpy flesh. She reached out, plucked two figs from the branches, and hid them in her pocket.

She entered the courtyard of a house. The gentle voice of a stranger told her not to be afraid, that there was nothing more to fear. She would be able to take a bath, eat, drink, and sleep.

Fragile wooden stairs creaked under Alice's feet as she climbed them. She gripped the banister and tried to tread as lightly as possible.

She entered a small room that smelled of beeswax. She took off her clothes, carefully folding them and piling them on a chair, and stepped naked into an iron bath. She looked at her face on the water's surface before the ripples erased it from sight.

She wanted to drink the bathwater. Her throat was dry and the room felt airless. Her cheeks burned. Her head felt as though it were gripped in a vise.

"Go back, Alice. You shouldn't have come. Go home, it's not too late."

Alice opened her eyes and sat up in bed. She was burning with fever, her body felt numb, and her legs were weak. A wave of nausea sent her running to the bathroom.

Back in bed, shivering, she called reception and asked them to fetch a doctor and to let Mr. Daldry know she was sick.

The doctor arrived, quickly made his diagnosis, and wrote a prescription that Daldry hurried off to buy in a pharmacy. Alice recovered quickly. Apparently such "digestive problems" were common among tourists, and there was no reason to be concerned.

The telephone in Alice's room rang early in the evening. It was Daldry.

"I never should have let you eat shellfish at lunch, I feel terribly guilty," he said.

"Oh, it's not your fault," said Alice. "You certainly didn't force me, but I hope you won't mind if I stay in my room tonight—the very thought of food turns my stomach."

"Then don't talk about it! I'll fast out of solidarity, it will do me good. A stiff bourbon and off to bed."

"You drink too much, Daldry."

"Considering your current state, you're not in much of a place to give me advice concerning my health. I don't mean to be cruel, but I'm in better shape than you are."

"Tonight perhaps, but on the average day it's quite the opposite."

"Why don't you get some rest and stop worrying about me. Take your medicine, sleep well, and if the doctor was right, you'll be fine in the morning."

"Have you heard anything from Can?"

"Not for the time being," said Daldry, "but I'm expecting his call. Speaking of which, I should probably free up the line and let you sleep."

"Good night, Ethan."

"Good night, Alice."

She hung up. When she reached out to turn off her bedside lamp, she was seized by an uneasy feeling, so she left it on and fell asleep shortly afterward. That night, for the first time in a long time, no nightmares troubled her sleep.

There was a perfume maker who lived in Cihangir. His house was perched on a weedy plot of land at the top of one of the highest hills in the neighborhood. A clothesline hung with shirts, trousers, smocks, and even a uniform was strung across the space between it and the neighboring house. It had been difficult for the *dolmu* they had taken to scale the steep cobbled street in the rain. The Chevrolet had slipped backward, the overheating engine stinking of burning rubber, and the driver, who had never before questioned the state of his balding tires, grumbled that there was nothing for tourists to see in the depths of Cihangir anyway. Daldry finally joined him in the front seat and slipped him a banknote, and the driver calmed down and got them to their destination.

Can guided Alice by the arm as they picked their way through the weedy plot, "so that she would not put her foot in a water-filled hole," as he put it.

The ground seemed dry enough, in spite of the mist that had fallen for much of the day, but Can was doing his best to show foresight. Alice was feeling better, but she was still weak and appreciated the attention. Daldry held his tongue.

They went into the house. The room where the perfume maker worked was spacious. Glowing embers smoldered beneath a large samovar, and the heat they gave off fogged up the windows of the dusty workshop.

The perfume maker did not understand why two people had come all the way from London to see him, although he was honored by their visit. He offered them tea and little Turkish pastries drizzled with syrup.

"My wife made them," he told Can, who translated in turn that the perfumer's wife was the most talented pastry maker in Cihangir.

Alice followed the perfumer to his organ. He had her smell some of his creations. The notes he was working with were sustained, the accords harmonious. They were well-made Oriental-style perfumes, but nothing very original.

At the end of the long table, Alice's eye fell upon a wooden case that piqued her curiosity.

"May I?" she asked, picking up a small bottle filled with a liquid of an odd green color she had never seen before.

The perfumer took the bottle from her hands and put it back in its place before Can had the time to finish translating her request.

"He says they aren't very interesting, just experiments for his amusement. A pastime."

"I'd still be curious to smell one of them."

The perfume maker shrugged and signaled that it was fine with him if she wanted to waste her time. Alice pulled out the stopper and was astonished. She took a strip of paper, dipped it in the liquid, and waved it under her nose. She put the bottle back and repeated the operation with a second bottle, then a third.

"So?" asked Daldry. He had been unusually silent up until then.

"It's incredible. He's recreated an entire forest in this box. I would have never come up with such an idea. Smell for yourself," she said, dipping a new strip of paper in another vial. "It's like being stretched out on the ground at the base of an old cedar tree."

She put it down, dipped another, and waved it in the air before presenting it to Daldry.

"This one is pine resin, and in the next bottle"—she opened it— "the smell of wet grass with a slight note of autumn crocus and bracken. And here's another, hazelnuts . . ."

"I've never met anyone who wanted to smell like a hazelnut," said Daldry.

"They're not for skin. I'd call them ambiance aromas."

"Do you really think there's a market for ambiance aromas? What the hell is an ambiance aroma anyway?"

"Imagine how wonderful it would be to have the scents of the natural world in one's home. We could fill our living spaces with the smells of the seasons."

"The smells of the seasons?"

"You could make autumn last a little longer when winter comes too soon, or move forward the date of spring's arrival when January seems like it will never end. A dining room that smelled ever so slightly like a lemon tree, or a bathroom scented with orange blossoms. Indoor perfumes that aren't incense . . . I think it's a wonderful idea."

"Well, if you say so. But first we need to make friends with this kind man, who seems rather astounded by your current state of excitement."

Alice turned to Can.

"Could you ask him how he makes the cedar note last so long?" She picked up the dipper and smelled it again.

"The note?"

"Ask him what he does to make the smell last so long in the open air."

While Can did his best to translate the conversation between Alice and the Turkish perfumer, Daldry walked over to the window and looked out at the Bosporus, blurred by the condensation on the windowpanes. This wasn't exactly what he'd had in mind when he organized their trip to Istanbul, he thought to himself. Alice might very well make a fortune in perfumes and, strangely enough, he couldn't care less.

Alice, Can, and Daldry thanked the perfumer for spending the morning with them. Alice promised to come back soon and told him she hoped they would be able to work together. The perfumer could never have imagined that his hobby of re-creating offbeat fragrances would interest another person so much. That evening he would be able to tell his wife that the late nights he spent in his workroom, and the Sundays he devoted to his walks through the hills to collect all sorts of flowers and vegetable matter in the woods and fields, were more than just an old fool's pastime, as she so often said: it was serious work that had caught the attention of an English perfume maker.

"It's not that I was bored," said Daldry as they stepped out onto the street. "I just haven't had anything to eat since yesterday at noon. I'm in need of a snack."

"Are you not joyous from this visit?" Can asked Alice, ignoring Daldry.

"Yes, I'm simply overcome with joy. That perfume organ was a veritable Ali Baba's cavern. You found exactly the sort of person I had been hoping to meet, Can."

"And I am enchanted that you are enchanted," said Can, blushing deep magenta.

"Hello? Did anybody hear what I just said?" Daldry was beginning to behave like an attention-starved child.

"I should inform you, Miss Alice, that some words of your vocabulary are new to me and very difficult to translate. And I did not see any baba cavern organ in this man's house."

"I'll have to explain all the perfume jargon. The organ is that set of shelves with all of the little bottles on it. You'll be the best perfumer's translator in Istanbul when I'm done with you."

"That is a specialty I would like very much. I would be eternally grateful, Miss Alice."

"Has nobody heard a word of what I just said?" asked Daldry. "I'm hungry! Can, could you kindly take us to a place where Miss Alice won't be poisoned?"

Can turned and looked at Daldry.

"I have the intention of driving you to a place that you will not be forgetting soon."

"Ah, just in time, you remembered I exist."

Alice leaned over to Daldry and whispered in his ear. "You're not being very pleasant."

"You've just noticed too? You think he's being pleasant to me? I'm hungry. I'd like to remind you that I fasted out of solidarity last night, but if you're going to take sides with our guide you can kiss that solidarity goodbye."

Alice gave Daldry a disapproving frown and returned to Can.

They picked their way down the steep and narrow streets to the lower part of Cihangir. Daldry hailed a taxi and asked Alice and Can if they were coming with him. He sat in the back seat and left Can no choice but to sit in front next to the driver.

Can gave the driver directions in Turkish and kept his back to them for the duration of the ride.

◆　◆　◆

A flock of seagulls sat motionless on the railings along the waterfront.

"We're going over there," said Can, gesturing to a wooden shack at the end of a wharf.

"I don't see any restaurants," said Daldry, preparing to protest.

"Because you don't know how to look," said Can, as politely as he could. "It's not a place for tourists. The room is not resplendent with luxuries, but you will have an excellent meal."

"You wouldn't happen to know of a place as promising as that greasy spoon, but with a little more charm? Maybe something over there?" Daldry pointed to the yalis, the grand homes that lined the waters of the Bosporus.

One of them caught Alice's eye. Painted entirely white, it stood out from the others.

"Something wrong?" said Daldry, teasing her. "You should see the look on your face."

"I lied," stammered Alice. "The other night I had a nightmare that felt more real than any of the others, and in that nightmare I saw a house like that one."

Can didn't understand what had come over Alice.

"Those are yalis," he said with the even voice of a tour guide. "Summer homes that are remains of the Ottoman Empire. They were very popular in the nineteenth century. Now they are less lucky. Their owners are mispossessed, and they are too expensive to heat in the winter. They need to be renovating."

Daldry took Alice by the shoulders and forced her to look away.

"I can only think of two possibilities. Perhaps your parents really did travel farther than the French Riviera and you were too young to remember them telling you about it. Or perhaps they had a picture book about Istanbul that you've forgotten about. One doesn't preclude the other."

Alice had no memory of her mother or father ever talking about Istanbul, and she could still remember every room in her childhood home . . . Her parents' room with its big bed covered in a gray bedspread . . . her father's bedside table, where he kept his reading glasses in a leather case and a small alarm clock . . . her mother's bedside table, with a picture of Alice at the age of five . . . the trunk at the foot of the bed and the red-and-brown-striped rug. There was the dining room, with its mahogany table and six mismatched chairs. The china cabinet, where the best porcelain was kept for special occasions, but which they never remembered to use. In the living room there was the chesterfield, where they sat as a family to listen to the evening radio dramas, and the little bookcase with the books that her mother read. None of it had anything to do with Istanbul.

"If your parents came to Turkey," said Can, "maybe traces of their passage remain in the authorities' archives. Tomorrow the British Consulate is organizing a ceremonious evening. The British Ambassador is coming especially from Ankara to welcome a long military delegation and many officers from my government." He seemed proud of this.

"And how do you know all that?" asked Daldry.

"Because I am the best guide in Istanbul. And, all right, because I read about it in the morning newspaper. As I'm also the best translator in Istanbul, I was inquisitioned to work at the ceremony."

"Are you trying to tell us that you won't be able to work for us tomorrow evening?" asked Daldry.

"I was going to invite you to come to this party."

"Don't show off. The consul surely won't be inviting all of the English people who happen to be staying in Istanbul."

"I am not showing anything off. The secretary who makes the invitation list would be very happy to do me a service and add your names. She never refuses Can. I will bring the invitations to your hotel."

"You're something else," said Daldry, almost in admiration. "Maybe you'd be interested in going, Alice? I suppose we could get introduced to the ambassador and ask him to enlist the consular services on our behalf . . . After all, what good is all that bureaucracy if we can't rope them into doing us a favor now and then?"

"I want to understand," said Alice. "I want to know why my nightmares seem so real."

"I promise we will do everything we can to get to the heart of this mystery. But first, I have to eat something and have a drink or I'll pass out."

Can pointed to the fisherman's restaurant at the end of the pier before going to sit on a piling.

"Bon appétit," he said, crossing his arms and gazing across the water.

Alice glared at Daldry to invite Can along with them.

"What are you doing? You can't sit by yourself out here in the cold," he said.

"I don't want to disconvenience," said Can. "I know I can be a bother. Go feeding yourselves. I am used to winter in Istanbul. And rain."

"Don't be ridiculous. If it's a local restaurant, I'll never be able to communicate if you don't come along. How do you expect me to survive without the best translator in town?"

Can lit up in response to the compliment and immediately accepted Daldry's invitation.

The generous welcome and the meal that followed surpassed Daldry's expectations. When they came to the coffee, he was suddenly overcome by a wave of sentimental melancholy that took Alice and Can by surprise. Aided by the alcohol, he finally admitted the guilt he felt at having so harshly judged the restaurant from a distance. Simple and excellent food could be served in even the most modest of establishments. He heaved a heavy sigh and finished his fourth glass of raki.

"I'm just getting emotional," he said. "When I think of the sauce that came with the fish and the delicacy of the dessert—do you think I could order a second?—it's just overwhelming. Please, Can, present my compliments to the owner, and promise me you'll take us to more places like this. Beginning this evening." He raised his glass as the waiter passed, asking for a refill.

"I think you've had enough to drink," said Alice, forcing him to lower his glass.

"I admit that the raki has gone to my head. But I came here on an empty stomach, and I was terribly thirsty when we arrived."

"You really ought to learn to quench your thirst with water," said Alice.

"Are you crazy? Do you want me to rust?"

Alice made a sign to Can, and they both stood and flanked Daldry, helping him to the door. Can paid and thanked the owner, who was amused by the scene.

The cool air made Daldry's head spin. He sat on a piling while Can tried to hail a taxi. Alice stood over him to make sure he didn't fall into the water.

"I think a little nap would do me some good," he slurred, gazing across the water.

"And all this time I thought you were going to be chaperoning me."

"I'm dreadfully sorry. I promise you I won't drink a drop tomorrow."

"You had best keep that promise."

Can managed to stop a *dolmu*. He came back to help Alice prop up Daldry in the back before taking a seat next to the driver.

"We'll take your friend to the doorway of the hotel and then I will go to the consulate to procure your invitations. I will present them, enveloped, to the concierge," he said as they drove.

"In an envelope," whispered Alice discreetly.

"Ah, yes. I had a feeling my phrase was deformed, but I was not certain in what way. Thank you for rectifying me."

Daldry had dozed off. He barely opened an eye when Alice and the doorman helped him back to his room and laid him out across his bed. He came back to life later in the day and called Alice's room. When she didn't respond, he called reception and learned that she had gone out. Embarrassed by his behavior, he slipped an apologetic note under her door asking if she would mind dining without him that evening.

Alice took advantage of her afternoon alone to walk through the Beyoğlu neighborhood. The hotel concierge had recommended visiting the Galata Tower and showed her how to get there, tracing the route on a map. On the way back she wandered down the broad thoroughfare of Istiklal and bought a few souvenirs for her friends. When she was finally too chilled by the cold, she took refuge in a little restaurant and had a bite to eat.

She returned to her room in the early evening and sat at the little desk to write a letter.

Dear Anton,

This morning I met a man who makes perfume like I do, but who is considerably more talented. I'll try to tell you about his thoroughly original creations when I'm home again, but they'll be difficult to explain. If you had been with me in the old perfume maker's drafty workshop this morning, you would understand why I'd feel guilty if I ever complained about the cold in my flat ever again.

When I went up the hill to Cihangir, where he lives, I discovered another side of the city, one very different from the view outside my hotel-room window. In the city center, the buildings are more or less the same as those that have been built in London since the war, but elsewhere there are much poorer, more authentic neighborhoods. Today in the narrow streets of Cihangir I saw children running barefoot in the cold, and later was also very moved by the weather-beaten faces of the street peddlers, standing in the rain along the shores of the Bosporus. The old women hawk their goods, working the crowds of locals waiting for the steamboat ferries.

As strange as it sounds, I feel deeply attached to these strange foreign places and people, to the troubling solitude of the old city squares and run-down churches, to the narrow passages whose worn stone steps lead up and down the hills. In spite of the melancholy atmosphere, the dust, and the filth, the cafés and restaurants are full of life. Istanbul is a beautiful city, a great city. Its people are generous and welcoming, and I love it for its nostalgia here, its crumbling grandeur.

This afternoon when I was walking near the Galata Tower, I saw a sleepy little cemetery behind an iron gate, right in the middle of the city. When I looked at those crooked gravestones, I felt I belonged here. With each passing hour an overwhelming love for the city grows inside me.

Excuse me for writing these scattered thoughts— I know this can't make much sense to you, but I can close my eyes and hear your trumpet echoing through the streets of Istanbul, coming all the way from some pub in faraway London. I'd like to have some news from Sam, Eddy, and Carol. I miss the four of you, and I hope you miss me too.

Warmest regards, from a room overlooking the roofs of a city I'm certain you'd adore.

Alice

8

At ten in the morning, somebody knocked on Alice's door. In spite of her shouting that she was in the bath, the knocking continued. But by the time she'd got out of the water and slipped into a bathrobe, it had stopped. A maid had let herself in, left some parcels on the bed, and slipped out. Alice opened the boxes to discover an evening gown carefully wrapped in tissue paper, a matching jacket, a pair of heels, and an adorable hat made out of felt. A note written in Daldry's handwriting was pinned to the lid of the hatbox.

See you this evening. I'll meet you in the lobby at six.

Alice stared in wonder at the beautiful clothes before slipping out of the bathrobe. She couldn't resist trying them on. It was as though they had come from heaven; she felt like she was in a dream.

The dress was carefully draped and fitted at the waist, then blossomed into a full skirt that fell below the calf. Since the war and all its restrictions, Alice had never seen so much fabric go into a single garment. She spun around and watched the skirt billow and float, whisking away the years of sacrifice and rations in a twirl of rustling silk. No more narrow skirts and meager, unlined jackets. The dress bared her shoulders, and defined her figure. The cut of the skirt added mystery and length to her legs, and its curves improved upon her narrow hips.

She sat on the bed to put on the shoes. When she stood again, she felt as though she towered over the room. She slipped on the long jacket, adjusted the hat, and then opened the wardrobe door to look in the mirror. She couldn't believe her eyes.

She carefully hung everything in the closet for later in the evening. The concierge called and said that a driver had arrived to take her to the salon.

"I'm sorry, you must have the wrong room," she said. "I didn't make any appointment."

"Miss Pendelbury, it says here that you're awaited at Chez Guido in twenty minutes. When you are done there, we'll send somebody to come and get you. Have an excellent day, madam."

The concierge hung up, and Alice stood with the receiver in her hand, stunned at the way her day had begun.

After the assistants had shampooed her hair and given her a manicure, Alice was presented to Guido, whose real name was Onur. He had taken classes and picked up his Italian *nom de guerre* at a beauty school in Rome. Guido/Onur explained that a man had come to the salon earlier in the morning and had given him instructions to put her hair in a clean chignon that would "hold up under a hat."

The appointment lasted about an hour, after which the driver came to take Alice back to the hotel. When she walked into the lobby, the concierge told her that Daldry was waiting for her in the bar.

She went in and found him sipping what looked to be a lemonade and reading a newspaper.

"Ravishing," he said, rising to his feet.

"I don't know what to say. I feel like I stepped into a fairy tale."

"I'm glad to hear it. You need to make a good impression this evening. There's an ambassador to seduce, and I don't think I'm the man for the job."

"I don't know how you managed, but everything fits perfectly."

"I'm a painter. Proportions are an important part of what I do."

"Well, you made an excellent choice. I've never worn anything so beautiful. I'll be very careful with everything. You rented it, I assume."

"It's a French model called the 'New Look.' They might not be much at the art of war, but I have to admit that the French have an undeniable genius for dressing women and fine cuisine."

"Well, I hope you'll like the look of the 'New Look.'"

"I'm sure I will. And I like your hair that way too. It shows off your neck. Quite charming."

"The neck or the hair?"

Daldry handed Alice a menu. "You should eat something. Party buffets are always a battle scene, and I'm afraid you won't be in combat gear."

Alice ordered some tea and finger sandwiches.

After taking tea, she retired to her room, where she opened the wardrobe and stretched out on the bed to admire the gown a second time.

A torrential rain began to pelt down outside. and she went to the window to look. The Bosporus had cloaked itself in a gray mist, and the ferries blew their foghorns as they chugged back and forth across the strait. In the street below, the people of Istanbul hurried to take refuge under streetcar shelters and awnings, while umbrellas tangled and butted against one another on the crowded pavement. Alice knew she was still part of the churning city that passed beneath the window, but for tonight, from behind the walls of her luxurious hotel and in the company of the beautiful gown, she felt as though she had been transported to another world altogether. She knew it was a privileged, ephemeral place. She would rub shoulders with its inhabitants for just one evening, and her ignorance of its customs made her all the more impatient to dive in and discover them.

Alice had called for the maid to come and zip her up. Hat in place, she left her room. When Daldry looked up and saw her in the elevator descending toward the lobby, his delight was even greater than he had anticipated. He offered his arm.

"Normally, I hate making formal compliments, but tonight I'm willing to break a rule. You look—"

"*Très* 'New Look,' don't you think?"

"That's one way of putting it. A car is waiting for us outside. We're in luck; the rain seems to have stopped."

They arrived just two minutes later because the consulate gate was more or less across the avenue from the hotel.

"I know the taxi was ridiculous, but you can't just walk up to this kind of place," he explained.

He went around the car to let Alice out but found that a valet had beaten him to it. As they walked up the grand steps, Alice was worried she might trip and stumble in her high heels. Daldry handed the invitations to the doorman, left his coat in the cloakroom, and accompanied Alice into the large reception hall that had been converted into a ballroom.

As they entered, many of the male guests turned to look. Some of them even halted their conversations. The women carefully inspected Alice from head to toe. The combination of her sleek hair, jacket, dress, and shoes made her seem the very image of modernity. The ambassador's wife smiled warmly, and Daldry went over to introduce himself.

He bowed, kissed her hand, and presented Alice, according to the protocol he had carefully studied in preparation for their evening. The ambassador's wife asked them what brought them so far from home.

"Perfume, Your Excellency," said Daldry. "Alice is one of England's most talented noses. Her creations are found in the best shops in Kensington."

"How fascinating," exclaimed the ambassador's wife. "I'll be sure to look for them when we've returned to London."

Daldry insisted she allow him to have some of Alice's perfumes sent directly.

"What an inspiration you are," she said, turning to Alice. "A professional and innovative woman with the courage to work in a business dominated by men. If you stay in Turkey long enough, you must come and visit us in Ankara." She added in a stage whisper, "I'm bored to death there." She blushed at her own unexpected honesty. "I would have liked to introduce you to my husband, but he's deep in conversation and I fear it may drag on. I'm pleased to have made your acquaintance."

The ambassador's wife slipped into the crowd to greet other guests, but everybody had noticed the attention she had given Alice, who now felt as though everybody was staring at her even more than when she had entered. It made her uncomfortable.

"I can't believe I let her go," said Daldry. "We were almost there. I should have kept talking to her."

Alice watched the ambassador's wife chatting with a group of guests. She left Daldry's side and crossed the room, doing her best to adopt a confident stride in the unfamiliar shoes.

She joined the circle that had surrounded the ambassadress and interrupted the conversation.

"I'm sorry, madam, I know it's unorthodox, but I absolutely must speak with you in private, just for a moment."

Daldry was dumbstruck to see Alice behaving so boldly.

"She is something else, is she not?" whispered Can.

Daldry jumped.

"Goodness, you startled me. I didn't even see you there."

"I know. I do this on purpose. So, are you satisfied with your good guide? The reception is of great exception, don't you think?"

"This sort of party bores me to tears, actually."

"Because you are not interested in other people," observed Can.

"I hired you as tour guide, not a spiritual guide."

"Must not a guide have a spirit?"

"Don't taunt me. I promised Alice I wouldn't drink tonight."

Can took the hint and disappeared as discreetly as he had arrived.

Daldry planted himself near the buffet, in a spot that was close enough to where Alice and the ambassador's wife were standing for him to catch the gist of their conversation.

"I'm terribly sorry to hear that you lost your parents in the war . . . Of course I understand your desire to know more about their origins . . . I'll call the consular services first thing in the morning and ask that they go through the files for you . . . When exactly do you think they might have come to Istanbul?"

"I don't really know, but probably before I was born. My parents didn't have anybody they could leave me with, apart from my aunt perhaps, but she would have told me about it if they had done so. I suppose they might have gone on a sort of honeymoon in 1909 or 1910. After that, Mother wouldn't have been in a condition to travel."

"I can't imagine that the research will be very complicated—that is, unless the fall of the Ottoman Empire and two World Wars have caused the papers to go missing. You know, my mother always said, 'When you already have a no, my girl, you might as well try getting a yes.' Let's be efficient and bother the consul about it now. I'll introduce you, and in exchange you must give me the name of your dressmaker."

"I think the label said Christian Dior, madam."

The ambassador's wife made a note to remember the name and took Alice by the hand to present her to the consul. She explained Alice's request, adding that it was a special favor for her new friend. The consul promised to receive Alice at the end of the afternoon the following day.

"Very well," said the ambassador's wife. "Now that you're in capable hands, I'm afraid I must return to my guests."

Alice bowed in thanks and left the ambassadress to her socializing.

"So?" asked Daldry, coming over to Alice.

"We have a meeting with the consul tomorrow at teatime."

"It's rather discouraging to see you succeed where I fail, but I suppose it's the results that count. Are you happy?"

"Yes, very. I still don't know how to thank you for everything you've done."

"You might begin by lifting your ban and allowing me to have a drink. Just one, I promise."

"I have your word?"

"My gentleman's honor," said Daldry, already on his way to the bar.

He came back with a glass of champagne, which he handed to Alice, and a tumbler filled with whisky.

"You call that one drink?" asked Alice.

"Do you see a second?"

The orchestra started playing a waltz, and Alice's eyes instantly lit up. She left her glass on the tray of a passing waiter and turned to Daldry.

"Would you dance with me? You can hardly refuse when I'm wearing a gown like this."

"It's just that . . ." Daldry glanced wistfully at his glass.

"Me or the whisky. Make up your mind."

Daldry sighed, put down his drink, and led Alice out onto the dance floor.

"You dance well," she observed after a moment.

"My mother taught me. She loved dancing, but my father didn't, so I was her partner."

"Well, she was an excellent teacher."

"I think that may be the first time you've given me a compliment."

"If you'd like a second: you're very handsome in a dinner jacket."

"You know, it's funny. The last time I wore it, I was at a very boring party in London where I ran into an old girlfriend who told me that black tie was so becoming on me she hadn't recognized me at first. I remember thinking that it didn't say much for her opinion of my everyday appearance."

"Have you already had somebody special in your life, Daldry? I mean, not just a run-of-the-mill girlfriend, but someone you really cared about?"

"Yes, but I'd rather not talk about it."

"Why not? We're friends, aren't we? You can confide in me."

"It's a bit early in the friendship for that sort of confidence. Besides, I'm not really the hero of the story."

"Oh dear. Does that mean she left you? Was it very difficult?"

"I don't know. Yes, I suppose it was."

"Do you still think of her?"

"Occasionally."

"Why aren't you together anymore?"

"Because we were never really together to begin with. It's a long story. One which, as I recall, I said I didn't feel like telling."

"Hmm, I don't remember that," said Alice, quickening her step.

"That's because you never listen. If we go any faster, I'm going to start stepping on your feet."

"I've never been dancing in such a beautiful dress, in such a grand and beautiful room, or to such a good orchestra. Please let's keep spinning as fast as possible."

Daldry smiled and acquiesced.

"You're a funny woman."

"And you're a funny fellow. You know, yesterday, when I was walking around town while you were sobering up, I came across a little intersection that I think you'd just love. As I was crossing, I could imagine you painting it all. There was a wagon being drawn by two magnificent horses, a place where two tram tracks crossed, about a dozen taxis, an old American car from before the war, people on foot all over the place, and a man pushing a wheelbarrow. You would have been in heaven."

"You thought of me at an intersection? It's lovely to think that crossroads are inspiring you now as well."

The waltz ended, and the crowd of dancing guests applauded the orchestra. Daldry returned to the bar.

"Don't look at me like that," he said. "The other glass didn't count. I hardly had time to get my lips wet . . ." Alice frowned. "Fine. A promise is a promise."

"I have a better idea," said Alice.

"Oh dear, I fear the worst."

"What if we left this party?"

"I have nothing against that—quite to the contrary—but where would we go?"

"We could take a walk in the city."

"Dressed like this?"

"Yes. Why not?" she asked.

"Well, if it makes you happy, why not?"

Daldry collected his coat from the cloakroom while Alice waited for him at the top of the steps outside.

"Do you want to see the intersection I was telling you about?" she asked.

"It probably isn't as interesting at night. Why don't we walk to the funicular and take it to the Bosporus near Karaköy?"

"I had no idea you knew the city so well."

"I don't, but I've spent a lot of time in my room over the past two days, and I don't have much to read apart from the guidebook I found on my bedside table."

They walked through the streets of Beyoğlu and took the funicular down the hill to Karaköy. As they left the station, Alice hurried to sit on the stone parapets.

"Let's forget about the walk and go to a café. You can drink as much as you like. I think I can see one from here."

"Your feet hurt?"

"These shoes may look pretty, but they're torture to wear."

"Well, lean on me for now. We'll take a taxi back later."

The cozy atmosphere inside the café was a dramatic contrast to the grand consulate ballroom. The clientele played cards, laughed, sang, and toasted to friendship, to the health of those seated around them, to the end of the day, or to the promise of a more profitable tomorrow. Others toasted to the particularly mild winter, and to the Bosporus, which had kept the city alive for centuries. Some of the regulars complained about the ferryboats that docked for too long, how expensive life had become, the packs of stray dogs, or that another *konak* had burned and that the old ways were going up in smoke thanks to ruthless property speculators. Then they toasted yet again, to brotherhood, to the Grand Bazaar, and to the tourists, who had started to return.

When Alice and Daldry walked in, the men turned from their card games to gawk for a moment at the foreigners in their evening wear. Daldry paid them no heed, chose a table with a commanding view, and ordered two rakis.

"Everybody is staring," whispered Alice.

"Everybody is staring at you, my dear. Just ignore them and drink up."

She gingerly sipped the raki and began to daydream out loud. "Do you think my parents used to walk in these streets?"

"Who knows? It's possible, I suppose. Maybe we'll know something tomorrow."

"I like to imagine the two of them visiting Istanbul, and that I'm following in their footsteps. Maybe they liked the view up in Beyoğlu, or wandered around in the little streets of Pera, or walked along the Bosporus. I know it's silly, but just imagining them here makes me miss them."

"There's nothing silly about it. If you don't mind my confiding in you, I must say that I actually miss my father too, if only for not being able to blame him anymore for all the things that go wrong in my life." He paused a moment, mulling over how to phrase his next question. "I never dared ask, but how did they . . ."

"It was a Saturday night in May 1941. The tenth of May. Back then, I lived in a studio flat just upstairs from my parents, and every Friday night I came downstairs and ate dinner with them. I was talking with my father in the sitting room. My mother was in bed with a cold. The air-raid sirens started going off and my father told me to go down into the shelter. He said he was going to help my mother get dressed and that they'd be right behind me. I wanted to help him, but he pushed me out of the door and told me to reserve a place in the shelter, where my mother would be comfortable if the alert dragged on through the night. So I obeyed. The first bomb hit when I was crossing the street, and the blast was so hard that it threw me to the ground and knocked the wind out of me. When I came to, I turned and saw our building was on fire. I had intended to go see my mother in her room after dinner but then decided not to, for fear of disturbing her. I never saw either of them again. I couldn't even bury them. When the firemen had put out the fire, I walked through the ashes, but nothing was left. Nothing from the lifetime we had spent together, not a single object from my childhood.

"After that, I left London to live with my aunt on the Isle of Wight and stayed there until the end of the war. Even once the war was over, it took me almost two years to be able to go back to London. I lived like a hermit on that island. I knew every little cove, beach, and hill. Finally, my aunt told me I needed to face my past, for my own good. She forced me to go back to the city and visit my old friends. They were all I had left in the world, apart from her. A new building had been put up on the spot where my parents and I used to live, and it was as though the whole awful event had never taken place. It seemed erased from existence, just like my parents themselves. The people who live there now probably have no idea what stood there before. Life just continued without them."

"I'm sorry," murmured Daldry.

"What about you? What did you do during the war?"

"I worked in army administration. Supposedly I wasn't considered fit enough for the front because of a childhood case of TB that had left me with lung damage. It made me furious, of course, and I suspect my father used his influence to arrange it all. But I fought tooth and nail to get transferred into active duty, and I finally managed to get put on an intelligence team in mid-forty-four."

"So you got your wish in the end," said Alice.

"No. It was always just office jobs. Nothing very glorious, I'm afraid. But let's not ruin the evening by talking about the war. It's my fault. I shouldn't have brought it up."

"I'm the one who started asking personal questions. But yes. Let's talk about something more cheerful. What was her name then?"

"Who's that?"

"The girl who left you and made you suffer so."

"That's your idea of cheerful?"

"Why so cagey? Was she much younger? Go on, tell me—blonde, redhead, or brunette?"

"She was green, from head to foot, with huge bulging eyes and immense hairy feet. Which is why I'd rather just forget about her. If you ask any more questions, I'm ordering myself another."

"Go on, and order two. We'll drink to her health."

It had got very late and the café was closing, but there were no taxis or *dolmu* to be found.

"Let me think," said Daldry. "There must be some solution."

The lights in the café went out behind them.

"I could walk home on my hands, but it might ruin my dress," said Alice, attempting to do a cartwheel. Daldry caught her just before she fell.

"My goodness. You're completely drunk."

"Don't exaggerate. I'm just a little tipsy. Blowing things out of proportion . . ."

"Did you hear yourself just now? I don't even recognize your voice. You sound like a fishwife after a long day."

"It's an honorable line of work, hawking fish." Alice did her best to put on a cockney accent and pretended to weigh invisible fish. "Two 'errings, a skate, an' a dozen oysters! There you are, guv'nor. Barely keeps me in knickers, but you're a nice chap, and it's time to close up."

"You're completely soused."

"Not at all. And with all you've had to drink since we arrived, you're in no position to judge." Alice turned in panic. "Where are you?"

"Next to you. The other side!"

She flailed and pivoted. "Ah, there you are. Shall we walk along the river?" She clutched a lamppost.

"It's more of a strait, really."

"Oh, that's fine. My feet hurt anyway. What time is it?"

"Past midnight, Cinderella, but I'm afraid our carriage is missing, and you've turned into a pumpkin instead."

"I don't want to go to the hotel yet. I want to go back and dance at the consulate. What pumpkin?"

"I see how it is. Desperate times call for desperate measures, as they say." Daldry threw her over his shoulder like a well-dressed but unruly sack of potatoes.

"What are you doing?" squealed Alice, giggling and squirming.

"I'm taking you back to the hotel."

"Will you present me, enveloped, to the concierge?" she asked, imitating Can's accent.

"If you like," said Daldry, rolling his eyes.

"But I don't want to be left with the concierge, okay? You promise?"

"Yes. Now if you wouldn't mind hushing up until we get there."

"There's a strand of blonde hair on the back of your jacket. Now how did that get there? Oh. I think I lost my hat."

Daldry turned to see the hat roll down the street and into the gutter.

"I'm afraid we'll have to write that one off," he grumbled.

When they got to the steepest part of the hill, he made Alice stagger beside him, keeping her upright by holding one of her arms over his shoulders. Her warm breath tickled his ear and neck, but there was nothing he could do about it.

The receptionist couldn't hide his astonishment to see them arrive in such a disheveled condition.

"Miss Pendelbury is extremely tired," said Daldry, with all the dignity he could muster. "If I might have my key and hers as well . . ."

The concierge offered his assistance, but Daldry refused.

He took Alice upstairs, laid her across her bed, took off her shoes, and covered her with a blanket.

He drew the curtains and watched her sleep for a moment before turning out the light and leaving.

He walked with his father and told him about his ambitions for the future. He wanted to do a large painting of the wheat fields that surrounded the family estate. His father thought it was a wonderful idea and offered to have the tractor pulled up so it could be featured in the picture. His father was proud of the tractor, a Ferguson that he had purchased new and which had just arrived from America by boat. Daldry imagined the wheat waving

150

in the wind in a huge golden mass in the lower half of the canvas, with a wash of different blues across the sky. But his father seemed so happy at the idea that his new tractor might have pride of place . . . Perhaps he could just make it a red mark ridden by a black speck to represent the farmer driving it.

A wheat field with a tractor in it under the sky. It really was a beautiful idea after all. His father smiled and waved. His face appeared in the clouds, and a bell began to ring incessantly.

The telephone woke Daldry from his dream, pulling him out of the English countryside and into the pale light of day in his hotel room.

"For the love of God," he groaned, sitting up in bed and leaning over to pick up the receiver.

"Daldry speaking."

"Were you asleep?"

"Not unless this is also part of the nightmare."

"Did I wake you? I'm sorry," said Alice.

"Don't be. I was just about to paint something that would have made me the landscape master of the second half of the twentieth century. It's better that I woke up before things went too far and broke my heart. What time is it?"

"Nearly noon. I just woke up too. Did we really come home that late?"

"Are you telling me that you don't remember?"

"I'm afraid not. What would you say to having lunch by the port before our appointment at the consulate?"

"Some fresh air would probably do me good, yes. What's the weather like? I haven't even opened the curtains."

"It's a glorious day. The city is positively shining," said Alice. "Get ready, and I'll meet you down in the *lobby*."

"In the bar. I need a coffee."

As he came down the stairs into the lobby, Daldry saw Can waiting with his arms folded across his chest. He had been watching Daldry.

"Been here long?" Daldry asked.

"Since eight in this morning, Your Excellency."

"I'm dreadfully sorry. I wasn't aware that we had an appointment."

"It's being normal that I come to my work in the morning. Your Excellency hired me as a guide."

"Are you going to keep up the 'Excellency' bit for much longer? It's rather annoying."

"As long as I am angry with you. I made another appointment with a perfume maker, but now it's too late. It's already past noon."

"Let me have some coffee and we can fight about it afterwards," said Daldry, leaving Can to stew in his own juices.

"Your Excellency has any other particular desirements for the rest of his day?" called Can to Daldry's back.

"That you leave me in peace."

Daldry took a seat at the bar and watched Can agitatedly pacing up and down the lobby. He got up and went back to talk to him.

"Listen, I didn't mean to be disagreeable just now. I'll make it up to you and just give you the rest of the day off. Paid, of course. Besides, Miss Alice and I are only going to lunch and then we have a meeting at the consulate. Why don't you come back tomorrow at a more civilized hour, say, around ten? We can go see the other perfume maker then."

Can agreed to this and left. Daldry went back to the bar. Alice came down and met him a good fifteen minutes later.

"I'm sorry to have taken so long. I was just looking for my hat."

"Did you find it?"

Alice bluffed. "Yes, of course. It was on the shelf in the wardrobe, right where it ought to be."

"Really. So, are you still up for lunch on the harbor?"

"Change of plans, I'm afraid. We don't have time for a coffee. Can is waiting for us in the lobby; he's set up a tour of the Grand Bazaar. Isn't that adorable?"

"I don't know if that's the word I'd use."

"I can't tell you how excited I am. I've dreamed about this for so long. Hurry up. We'll wait for you outside."

Daldry clenched his teeth as Alice walked away. "If we're lucky, I'll find a quiet little spot where I can strangle our guide."

They stepped out of the tram, and Can led them toward the northern side of the Bayezid Mosque. On the other side of the square, they walked down a narrow street cluttered with the stands of second-hand booksellers and engravers' shops and into the bazaar. Nearly an hour passed as they browsed. Daldry remained silent, while the radiant Alice listened attentively to Can's explanations and anecdotes.

"This is the biggest and oldest covered market in the world," Can said with pride. "'Bazaar' is a word that comes from Arabic. We used to be calling this *bedesten*, because *bedes* means wool in Arabic, and here was where we were selling wool."

"And I'm the sheep following my shepherd," grumbled Daldry.

"Did you say something, Your Excellency?" asked Can, turning around.

"Just drinking in your words."

"The old *bedesten* is at the heart of the Grand Bazaar, but today this is where they are selling old firearms, bronzes, and some very exceptional porcelains. It used to be made entirely of wood, but sadly it burned in the early eighteenth century. This is like a city with one gigantic roof. It is covered by enormous domes. You can find anything here—jewelry, furs, rugs, art. There are many counterfakes, but also some very magnificent pieces for an expert's eye who can undiscover them in the middle of—"

"This enormous, chaotic rubbish heap," muttered Daldry.

"What's the matter with you?" asked Alice. "This is a fascinating place. You're in a terrible mood, aren't you?"

"I'm just hungry, that's all."

"You would need at least two days to explore all of the streets in the Bazaar," continued Can, mercilessly ignoring Daldry. "But to help you spend a few hours in leisure, you must know that the Bazaar is divided into neighborhoods, magnificently kept, as you can see. Each neighborhood is home to different items. We can even enjoy a meal in an excellent place because we are now in an area where we will find the only foods susceptible to please Your Excellency."

Alice whispered in Daldry's ear, "Strange how he's started calling you that. Although 'Excellency' suits you somehow, when you think about it."

"Not really, but if the two of you are having fun, I certainly don't want to ruin it for you."

"Did something happen? You seem to be getting on like oil and water."

"Nothing at all." Daldry pouted.

"You really are impossible. Can is such a devoted guide. If you're as hungry as that, let's find something to eat. I'll give up my walk through the Bazaar if it means you'll stop behaving like a child."

Daldry shrugged and walked ahead of Alice and Can.

Alice stopped in front of a store selling musical instruments. An old brass trumpet had caught her eye. She asked the shopkeeper if she could have a closer look at it.

"Armstrong has the same model," said the salesman. "This one is unique. I don't know how to play, but a friend tried it and wanted to buy it. It's an exceptional deal."

Can looked at the trumpet and leaned over to whisper. "This is junk. If you are looking to buy a beautiful trumpet, I know where to go. Put it down and come with me."

Daldry rolled his eyes in exasperation as he watched Alice follow Can.

Can took her to another shop selling musical instruments in a neighboring street. He asked the salesman to show his friend the best of his wares, not just the most expensive. In the meantime, Alice had already found a trumpet to her liking in a display case.

"Is this a real Selmer?" she asked, once it was out of the case and in her hands.

"Entirely authentic. Try it if you don't believe me," said the salesman. Alice looked over the instrument carefully. "Sterling silver and four pistons. It must be completely out of my price range."

"That's not how you should negotiate prices in the Bazaar, miss," said the salesman, chuckling at Alice's innocence. "I also have a Vincent Bach I can show you. The Stradivarius of trumpets. The only one you will find in Turkey."

But Alice only had eyes for the Selmer. It made her think of Anton, whom she remembered had admired a model much like it. He had stood for what seemed like hours gazing through the window of a shop in Battersea like a motorcar enthusiast lusting after a Jaguar convertible. Anton had taught her a great deal about trumpets: the difference between the models, their keys, valves, and pistons, the various patinas and finishes, and the different alloys that could have an effect on the sound of the instrument.

"I can sell it to you for a reasonable price," offered the shopkeeper.

Can said a few words in Turkish.

"A very good price," he corrected. "Can's friend is my friend. I will even give you a case."

Alice paid the salesman and left the shop with her purchase.

Daldry was skeptical. "I didn't know you were a trumpet expert," he said, following her. "You looked like you knew what you were doing."

"You don't know everything about me," said Alice teasingly.

"Well, I've certainly never heard you play, and Lord knows, I would if you did."

"And you still insist that you don't play the piano?"

"I told you, it's the woman downstairs. So what is it? You practice under railway arches to avoid bothering the neighbors?"

"I thought you were hungry, Daldry." She stopped in front of a restaurant. "This place doesn't look half bad."

Can went into the restaurant ahead of them and managed to get a table in spite of the queue of customers waiting to be seated.

"Are you a shareholder in the Bazaar, or is it that your father owns the entire place?" asked Daldry as they sat down.

"Just a guide, Your Excellency."

"I know, I know. 'The best in Istanbul.'"

"I'm thrilled to hear you finally say so. Let me order. Our time is limited and you have a meeting soon."

Can approached the counter.

9

The consulate had reassumed its everyday appearance. The elaborate flower arrangements were gone, the crystal had been packed away, and the ballroom doors were closed.

Alice and Daldry showed their papers to a uniformed officer, who took them to the second floor, where they walked down a long corridor and waited for a secretary to call them.

Not long afterward, they entered the consul's office. He had an austere appearance, but a pleasant voice.

"Miss Pendelbury, I gather you're a friend of His Excellency's wife."

Alice turned and looked at Daldry quizzically.

"Not me," said Daldry. "The real one."

"Oh yes, quite," said Alice to the consul.

"You must be rather close indeed for her to have asked for this appointment on such short notice. How might I be of service?"

Alice explained her request to the consul as he continued his work, signing and initialing a series of official documents in a leather portfolio.

"Supposing, Miss Pendelbury, that your parents asked for an official visa, it would be more likely that you would find the information you're looking for in the archives of the old Ottoman regime, not with us. Before the Republic of Turkey was founded in 1923, this consulate used to be our embassy, but I see no reason why the papers you are looking for would have found their way here. Only the Turkish foreign minister might have something in his archives that would interest you, but even supposing that such minor paperwork has been kept, I highly doubt that they would undertake such complicated research on behalf of a private party."

Here Daldry interjected. "Unless, perhaps, the British Consulate contacted the Turkish authorities and made it clear that the request came from a close personal friend of the British Ambassador's wife. You might be surprised at what the desire to please an ally and economic partner can do to lift administrative roadblocks. I know from personal experience. One of my uncles on my father's side is a close advisor to our Foreign Secretary. I'm sure he'd be glad to hear about your efficient assistance in this matter."

The consul looked up from his work. "I understand entirely, Mr. Daldry. I'll be in touch with the Turkish authorities and I'll do my best to get an answer for you. Still, I wouldn't be too optimistic if I were you. It strikes me as highly unlikely that they would have kept something so simple as a visa request for such a long time. You said, Miss Pendelbury, that your parents might have come to Istanbul sometime between 1900 and 1910?"

"Yes, that's right." Her face had flushed a particularly deep shade of red during Daldry's bald-faced lie.

"Enjoy your stay in Istanbul. It's a wonderful city. If I hear anything back from the Turks, I'll send a message to your hotel." He rose and showed them to the door. Alice thanked him for his time.

"I suppose your uncle must also be named Daldry, if he's your father's brother, isn't that so?" asked the consul, shaking Daldry's hand.

"No, actually, it's not," said Daldry, remaining composed. "As an artist, I chose to take my mother's maiden name because it seemed much more original at the time. My uncle's name is Davies, as was my father's."

Alice and Daldry left the consulate and returned to the hotel to take the tea that the consul never got around to offering them.

"Is Daldry really your mother's maiden name?" she asked, settling into a chair.

"Not at all. But chances are that you'll find a Davies or two in every branch of the government."

"You really aren't afraid of anything, are you?"

"You ought to be congratulating me. We made out rather well."

The Karayel, a cold wind from the Balkans, began to blow as evening fell, bringing with it a snowstorm that effectively ended the unusually mild winter Istanbul had been enjoying that year. When Alice woke up the following morning, the pavement was as white as the percale curtains hanging on either side of her window, and the roofs of Istanbul looked no different than those she had left behind in London. The snowstorm continued throughout the day, keeping people indoors and nearly obscuring the view of the Bosporus. After eating breakfast in the hotel dining room, Alice went back to her room and sat at the desk, where she had developed a habit of writing a letter nearly every evening.

> Dear Anton,
> Winter has struck and given us an excuse to take a break from touring the city. I met the British consul here yesterday, but he didn't leave me feeling very optimistic about my chances of finding out whether my parents ever came here. I think about them all the time. I often wonder whether it was the fortune-teller's predictions or the dream of discovering a new fragrance that took me away from London. Perhaps it was you. If I'm writing you, it's because I miss you. Why did I hide my feelings? Maybe I was afraid of putting our friendship at risk. When my parents died,

you were one of the few remaining links to my past. I'll never forget the letters I received from you every week during the long years that I lived with my aunt.

I wish you'd write me letters again so that I could read about what's new in your life and know how you pass your days. I'm having a wonderful time. Daldry sometimes acts like a spoiled child, but he's a gentleman at heart. And Istanbul continues to be a beautiful, fascinating place. Today I found something in the Bazaar that I think you'll like very much. That's all I'll tell you for now . . . I've sworn to myself that I'll manage to keep a secret for once. When I come home, we'll go for a walk along the Thames and you'll play . . .

Alice paused for a moment and chewed on the tip of her pen. She scribbled out the last sentence until it was illegible.

. . . we'll walk along the Thames and you'll tell me everything that happened while I was away.

Don't think I've come all this way just to be an idle tourist. My ideas for a new perfume are also coming along, or rather, I've got ideas for several different projects. The next step, as soon as I have some time, is to visit the spice market. Last night, I decided to create a series of fragrances for people's homes. I know it's not a completely new idea, but this particular variation is promising, and it came to me thanks to the perfume maker I told you about in my last letter.

As I was falling asleep last night, I thought about my parents, and each memory was linked to a scent. I'm not talking about my father's cologne or my mother's perfume, but other things, like the smell of a leather satchel, of chalk dust and hot chocolate. It always smelled like cinnamon in our house when my mother was baking. She put it in nearly all of her desserts. And when I think back to the winters of my childhood when we went out to the countryside, I can smell the firewood my father collected in the forest and burned in our fireplace. In late spring there were the wild roses he gave to my mother, filling the sitting room with their fragrance. Mother always knew about my interest in and sensitivity to smells, but I never explained to her how odors mark every minute of my life and form a sort of language, a way of understanding the world. I smell the passage of time the way that others watch the changing colors of a sunset, distinguishing dozens of notes—rain dripping off leaves and filtering through moss, grass drying in the summer sun, the straw in the barns where we used to play hide-and-seek, the manure pile you pushed me into that time, or the branch of lilac blossoms you gave me on my sixteenth birthday.

The memories of our teenage years and our adult lives recall other odors. Did you know that your hands have a peppery scent, for example, something between brass, soap, and tobacco?

Take care of yourself, Anton, I hope you miss me, at least a little bit.

I'll write to you again next week.

Fondly,

Alice

◆　◆　◆

The following day a steady rain melted the snow. It was the first of several days that Can took Alice and Daldry around the city to see monuments such as the Topkapi Palace, the Süleymaniye Mosque, and the tombs of Süleyman and Roxelana. For hours on end they wandered the animated streets around the Galata Bridge and shopped in the Egyptian Bazaar. In the spice market, Alice stopped at each stall, breathing in the varied scents of the powders, dried flowers, and vials of essential oils. Daldry went into raptures at the sight of the intricately painted tiles in the Rüstem Pasha Mosque, and again before the frescoes in the former Church of the Holy Saviour in Chora. Only on one occasion, when they were in an old neighborhood where the timeworn wooden houses had escaped the great fires, did Alice feel ill at ease and ask to go elsewhere. She later took Daldry to the top of the Galata Tower, which she had first visited without him.

For Alice, the most memorable visit was a morning trip to the Flower Passage and its covered market, followed by lunch in a charming little waterside restaurant. On Thursday they toured the Dolmabahçe neighborhood, and on Friday they went to Eyüp, a district stretching from the Golden Horn to the Black Sea. After admiring the tomb of the Prophet Mohammed's companion Abu Ayyub, they walked up the steps to the cemetery and paused for a drink at the Pierre Loti Café. From the windows of the old house where the French author came to relax, one could see over the Ottoman tombs to the broad horizon and the shores of the Bosporus beyond.

It was here, during a moment alone, that Alice confided in Daldry and told him that she thought the time had come to start thinking about returning to London.

"You want to give up?"

"We came in the wrong season. We should have waited at least for the flowers to bloom before rushing over. Besides, if I ever want to be able to pay you for all the costs we've incurred, I've got to get back to work. This has been an extraordinary journey, and I'll go home my head buzzing with new ideas, but I have to turn them into something concrete."

"You know full well that we didn't come here for your perfumes."

"That's not true . . . I'm not sure what brought me here. Was it the fortune-teller? My nightmares? Your insistence? The opportunity to escape my daily life for a while? In the beginning, I wanted to believe that my parents had come to Istanbul. The idea of following in their footsteps made them seem closer. But we haven't heard anything from the consulate, and it's time I started acting like an adult. Even if my entire being is resisting it, I have to face the facts. So do you, for that matter."

"I disagree. I admit we may have overestimated the consul's capacities, but think about the life the fortune-teller promised, about the man waiting at the end of your journey. I'm the one who promised to take you to him, or at least to the second link in the chain. I'm a man of honor. I keep my promises. It's out of the question to give up in the face of adversity. We haven't lost any time. On the contrary, you have new ideas, and I'm sure others will soon follow. One of these days we'll find that second person."

"Be reasonable. I'm not asking for us to go home tomorrow—I just think we should start thinking about it."

"I've thought about it. And since you ask, I'll think about it some more."

As Daldry spoke, Can returned, cutting short their conversation. It was time to go back to the hotel.

Day in and day out, from churches to synagogues, from synagogues to mosques, from sleepy old cemeteries to lively streets, and in the tearooms and restaurants where they ate every evening, Alice, Daldry, and Can shared a little more about themselves and about their pasts. Daldry and Can had come to an understanding. A certain camaraderie had even developed between them, thanks to their common endeavor.

The following Monday, the hotel concierge caught Alice's attention as she was returning from a busy day in the city to tell her a consular courier had delivered a message at the end of the morning.

Alice turned to Daldry with feverish excitement.

"Well, go on. Open it."

"Not here. Let's go to the bar."

They took a table at the back of the room, and Daldry sent away the approaching waiter.

"So?" He was bubbling over with impatience.

Alice pulled open the flap, read the few lines of text, and put the note on the table.

Daldry looked back and forth between Alice and the telegram.

"It would be indelicate of me to read your private correspondence, but it's cruel to make me wait a second longer."

"What time is it?"

"Five o'clock. Why?"

"Because the consul is about to show up at any minute."

"Here?"

"That's what he says. He has something he wants to tell me."

"Well, in that case, I'll leave you to it."

Daldry started to get up, but Alice put her hand on his arm to show he could stay. She didn't have to ask twice.

A short while later, the consul walked into the lobby, saw Alice in the bar, and came to meet her.

"You received my message in time," he said, taking off his coat, which he passed, along with his hat, to the waiter. He took a seat in a club chair between the two of them.

"Something to drink?" asked Daldry.

The consul glanced at his watch and asked for a bourbon, which the waiter swiftly brought to him.

"I've got an appointment in the neighborhood in about half an hour. The consulate isn't far, as you know, and since I had news for you, I thought I'd deliver it in person."

"That's very kind of you," said Alice.

"As I had anticipated, our friends the Turks weren't much help. It's not that they didn't want to be helpful. A connection of mine at the Turkish equivalent of our Foreign Office called me the day before yesterday to say that they had tried everything, but that visa requests from the old Ottoman days were never even archived."

"A dead end," said Daldry.

"Not quite. I happened to ask one of my intelligence officers to look into your affair. He's a young fellow, but extremely effective. He said that with a bit of luck—for us, not them, of course—one of your parents might have lost their passport during their stay, or perhaps had it stolen. If you think Istanbul is chaotic today, I assure you it was far worse forty years ago. Had this been the case, your parents would have certainly gone to what was, back then, the British Embassy."

"Somebody stole their passports?" Daldry was more impatient than ever.

"No, I'm afraid not." The consul swirled his drink in its tumbler, making the ice cubes tinkle. "However, they did come to the embassy during their stay. Your parents were in Istanbul, not in 1909 or 1910, as you initially thought, but at the end of 1913. Your father was finishing a study on Turkish medicinal plants for his pharmacology degree. They lived in a little apartment in Beyoğlu, not far from here, as it happens."

"How did you learn all that?" asked Daldry.

"Well, I don't have to remind you of the chaotic state of affairs leading up to the beginning of the war in August 1914, or the unfortunate decision made by the Ottoman rulers in November to side with Germany and the Central Powers. As subjects of His Majesty, your parents found themselves, ipso facto, enemies of the Turkish regime. Your father anticipated the risk he and his wife were taking and signaled their presence to the embassy in hopes that they might be repatriated. Alas, in wartime, travel was not without risk, and they had to wait a long time before they were able to return to England. Their request to take refuge in the embassy in the event of an emergency created a paper trail that allows me to tell you all this today."

Alice's face had grown progressively paler as she listened to the consul's story. Daldry was beginning to worry about her.

"Are you all right?" he asked, taking her hand.

"Should we call a doctor?" asked the consul.

"No, it's nothing. I'm fine," she murmured, trembling slightly. "Please, do go on."

"In the spring of 1916, our embassy managed to exfiltrate about a hundred British citizens by hiding them aboard a cargo ship flying the Spanish flag. Spain was a neutral power, and the ship made it all the way to Gibraltar without a scratch. From that point onward I don't have any information, but your presence here today would seem to indicate that they made it home safe and sound." He took a sip of his drink. "Now you know as much as I do, Miss Pendelbury."

"It's impossible," she said, her voice broken.

"Miss Pendelbury, I'm afraid everything I've just told you is quite official."

"But I was already born. I must have been with them."

The consul eyed her skeptically. "If you say so, but I'd be surprised. There's no trace of you in the ledgers and logbooks we consulted. Perhaps your father simply didn't mention you when he contacted our services."

Daldry couldn't resist interjecting. "I'd be surprised if her father bothered going to the embassy to seek protection for himself and his wife without mentioning their only child. Were children recorded in the books at all?"

"Well, of course. We are a civilized country, after all. The children were listed along with their parents."

Daldry turned to Alice. "Perhaps your father purposefully omitted mentioning you for fear that the authorities would consider the voyage too risky for a young child."

"I don't think so," said the consul. "Women and children first, you know. There is clear evidence that there were many families with small children aboard the ship. They were the priority."

"Well, I don't want to get carried away arguing about the hypothetical," said Daldry. "I don't know how to thank you, sir. The information you uncovered goes far beyond what we initially hoped for."

Alice was not so easily placated. "And I don't remember any of it? Not even the slightest memory?"

"I don't mean to be indiscreet, but how old are you, Miss Pendelbury?"

"Thirty-nine. I would have been four years old on March 25, 1915."

The consul tried to reason with her. "And five years old in the spring of 1916. You know, I feel a great deal of affection for my parents, and I'm very thankful for the upbringing and love they gave me, but I do think I would be entirely incapable of remembering anything from that early in my life." He patted Alice's hand. "If I can be of any further assistance, please don't hesitate to come and see me. You know where I can be found. I'm afraid I must leave now or I'll be late for my appointment."

"Do you remember their address?" asked Alice.

"I wrote it down on a piece of paper, thinking you might ask." He rummaged around in his coat pocket. "Here it is. They lived quite nearby, on Istiklal, the big avenue. It was called Pera then. They were on the third floor of the Rumelia building, just next to the famous Flower Passage."

The consul rose to his feet and kissed Alice's hand.

"Would you mind seeing me to the door?" he asked Daldry. "I have one or two things I'd like to speak to you about. Nothing important."

Daldry stood and followed the consul as he put on his coat. They crossed the lobby and paused in front of the receptionist.

"While I was doing all that research for your friend, out of curiosity I also happened to look into the presence of your relative in the Foreign Office."

"Oh?"

"It happens that the only employee we have who answers to the name of Davies is a boy who works in the post room. I think he's most likely too young to be your uncle. Isn't that so?"

"Yes, probably," said Daldry, looking at his feet.

"That's what I thought. Have a pleasant stay in Istanbul, Mr. Daldry," said the consul before stepping into the revolving door and out into the evening.

10

Daldry returned to the bar, where Alice was waiting for him. He kept her company for half an hour, sipping his drink and watching her stare in silence at the black piano that stood in the corner of the room.

"If you like, tomorrow we could take a walk and see the building where they lived," Daldry said.

"Why didn't they tell me?"

"I don't know, Alice. Maybe they wanted to protect you? They must have gone through a difficult time at the end. Maybe it was just too painful to speak of. My father was in the First World War and he never wanted to talk about it."

"But why didn't they declare me at the embassy?"

"Perhaps they did, and perhaps the embassy official just didn't write it down correctly. It was a chaotic period. Some details might have slipped through the cracks."

"That makes for a lot of 'perhaps,' don't you think?"

"Yes, well, I suppose it does, but what else can I say? We weren't there."

"As it happens, I was there."

"Then let's look into it further."

"I don't even know where to begin."

"We could go back to the neighborhood and ask if anybody remembers them."

"Nearly forty years later?"

"You never know. We've hired the best guide in Istanbul; let's ask him to help us."

"You want to get Can involved?"

"Why not? He's going to turn up at any minute, you know. After the ballet we can invite him to have dinner with us."

"I don't feel like going to the ballet anymore. Why don't the two of you go without me?"

"I don't think you should be alone this evening. You'll just worry about far-flung possibilities and keep yourself awake all night. Come with us, and afterwards we'll discuss the situation with Can over dinner."

"I'm not hungry, and I know in advance that I won't be pleasant company. I just need to be alone for a while. I need time to think."

"Alice, I don't mean to minimize the shock of what you've just heard, but none of it changes the essentials. Your parents, as it's clear from the stories you've told me, loved you very much. For whatever reason, they just didn't tell you about the time the three of you spent in Istanbul. It's not worth putting yourself in a state. You look so shaken up that you're even beginning to worry me."

Alice looked up and smiled reassuringly.

"You're right," she said. "But I'm still quite sure I won't be any fun this evening. Go on. Enjoy the show and have dinner with Can, just you boys. I promise I won't stay up all night thinking. A good night's rest, and tomorrow we can decide whether or not we really feel like playing detective."

Can had come into the lobby and was now tapping on his watch to say that it was time to go.

"Go," said Alice, seeing Daldry hesitate.

"Are you sure?"

Alice shooed Daldry away with a gesture. He said goodbye and then joined Can in the lobby.

"Miss Alice isn't pairing with us?"

"No, she's not pairing with us. But I'm sure we'll still manage to have an unforgettable evening, just the two of us."

Daldry fell asleep during the second act. When his snoring grew too noticeable, Can would jab him with his elbow, making Daldry jump before he dozed off again a few moments later.

After the final curtain, they left the old French theatre on Istiklal Avenue, and Can took Daldry to dinner at the Regency in Olivo Passage. The food was refined, and Daldry ate even more than usual, finally beginning to relax after the third glass of wine.

"Why did Miss Alice not accompany us this evening?" Can asked.

"Oh, I think she was a bit tired."

"The two of you had a bickering?"

"I beg your pardon?"

"A spatting?"

"An argument? No, not this time."

"All the better," said Can, without really seeming convinced. Daldry topped up their glasses and told him what the consul had revealed just before Can's arrival at the hotel.

"What an incredible story. And from the consul's own mouth? I understand why Miss Alice is so topsy-turvy. In her place I would feel the same way. What will you do?"

"Try to see her through it, I suppose. If that's possible."

"In Istanbul, nothing is impossible with Can. How can we enlighten Miss Alice?"

"Well, a good start would be to find people in the neighborhood where her parents lived who still remember them."

"This is possible. I will find somebody who remembers."

"Well, do your best, but don't tell her until we've found something concrete. She's sufficiently stirred up as it is."

"Very wise. No need to be stirring."

Daldry raised his eyebrows, but said nothing.

"May I ask you a question?" asked Can, lowering his voice.

"Ask, and we'll see."

"Is there something . . . picturesque between you and Miss Alice?"

"Come now. You're not even trying!"

"Something special? In a romantic way?"

"And how would that be any of your business?"

"I have my answer. You just told me."

"No, I haven't just told you, Guide Know-It-All."

"I have hit a tender spot for you to be sputtering like a chicken."

"I'm not sputtering like a chicken for the very good reason that chickens don't sputter."

"Well, anyway, you answered my question."

Daldry refilled his glass and took a long sip. Can imitated him.

"There's nothing between Miss Alice and me, apart from a mutual understanding. A friendship."

"It is a strange friendship where you plan to deceive her."

"We're doing each other a favor. She needed a change in her life, and I needed a studio with decent light. It's a fair trade between friends."

"It would be, if both friends were aware of the trade."

"I can't tell you how utterly boring I find your morality lessons."

"You don't find her attractive?" Can asked.

"She's not my type of woman, and I'm not her type of man. It's a very equitable arrangement."

"What don't you like about her?"

"Tell me, you wouldn't happen to be casing out the territory for a personal campaign, would you?"

"It would be degrading to be . . . casing her territory." Can was clearly drunk.

"How else shall I put it? Do you have a crush on Alice?"

"I have not begun my investigation. How can I already find a crush?"

"Stop playing the fool when it suits you. I'm just asking whether you're attracted to her."

"Well, excuse me for saying it," said Can, "but I'm the one who asked first."

"And I told you."

"Absolutely not. You were avoiding to answer."

"The thought has never even crossed my mind. How do you expect me to respond?"

"Liar."

"Don't take that tone with me. I've never lied in my life!" Daldry exclaimed.

"You lie to Alice."

"You just gave the game away, my friend. You called her Alice."

"What does it prove if I forgot to say 'Miss'? Just a mistake on my part. I drank too much."

"Just a little?"

"You should talk!"

"Fine, since we agree that we're both drunk, what would you say to maintaining the status quo?"

Daldry ordered them a very fine and very old cognac.

"If I ever did fall in love with a woman like her, the only way I could show my feelings would be to go as far away from her as possible. To the other side of the world."

"I don't understand how that would show your love," said Can.

"Because I would save her from meeting a fellow like me. I'm a loner, a bitter bachelor. I'm set in my ways and I hate it when the outside world tries to make me change. I hate noise, and she's noisy. I hate socializing, and she's right across the corridor. Besides, all the noble sentiments associated with love always end up threadbare and debased. In love, you have to know when to make an exit before it's too late.

For me, that means restraining myself from making any declarations to begin with." He paused. "Why are you smiling like that?"

"Because we both agree that you're a rather sorry fellow."

"I'm just like my father in so many ways, even if I pretend to be everything to the contrary. I know what I'm talking about—I grew up with him, and now I have to see him in the mirror every morning."

"Your mother was never happy with your father?"

"I'll need another drink to answer that. That story lies at a depth that we haven't reached."

Three cognacs later, the restaurant was starting to close. Daldry asked Can to take him to a bar worthy of such a title, and Can suggested a place that didn't close until very early in the morning.

They followed the rails of the tramway down the hill. Can teetered on the right rail, Daldry on the left. When a tram tried to pass, they waited until the last moment to get out of the way, in spite of the conductor's insistent ringing of the bell.

"If you had met my mother when she was Alice's age, you would have thought she was the happiest woman in the world. She was so good at acting that I think she missed her true calling. She could have made a lot of money on the stage. But on Saturdays she didn't have to act. On Saturdays I think she was truly happy."

"Why Saturdays?" Can slouched onto a bench.

"Because on Saturday, my father paid attention to her," said Daldry, joining him. "He probably only did it so that she'd forgive him for his sins, and for ignoring her the rest of the time, but he did pay her attention."

"His sins?"

"I'll get to that. Why didn't you ask, 'Why not Sundays? Wouldn't that be more logical?' Well, because on Saturday, my mother was distracted enough to forget that he would be leaving soon. But when Sunday Mass was over, she grew more and more depressed as the hours wore on. Sunday evenings were horrible. When I think that he even had the nerve to take her to Mass."

"What did he do that was so bad on Monday?"

"After washing and shaving, he put on his finest suit, tied his bow tie, polished his pocket watch, arranged his hair, perfumed himself, and called for his carriage to be prepared to take him into town. Every Monday afternoon he had a meeting with his solicitor and he slept in town because the roads were supposedly dangerous at night. He would return the following day."

"But he was going to see his mistress?"

"No, he really did have a meeting with his solicitor. They were old friends from school. But they spent the night together, so I suppose it was more or less the same thing."

"And your mother knew?"

"That her husband was cheating on her with a man? Yes, she knew. She knew, and the driver knew, and the chambermaids and the cook and the governess knew . . . everybody apart from me. For a long time, I thought he was seeing another woman, but I'm a bit of a fool by nature."

"You know, in the days of the sultans . . ."

"I know what you're going to say, and it's very kind of you, but in England we have a king and a queen and a palace. No harem. Don't think I'm being judgmental. It's a question of tradition. And to tell you the truth, I couldn't have cared less about my father's private life; it was the suffering he caused my mother that hurt me. My father certainly wasn't the first man on earth to sleep with someone other than his wife, but he sullied her love by doing it. When I finally got up the courage to talk to her about it, she was on the verge of tears but explained everything with a calm dignity that chilled my blood. She defended my father and explained that it was all part of the order of things, that it was necessary for him, something she had never been angry about. For somebody who was usually such a good actress, she really bungled up her lines that day."

"But if you hate your father for what he did to your mother, why do you let yourself behave like him?"

"Well, I try not to be like him. In watching the way he made my mother suffer, I came to understand that for a man, loving a woman is taking her beauty and putting it under a glass, where she feels sheltered and cherished . . . until it wilts and fades away. Then he turns elsewhere, to other flowers. I promised myself that if I ever came to love a woman, to love her truly, that I would leave her alone, refuse to take her and put her under glass.

"And here we are. I've had too much to drink and told you too much. I'm going to regret it in the morning. If you repeat a single word I've said, I'll drown you in the Bosporus with my own bare hands." He sighed. "The real question is, How on earth are we to get back to the hotel? I think I'm too drunk to walk."

Can was no more sober than Daldry. Together they helped each other stagger up Istiklal, hanging on each other's shoulders like two old drunks.

The next morning, Alice settled in the sitting area next to the bar while the hotel maid was tidying up her room. She was writing another letter that she probably wouldn't send. She glanced in the mirror and saw Daldry coming down the grand staircase. He came and collapsed into an armchair next to hers.

"Long night out?" she asked, without looking up from her letter.

"What makes you say that?"

"Well, your jacket is buttoned up crooked and you missed a few patches shaving."

"Yes, well, I had a few drinks. We missed you."

"I don't doubt it for a second."

"Writing a letter?"

"To a friend in London." She folded the paper in half and put it in her pocket.

"I've got a ghastly headache. Would you like to go for a walk and get some fresh air? What friend in London?"

She ignored the last question. "Yes, let's go for a walk. I wondered what time you might resurface this morning. I've been up since dawn and was starting to get bored. Where should we go?"

"The Bosporus? Old habits die hard, you know."

Along the way, Alice dawdled in front of a cobbler's shop and watched the drive belts spin on a machine.

"Need to resole some shoes?"

"No . . . But don't you ever come across places that make you feel peaceful inside, without entirely understanding why?"

"As a person who paints intersections, it would be difficult for me to pretend otherwise. I could watch double-decker buses drive past for an entire day. I like the sound they make when they brake and change gear, and the bell that the conductor rings before they set off."

"All very poetic, what you just said."

"Are you poking fun at me?"

"Just a little bit."

"I suppose you think this shop is a much more romantic subject."

"Well, there is a certain poetry in the way he uses his hands. And I've always loved the smell at the cobbler's—leather, glue, wax . . ."

"That's just because you like shoes. I'm more of a bakery man myself, but I don't think I have to explain."

A short while later they were walking along the water. Daldry sat down on a bench.

"What are you looking at?" asked Alice.

"That old woman near the railing talking to the man with the terrier. It's fascinating."

"She likes animals. What's so fascinating about that?"

"Keep watching; you'll see what I mean."

After exchanging a few words with the terrier's owner, the old woman went over to another dog. She knelt and caressed its muzzle.

"You see?"

"She's patting another dog?"

"She's not interested in the dogs; she's interested in the leash."

"The leash?"

"The leash that attaches the dog to its owner—the fellow fishing. The leash is what allows her to have a little conversation. She's probably dying of loneliness, but she's come up with a way of getting a few words out of complete strangers. I'll bet she comes here every day for a little dose of humanity."

This time, Daldry seemed to be right. When the old lady didn't manage to get the attention of the dog's owner, she walked a little farther down the waterfront and took some crumbs from her pocket, throwing them to the pigeons. Soon she was chatting with another fisherman.

"A sad, solitary existence, don't you think?" asked Daldry.

Alice turned and looked him in the eye. "Why did you come all this way? Why did you come on this trip with me?"

Alice had caught Daldry off guard. "You know why . . . We made a deal. I'm helping you find the love of your life, or at least putting you on the right track. While you're on the trail, I'll paint under your skylight."

"Is that really why?"

Daldry gazed out over the water and seemed to contemplate the minaret on the Asian side of the Bosporus.

"You remember the café at the end of our street?" asked Daldry.

"Yes, of course. The one where we had breakfast together."

"I used to go there every day and sit at the same table with my newspaper. One day, when the article I was reading was particularly boring, I looked up, saw myself in the mirror, and suddenly realized how the years had been dragging on. I needed a change of scenery too. But I've started to miss London these past few days. Nothing's perfect."

"You're thinking about going home?"

"You were thinking about it yourself, not so long ago."

"Not anymore."

"The fortune-teller's predictions are starting to seem more plausible. You have a reason to stay now. But I've accomplished my mission. I think the consul was the second person in the chain of six, perhaps even the third, if we consider Can the second."

"You're going to abandon me?"

"That's what we agreed to, isn't it? Oh, don't worry, I'll pay for your hotel room and Can's services for three more months. He's very devoted. I'll also leave him a generous advance on his expenses. I'll open an account for you in the Banca di Roma—the branch is right on Istiklal and they're used to receiving foreign clients."

"You expect me to stay in Istanbul three months longer?"

"You still have a long way to go if you want to get to the end of your journey, Alice. Besides, you don't want to miss springtime in Turkey. Think of all the flowers you'll be able to use in your perfumes . . . Think of our business venture."

"When did you decide it was time for you to leave?"

"When I woke up this morning."

"And what if I asked you to stay, just a little while longer?"

"You don't even have to ask. The next flight for London doesn't leave until Saturday. We still have a few days ahead of us." Alice's face fell. "Oh, come now. Don't be like that . . . My mother's health isn't very good, I can't stay away for too long."

Daldry got up and walked over to the crash barrier, where the old woman they had watched earlier was sidling up to a large white dog.

"Be careful," he said to her. "That one looks like a biter."

◆　◆　◆

Can arrived at the hotel in time for tea. He looked very pleased with himself.

"I have fascinating news to deliver you," he said as he joined Alice and Daldry in the bar.

Alice put her cup on the table and gave Can her full attention.

"In a building near to the one where your father and mother lived, I met an old man who knew them. He invited us to come see him."

"When?" asked Alice, turning to Daldry to see his expression.

"Now."

11

Mr. Zemirli's apartment occupied the third floor of a reasonably well-to-do building on Istiklal Avenue. His door opened onto a hall whose walls were lined with countless stacks of old books.

Ogüz Zemirli wore flannel trousers, a white shirt, a silk dressing gown, and two pairs of glasses. One of them remained fixed to his forehead as if by magic, and the other rested on the tip of his nose. He alternated between them depending on what he needed to see. His face was closely shaven, apart from a few gray hairs on the tip of his chin that seemed to have escaped the barber's attention.

He led his guests into a sitting room furnished with a mix of French and Ottoman furniture and disappeared into the kitchen, returning in the company of a curvaceous woman. She served them glasses of mint tea and Turkish pastries. Mr. Zemirli thanked her and she went back into the kitchen.

"She is my cook," he said in an accented English. "Her cakes are delicious. Please help yourselves."

Daldry didn't have to be asked twice.

"So, you are the little girl of Cömert Eczaci . . ."

"No, sir, my father was named Pendelbury." Alice glanced at Daldry in disappointment.

"Pendelbury? I don't think he told me . . . Maybe my memory isn't as good as it once was."

Daldry wondered for a moment if their host still had all his wits about him. He mentally cursed Can for bringing them into a stranger's home and getting Alice's hopes up.

"In the neighborhood we never called him Pendelbury, especially back then. We called him Cömert Eczaci."

Can interjected. "It means 'generous pharmacist.'" Alice's heart started beating faster with Can's explanation.

"He was indeed your father?" Mr. Zemirli asked.

"It's quite possible. My father was both generous and a pharmacist."

"I remember him well. Your mother too, a woman of character. They worked together at the university." Mr. Zemirli got up from his chair, not without some difficulty. "Follow me," he instructed, going over to the window and pointing out an apartment on the second floor of the building across the street from his. "They lived there."

"The consul said that they lived on the third floor."

"Well, I'm telling you they lived on the second. Believe him if you like, but it was my aunt who rented them the apartment. You see, the window on the left was their sitting room, and the window on the right was their bedroom. There was a kitchen at the back that looked out over the courtyard, just like in this building. Let's sit. My leg is bothering me." They sat. "In fact, my leg is what led me to meet your parents."

Mr. Zemirli explained how, as a teenager, like many of the other boys his age, he liked to come home from school by jumping on a passing tram and riding astride the single taillight on the back of the wagon. One rainy day, Ogüz missed his mark and got his leg caught between the wheel and the wheel guard. The tram dragged him for several meters before he fell free. The surgeons did their best to stitch up his wounds and saved him from needing an amputation, but he couldn't do his military service, and his leg always throbbed with pain when it rained.

"The medicine was very expensive, much too expensive in the pharmacy, but your father brought it home from the university hospital, as he did for many of the needy families in the neighborhood. It was during the war, and many people were falling ill. In their little apartment, your parents established a sort of clandestine dispensary. When they got home from the hospital, your mother would care for patients, while your father handed out the medicine he had found, as well as remedies he created himself from medicinal plants. In the winter, when many children came down with fevers, sometimes the line of mothers and grandmothers stretched into the street. The local police knew what was going on, but since it was entirely voluntary and for the public's good, they looked the other way. Besides, they sent their own children when they fell sick. I can't imagine any policeman brave enough to confront his wife with the news that he had arrested the source of the family's medical care. And believe me, as a child, I knew all the local policemen!" He chuckled.

"One evening, your father handed out much more medicine than he usually did. He gave away everything he had. The next day, your parents had disappeared. They had been gone for two months before my aunt dared take the key and go see what had become of the apartment. Everything was perfectly arranged and in its place. Not a single dish or spoon was missing. On the kitchen table they had left the rest of the rent they owed and a note saying they had gone back to England. That note came as a huge relief to the people of the neighborhood. We had all been very worried about Cömert Eczaci and his wife, and also worried that our policemen had done something terrible to them and hidden it from us. You know, thirty-five years later, every time I go to the pharmacy to get the medicine for this cursed leg of mine, I can feel them around me. I look up and see Cömert Eczaci's face in the window of my aunt's apartment. So you can imagine what an emotional experience it is to see his daughter here before me this evening."

Alice could see the tears welling behind the thick lenses of Mr. Zemirli's glasses, and it made her feel a little less embarrassed about not having been able to keep her own from streaming down her cheeks.

The flood of emotions had also taken Can and Daldry by surprise. Mr. Zemirli took a handkerchief from his pocket and dabbed the tip of his nose before leaning over and refilling their glasses.

"We should drink to the memory of the generous pharmacist of Beyoğlu and his dear wife."

They raised their glasses of mint tea in an improbable but heartfelt toast to Alice's parents.

"Do you remember me from those times?" asked Alice.

"No, I don't recall having seen you. I wish I could tell you otherwise, but I would be lying. How old were you?"

"Five."

"Well, that's normal. Your parents worked and you must have been at school."

"That makes sense," said Daldry.

"What school do you think I went to?" asked Alice.

"You really have no memory of it yourself?" asked Mr. Zemirli.

"Not the slightest. That period is like a black hole. I only remember my childhood in London."

"They're strange things, our first memories. This is different with everybody, and some people remember more than others. And you can ask: Are those memories real, or have we just created them from what people told us? I personally don't think I remember much from before I was seven, and still, I might have been eight . . . I do remember telling my mother this once, and it made her very distressed. 'What? All those years taking care of you, and you don't remember a thing?'" He paused. "But you were asking about the school. Your parents probably sent you to Saint Michel's; it's not very far from here and they taught some English. It was a very strict school with a good reputation, and I'm sure they keep very careful records of their pupils. You should visit them."

Mr. Zemirli suddenly seemed very tired. Can coughed and signaled that it was time for them to go.

Alice rose to her feet and thanked the old man for his hospitality.

Mr. Zemirli put his hand on his heart. "Your parents were humble, courageous people. They were heroes. I'm glad to know for certain that they made it back to their home country in safety, and even happier to meet their daughter. If they never told you about their time in Turkey, I'm sure it was pure modesty. I hope that you will stay long enough in Istanbul to understand what I am talking about. Godspeed to you, *Cömert Eczaci' nin kizi.*"

When they were back in the street, Can explained that he had called Alice "daughter of the generous pharmacist."

It was too late to go directly to Saint Michel's School, but Can promised to make an appointment for them the following day.

Alice and Daldry had dinner together in the hotel dining room. They spoke little over the course of the meal, and Daldry respected Alice's silence. From time to time he tried to amuse her by telling stories from his school days, but Alice's mind was elsewhere, and her smiles seemed half-hearted and distracted.

As they were saying good night in the hall, Daldry remarked that Alice had every reason to be happy. Oğüz Zemirli was probably the third, if not the fourth, link in the chain.

Back in her room, Alice sat at the writing desk next to the window.

> Dear Anton,
> Every evening when I cross the hotel lobby, I hope the concierge will give me a letter from you. It's a silly thing to hope for. After all, why would you write?
>
> I've made a decision. It's taken a lot of courage for me to promise such a thing to myself, or rather, it will take a lot of courage to keep the promise. The day I come back to London, I'll ring your doorbell and leave a packet of all the letters I've written in a little box in front of your door. I'll buy the box in the Bazaar this week.

Maybe you'll read them through the night, and maybe the next day you'll come to my door. I know that makes for a lot of maybes, but maybe has recently become a big part of my life.

I may have finally found the source of the nightmares that have been plaguing my sleep.

The fortune-teller in Brighton was right, at least about one thing. My childhood began here, on the second floor of an apartment building in Istanbul. I spent two years here, and I must have played in a little street with a long flight of steps at its end. I don't remember it, but these images from another life keep coming back to me in the night. If I'm going to understand the mystery that surrounds those early years of my life, I have to keep searching. I'm starting to guess at the reasons my parents never told me anything. If I had been my mother, I would have done the same thing and kept any memories to myself that were too painful to recount.

This afternoon, I was shown the windows of the apartment we used to live in, where my mother must have watched people passing in the street below. I could almost make out the little kitchen where she cooked our meals, and the parlor where I must have sat on my father's lap. I thought time had healed the pain of their deaths, but nothing could be further from the truth.

I'd like to show you around Istanbul one day. We'll take a walk down Istiklal Avenue, and I'll show you the building I once lived in. We'll go for a walk along the Bosporus, you'll play your trumpet, and the people will be able to hear the music all the way across the water in the hills of Üsküdar.

See you soon, Anton.

Fondly,

Alice

Alice woke as the sun was rising. Watching the waters of the Bosporus light up and sparkle made her want to escape into the morning.

The hotel dining room was still empty, and the waiters in their silver-trimmed uniforms were still setting the tables. Alice sat in the corner and read an old newspaper she had found on a side table. The news from London slowly slipped from her hands and into her lap as Alice's thoughts wandered from the luxurious hotel dining room in Istanbul to Primrose Hill in London.

She imagined Carol walking down Regent's Park Road to catch the bus to work, and she could see her jumping onto the rear platform and chatting up the conductor so that he'd forget to charge her fare. Carol would tell him he looked pale, introduce herself, and then tell him to come visit her at the hospital. About half the time it worked, and she'd get off the bus in front of the hospital having had a free ride.

Alice thought of Anton walking with his knapsack over his shoulder and his coat open, even in the cold of winter, his hair disheveled and his eyes still half-closed with sleep. She saw him cross the courtyard of the building where he had his workshop, set up the stool in front of his carpenter's bench, and look over his tools, sorting through the chisels, caressing the rounded handle of a plane, before glancing at the clock and setting to work. She thought about Sam, entering the back door of the bookshop in Camden, taking off his overcoat, and putting on his gray smock before going to dust off the rows of books and stock take while waiting for the first customers to arrive.

Finally, she imagined Eddy, sprawled across his bed and snoring his head off. It made her smile.

"Am I bothering you?"

Alice jumped and looked up to see Daldry standing in front of her.

"I was just reading the paper."

"You must have pretty good vision; it's lying on the floor."

"My thoughts drifted elsewhere."

"Might I ask where?"

"Oh, to London."

Daldry turned to the bar and tried to flag down a waiter.

"Tonight I'm going to take you somewhere incredible. One of the best restaurants in Istanbul."

"Are we celebrating something?"

"In a sense. Our trip together began in one of London's finest restaurants, and I thought it would be fitting if my leg of the journey ended in a similar manner."

"But you're not leaving until—"

"My plane takes off."

"Yes. And it doesn't take off until—"

Daldry interrupted her again. "What does a man have to do to get a coffee around here?" He waved until a waiter came to their table and took Daldry's order for an enormous breakfast.

"Since our morning is free, what do you say to going to the Bazaar? I have to find my mother a present, and I'm sure you'd be of great assistance in helping me decide. I haven't the faintest idea what she'd like."

"Maybe some jewelry?"

"I doubt the jewelry here would be to her taste."

"Perfume?"

"She's worn the same perfume all her life."

"An antique?"

"What kind of antique?"

"A jewelry box? I saw some that were inlaid with mother-of-pearl that were very pretty."

"Why not? Though I'm sure she'll tell me she much prefers English things."

"Or a piece of silver?"

"She's more of a porcelain person."

"You should just stay a few days longer and paint her something. You could work on the big intersection at the Galata Bridge."

"Yes, that's not a bad idea. I'll make a few sketches today and I can start work on it when I'm back in London."

"Or you could do it that way." Alice sighed, disappointed her ruse to keep him in Istanbul a bit longer hadn't worked.

"It's settled then. We'll take a walk on the Galata Bridge."

As soon as they were done with breakfast, Alice and Daldry took the tram to Karaköy and got off near the end of the bridge that stretched out over the water and connected Galata, across the Golden Horn to Eminönü.

Daldry took a little black notebook and a pencil from his pocket and made a careful sketch of their surroundings, noting the taxi rank and capturing a few lines of the quay where the ferries for Kadiköy and the Princes' Islands docked, as well as the coast of Üsküdar. He added the little pier where the boats that went back and forth across the water drew up on the other side of the bridge, and the oval-shaped plaza where the trams for Bebek and Beyoğlu stopped. He took Alice over to a bench, where they sat together as he continued to cover the pages of his notebook, drawing people's faces, a peddler selling watermelon, a shoeshine man seated on an old wooden crate, a knife grinder turning the wheel of his sharpener. Then he drew a little cart drawn by a potbellied mule and a car that had broken down, with its owner bent over the bonnet trying to repair it.

After about an hour, he put away his notebook, remarking that he had captured the essentials. The rest was in his head. Just in case the painting didn't work out, they decided to go shopping for a gift in the Bazaar as well.

Alice and Daldry navigated the narrow streets of the Grand Bazaar until about midday. Alice bought a little box with a lacy mother-of-pearl inlay, and Daldry found a pretty ring, set with a piece of lapis lazuli. Perhaps his mother would wear it; she liked the color blue.

They had kebabs for lunch and went back to the hotel at the beginning of the afternoon. When they arrived, Can was waiting for them in the lobby. He looked disappointed.

"I'm sorry; my work is without success," said Can.

"What?" Daldry wasn't in the mood.

Alice translated. "He didn't find anything."

"How do you expect me to understand that?"

"With a little patience and tolerance?" Alice suggested.

"As I promised you, I found myself this morning in the Saint Michel School, where I met the headmaster. He was very sociable with me and I consulted his books. We looked at every class for every year, and it wasn't easy with the old writing and old paper. It was very dusty, and we were always sneezing. But we looked at every page and read every name and there was no rewarding our efforts. No Pendelbury, no Eczaci. We separated very disappointed. I am sorry you never went to Saint Michel School. The headmaster is incontestable."

Can's story finished, Daldry spoke to Alice under his breath. "I don't know how you keep calm."

"I'd like to see how you'd fare in Turkish," Alice said to Daldry.

"You always take his side anyway."

Alice turned back to Can. "Maybe I was in a different school?" she suggested.

"That is exactly what I thought when I left the headmaster. In fact, I organized a list. I will go this afternoon to the Chalcedony School in Kadiköy, and if I don't find anything, tomorrow I will go to Saint Joseph's, in the same area. There is also the girls' school in Nişantaşi. We still have many resources ahead of us, and it is precocious to imagine failure."

"With all the hours he's going to spend in these schools, maybe you could suggest ducking in on a few English classes," said Daldry.

"You're the one who should go back to school," Alice replied.

"I don't claim to be the best interpreter in town . . ."

"No, but you're the right maturity level."

"As I was saying, you always take his side. It's reassuring, really. At least when I'm gone, you won't miss me much. The two of you get along so well."

"How can you say that?"

"I think the two of you should spend the afternoon together. Go with Can to that school. Who knows, maybe the place will stir up a few dusty old memories for you."

"Because you didn't get your way? You really are a child."

"Not in the least. I have two or three things I want to attend to that would only bore you. Let's do what we have to do, and I'll see you at dinner. Can is welcome to join us if you'd like."

"Are you jealous, Daldry?"

"Jealous of Can? What next? I can't believe I came all this way to hear such nonsense."

Daldry told Alice to meet him in the lobby at seven and left without saying goodbye.

An iron gate set in a high stone wall opened onto a courtyard, where an old fig tree languished next to rows of worn wooden benches lined up under a glass awning. Can knocked at the caretaker's door and asked to see the headmaster. The caretaker pointed them toward his office and went back to his newspaper.

They walked down a corridor, past a series of classrooms that were all occupied by children hard at work. The school supervisor had them wait in a little office.

"Ah, the smells!" said Alice, inhaling.

"What smells?"

"The smells of childhood! The vinegar they use to clean the windows, the chalk dust, the floor wax. It takes me right back."

"My childhood didn't smell like those things. There was no vinegar or chalk or wax. It smelled like cramped apartments in the early evening, people walking home from work with their heads hanging low, darkness on dirt paths, and filthy slums. But I'm not complaining. My parents were good people. Not all my friends were good people."

"I'm sorry," said Alice. "I didn't realize you had such a difficult childhood. You've come a long way." Alice paused and realized Can hadn't made any of his usual grammatical errors. "Why don't you speak English like that around Mr. Daldry?"

"Because it is so amusing to tease him."

The supervisor tapped on his desk for them to be quiet. Alice couldn't help but sit up a little straighter in her chair. This made Can chuckle. The headmaster appeared and invited them to come into his office.

Eager to show that he spoke English fluently, the headmaster ignored Can and spoke directly to Alice. Can winked at Alice and smiled; after all, the results were all that counted. As soon as Alice had explained her request, the director told her that he was sorry, but the school was still boys only in 1915. He accompanied them to the gate and saw them off, saying that he hoped to visit England one day. Maybe when he was retired.

They made their way to Saint Joseph's, where they met with the priest in charge of the school. There was something alluring about his austerity. He listened attentively while Can explained why they had come, before rising from his desk and pacing the room with his hands clasped behind his back. He went and looked out of the window into the courtyard, where a group of boys was squabbling.

"Why do they always have to fight?" he wondered out loud. "Do you think that violence is an inherent part of human nature? I could ask them in class, I suppose. It would make a good essay topic, don't you think?" He talked to them without turning away from his view of the playground.

"Probably," said Can. "It's a good way to make them think about how they behave."

"I was asking your friend," said the priest.

"I don't think it would serve any purpose," said Alice, without pausing to reflect. "The response is clear. Boys like to fight, and of course, it's in their nature. But as they grow up and their vocabulary expands, they will find the right words to express themselves and the violence will subside. Brutality is just the result of frustration, the incapacity to express oneself in words. Without words, people often resort to fists."

The priest turned around.

"You would have got a good grade. Did you like school?"

"I mostly liked going home from school."

"I'm not surprised. I don't have time to look through our records, and I don't have anybody else to do it for me. If you'd like, you may consult the ledgers in the study hall. Of course, talking is forbidden, and you'll be sent away if you do."

"Of course," said Can, trying to participate.

"I was still addressing your friend."

Can gave up and looked at the floor.

"Very good, come with me. The caretaker will bring you the admissions ledgers as soon as he's found them. You have until six this evening, and not a minute longer, so work efficiently."

"We will," said Alice. "I promise."

"Well then, come along."

He stood aside for Alice to pass and turned to Can.

"You too. Come on."

"I didn't realize you were talking to me, headmaster."

The walls in the study hall were painted gray halfway up from the floor and then blue to the ceiling, from which there hung two rows of flickering fluorescent lights. Most of the students were there as punishment, and they giggled when they saw two adults join them on the bench at the back of the room. The headmaster stomped his foot and silence immediately returned. Soon the caretaker brought them two large black books that were tied shut with ribbon. He explained to Can that everything could be found in them: admissions, expulsions, and grades from the end of the school year. The students' names were grouped by class.

Each page was divided down the middle. On the left the student's name was written in Latin characters, and on the right in Ottoman script. Can traced each line with his finger and studied the ledgers page by page. When the wall clock showed that it was five thirty, he closed the second volume and turned to Alice with a look of disappointment.

They took the books under their arms and returned them to the caretaker. As they headed out of the gate, Alice turned and waved at the headmaster, who was watching them go from his window.

"How did you know he was there?" Can asked when they were back on the street.

"The headmaster I had at school was exactly the same sort of man."

"Tomorrow, we'll succeed. I'm sure of it."

"I suppose we'll find out tomorrow."

Can took her back to the hotel.

Daldry had reserved them a table at Markiz, but when they arrived at the restaurant, Alice stopped him from going in. She didn't want to have a formal dinner. The evening air was warm, so she suggested they walk along the Bosporus instead of sitting in a noisy and smoky room for hours on end. If they were hungry, they could always find a place to stop and eat later in the evening.

Daldry agreed. Remarkably, he wasn't hungry either.

Down by the water, a few other people were out for walks as well. Some were trying their luck at fishing, casting their bait into the black water. A newspaper vendor was selling the morning news at a reduced price, and a shoeshine boy was hard at work on a soldier's boots.

"You look worried," said Alice, gazing across the water at Üsküdar Hill.

"Just a few things on my mind; nothing serious." He turned to face her. "How was your day?"

Alice told him about the schools they had visited that afternoon.

"Do you remember our trip to Brighton?" asked Daldry. He lit a cigarette. "On the way back to London, neither one of us wanted to give any credit to that woman. Even though you never said anything—you were being polite, I suppose—I think you were wondering why we were driving so far for nothing, why we were spending Christmas Eve on icy roads in an unheated car. But we've traveled together quite a bit since then, and a lot of unexpected things have happened . . . I'd like to continue believing in what she told you, to think that the trouble we've taken hasn't been in vain. Istanbul has already revealed so many secrets, things neither you nor I would have ever imagined. Who knows? Maybe in a few weeks you'll meet the man who will become your husband and make you the happiest woman in the world. Speaking of which, there's something I'd like to tell you about that's been bothering my conscience."

"But I already am a happy woman, Daldry. Thanks to you I've been able to come on this incredible journey. You know I was having trouble with my work, and now, also thanks to you, my head is full of ideas. I don't really care whether everything that woman told me actually comes true. To be honest, there was something rather hateful and vulgar about it all . . . making the sorts of assumptions she did, imagining me as a desperate and lonely woman chasing after the mirage of a man who would magically change my life. I've already met a man who has changed my life."

"Oh really?"

"The perfume maker in Cihangir. His work has allowed me to imagine a different sort of project. I've been thinking about it since our visit. It's not just interior fragrances, but the smells attached to places that mark our lives, the kinds of scents that call up lost or forgotten moments from our past. You know, our olfactory memories are the last ones to go. We may begin to forget the faces and voices of our loved ones, but never the smells. You love food so much—I'm sure that smelling a favorite food from your childhood must take you back to the past in vivid detail.

"Last year a man who particularly liked one of my perfumes got my address from a shopkeeper and came to see me. He brought along a little box that contained a bit of braided leather cord, a tin soldier whose painted uniform was chipped off, an agate marble, and a ragged little flag. It was the summary of his childhood all in a tiny metal box. He told me that when he first smelled my perfume, he was overcome by the strange and inexplicable desire to go home and go through his attic to find that box, one he'd completely forgotten about until then. He had me smell the interior of the box and asked if I could reproduce the mix of odors before it faded away. I rather stupidly told him that it was impossible, but after he left, I wrote down what I had smelled. The rust on the inside of the lid, the hemp of the cord, the tin, the old oil paint, the oak that had been used to sculpt the little toy, the dusty silk of the flag, the agate marble . . . I think I still have that list somewhere. I kept it, not knowing what to do with it. But today, with some more experience, by continuing to observe and study, like the way you made all those sketches this afternoon, I think I know what to do. I have an idea about how to make a perfume that could combine many different materials. You seem to be inspired by forms and colors, but for me, it's odors.

"I'm going to go see the man in Cihangir again and ask to spend some time with him, to watch how he works. I could show him my techniques too . . . It could be a sort of exchange. I'd like to be able to recreate forgotten moments and places. I know it all sounds very mixed-up right now, but try to imagine if you were to stay on here, and you really started to miss London, what it would be like to suddenly smell the rain in the city you'd left behind. The streets back home have a particular odor, and it changes from morning to evening. Every important moment in our lives has a particular scent."

Daldry thought about this. "It's an odd idea, indeed," he said, "but it's true that I'd like to rediscover the smell of my father's office. I think it was more complex than I realize. There was the smell of the fire in the fireplace, and his pipe tobacco, the leather of his chair and the blotter on the desk where he worked. I can't describe them all, but I also remember the smell of the rug where I used to play with my tin soldiers. The red stripes marked the positions of Napoleon's armies, and the green borders, our English troops. It had a very comforting scent of dust and wool. I don't know if you'll make much money with your idea. Who would buy a bottle of dusty rug or rainy street? But it's very poetic."

"Yes, perhaps not street smells, but childhood smells? Right now I'd cross all of Istanbul just for a little bottle of the smell of the first days of autumn in Hyde Park. It would probably take me months, even years, to create something worthwhile, something sufficiently universal. But for the first time in my life, I'm starting to feel comforted by my line of work. I've been doubting myself, even though perfume making is the only profession I've ever wanted. I'll be eternally grateful to you and to that fortune-teller for having encouraged me to come here. Even though the things we discovered about my parents are disturbing, they also make me very happy—it's a sort of gentle, nostalgic feeling, something between crying and laughing. Every time I went past the street where we used to live in London, I didn't recognize a thing. Our house and even the shops nearby were all destroyed. But now I know that there's still a place in the world where my parents and I lived together. The smells of Istiklal, the stone of the buildings, the rumbling tramways, and a thousand other things belong to me as well. Even if I don't remember anything from those days, I know we had them together, and when I'm trying to fall asleep at night, I don't think about how my parents are gone, but about what their lives must have been like here. It's a wonderful change."

"You're not going to give up searching, are you?"

"No, I promise I won't. But it's not going to be the same without you."

"I certainly hope not! Even though I'm sure you'll find it is. You and Can get along so well. I know that sometimes I act as though it bothers me, but deep inside I'm glad the two of you have a bond, a certain understanding. He may speak a strange sort of English, but he's an excellent guide."

"You wanted to tell me something earlier. What was it?"

"It can't have been very important. I've already forgotten."

"You're leaving soon."

"Yes, I'm afraid I am."

They continued their walk along the water. When they arrived at the dock, where the last ferry for the evening was setting off, Daldry's hand brushed against Alice's. She turned and took it in hers.

"Two friends can hold each other by the hand, can't they?" she asked.

"I suppose they can."

"Let's walk a little farther together. Do you mind?"

"Yes. Let's walk a little farther together."

12

Dear Alice,

I hope you'll excuse me for leaving so unexpectedly. I didn't feel like making us both suffer through another goodbye. I thought about it every night this week as I said good night, and every time the idea of saying goodbye to you in the hotel lobby with my suitcase in hand seemed too awful for words. I wanted to tell you last night, but decided not to ruin those last few delightful moments of your company. I'd rather we remember our last walk together along the Bosporus. You seemed happy and I was too. What more could one ask for at the end of a long journey?

During the time we've spent together, I've got to know you better. I can say without hesitation that you're a marvelous woman, and that I'm proud to have you as a friend—at least I hope I can consider you my friend. You are a friend to me. Our stay in Istanbul will certainly remain one of the happiest times of my life. I hope with all my heart that you'll reach the end of your journey and meet a man who loves you and accepts you for who you are, for your virtues as well as your flaws. (A friend can say such things to another friend without getting in trouble, can't he?) He'll find a woman by his side whose laughter will chase the worries right out of his life.

I'm very happy to have had you as my neighbor, and I already know as I write you this letter that your presence in the house, noisy though it sometimes was, will be missed.

Godspeed to you, daughter of the generous pharmacist, keep chasing after the happiness that suits you so well.

Your devoted friend,
Daldry

◆ ◆ ◆

Dear Ethan,

I found your letter this morning and I'll send you mine this afternoon. I wonder how long it will take to reach you. The sound of the envelope slipping under the door made me get out of bed, and I immediately understood you were leaving. I watched you get in the taxi from my window, and when you looked up at the hotel, I stepped back—probably for the same reasons you chose to leave without saying goodbye. And yet, as your taxi headed off, I wanted to say goodbye and thank you for your company. You're not always an easy man to get along with (a true friend can say that without vexing you, can't she?), but you're also remarkable, generous, amusing, and talented. You came into my life and became my friend in an unexpected manner. We've only spent the past few weeks in Istanbul together, but still I felt a need to talk to you this morning.

Of course, I forgive you for leaving as you did. I even think that you were probably right for having done so. I don't like goodbyes much either. Part of me is jealous to think that you'll be back in London soon. I miss our old house, and my apartment . . . I'll stay here until spring comes, as you suggest. Can has promised to take me to the Princes' Islands, something we missed out on doing together. I'll write to you about it, and if I happen across an intersection worthy of note, I'll describe every detail. Apparently going to the islands is like stepping back in time—there are only horses and donkeys for transport. Tomorrow we're going to go back to see the perfume maker in Cihangir. I'll tell you how it goes and keep you up to date on the developments in my work.

I hope the trip home wasn't too exhausting and that your mother is in good health. Take care of her, and take care of yourself as well.

Your friend,
Alice

My dearest Alice,
Your letter took exactly six days to arrive. The postman handed it to me this morning as I was going out. I suppose that it also must have taken the plane, but the postmark didn't indicate which line, or whether it had stopped in Vienna. The day following my return, after having put things in order in my flat, I went next

door and did the same in yours. I promise I haven't moved a thing, I just chased away some of the dust that had taken up residence in your absence. If you had seen me, like an old charwoman in an apron with a handkerchief tied over my head, bumbling around with a broom and a bucket, I'm sure I would have never heard the end of it. I did happen to run into the woman downstairs as I was taking out the rubbish, and she gave me a very strange look indeed.

There's so much light in your place that it already feels like springtime, a season that I hope will arrive in the rest of the world sooner rather than later. It's useless for me to remind you that England is a very cold and damp place, and though the weather is one of my favorite subjects of conversation, I won't bore you with the meteorological details, apart from letting you know that it has rained every day since my return, and that according to the people in the café where I've taken up my old habit of having breakfast, it has been raining the entire month. The gentle winter on the Bosporus seems very far away indeed.

Yesterday, I took a walk along the Thames, and you're right, the smell is certainly very different from those you had me analyze on our walks near the Galata Bridge. Even the manure here smells different, though perhaps that isn't the most elegant example to support my observation.

I feel guilty for having left without saying goodbye. I had a heavy heart that morning. I don't understand myself what you did to me—of course, you'll never understand what it's like to be me, but that matters little. During that last night we spent together in

Istanbul, you became my friend. In some inexplicable way, you made me a better painter, and perhaps even a better man. Don't take this the wrong way—this is not a confession of mixed-up feelings for you, but a true and simple declaration of friendship. Friends can say such things to each other, can't they?

I miss you, Alice. The pleasure of setting up my easel under your skylight amidst all the perfumes you taught me to appreciate is almost like being in your presence again. It pushes me to work and gives me the courage to paint the intersection that we admired together. It's an ambitious project, and I've already thrown out a huge number of studies that weren't good enough, but I'll get there with patience.

Take care of yourself and give my regards to Can. On second thoughts, don't—keep my regards for yourself.

Daldry

Dear Daldry,
I just received your very kind and touching letter. Thank you for all the lovely things you wrote.

I should tell you about the events of the past week. The day after you left, Can and I took the bus from Taksim to Nişantaşi. We visited all the schools in the area, but found nothing. Every visit was more or less the same. We spent hours poring over old ledgers, from which my name was always missing. Sometimes we didn't have to bother because the school hadn't kept its records or didn't allow girls in the Ottoman

days. I'm starting to think that my parents never sent
me to school at all. Can thought that maybe they kept
me at home because of the war. Still, it's strange not
to find my name anywhere—I'm starting to wonder
if I even existed! I know there's no sense in thinking
that way, so yesterday I decided to give up looking for
a while. The whole search has become rather tiresome.

The past two days we've gone back to visit the
perfume maker in Cihangir. Each moment working
with him is more fascinating than the last. Thanks to
Can, whose English has greatly improved since your
departure, I'm able to explain all of my ideas. In the
beginning, the perfume maker thought I was crazy,
but I got him to understand by asking him to imagine
all of the people who would never climb the hill to
Cihangir, who would never hear the foghorns of the
ferries sailing back and forth, and who would only see
the moon's silvery reflection in the Bosporus in books
and postcards. I tried to explain to him how wonderful it would be if we could offer them the possibility of
imagining the magic of Istanbul through a fragrance
telling the story of the city's beauty. Since he loves his
city more than anything, he stopped laughing at my
ideas and started paying closer attention. I wrote out
a list of the odors I had noticed in the little streets of
Cihangir, Can read them out, and the old man was
impressed. I know that it's an ambitious project, but
I've started daydreaming about the day that a perfume
shop in Kensington or Piccadilly will display a bottle
of perfume called "Istanbul" in its window. Don't make
fun of me now—I've managed to convince the old perfume maker, but I still need all the support I can get.

Our approaches to making perfume are very different. He thinks in terms of absolutes, and I think more like a chemist, but his techniques have brought me back to the essentials of our craft and have opened new horizons. Our methods seem to become more and more complementary each day. To me, creating a perfume isn't just mixing molecules. I always begin by writing down what my nose dictates to me, all of the impressions it senses, the way a needle etches sound on a blank gramophone record.

If I'm telling you all this, it's not just to talk about myself (although I've got quite used to that), but also because I'd like to know how your own work is coming along.

Since we're business associates, it's out of the question that I should be the only one with my nose to the grindstone. Unless you've forgotten the agreement we made in that lovely restaurant, you will recall that your duty was to paint one of Istanbul's most beautiful intersections. Tell me what you're focusing on among all the things you sketched on our last day together near the Galata Bridge. I haven't forgotten a moment of it, and I hope you won't have forgotten any of the details. Think of it as a written test, and don't roll your eyes, even though I can practically see you doing it now. I've spent too much time in schools lately.

Maybe you'd rather think of my request as a challenge. When I come back to London, I promise to bring you a perfume. When you smell it, you'll immediately be taken back to all of the places we visited together. I hope that when I arrive, the painting will be done as well. They'll have something in common because both of them will tell something of the time we spent together between Cihangir and Galata.

Now it's my turn to ask you to forgive me for this convoluted way of telling you that I'm going to stay here a little longer than I initially planned. I feel both a need and a desire to do so. I'm very happy here. I think I've never felt so free, and the sensation has become addictive. That doesn't mean that I want to continue living off your inheritance. I don't need or want to keep living in such luxurious conditions. Can has been tremendously helpful and has helped me find a pretty room in a house in Üsküdar, not far from where he lives. One of his aunts is renting it to me. I can't tell you how excited I am. Tomorrow I'll leave the hotel and start living the life of a real native of Istanbul. It will take me about an hour to get to the perfume maker's house in Cihangir every morning, and a little longer to come home in the evening, but I'm not complaining, quite to the contrary. Crossing the Bosporus on a vapur isn't nearly as wearing as descending into the depths of the Tube in London. Can's aunt has even offered me a job as a waitress in her restaurant, where her husband is the chef. It's the best restaurant in Üsküdar and there are more and more tourists, so it's helpful for her to have somebody who speaks English. Can has explained the menu and taught me the Turkish for the different dishes. I'll work there three days a week and my earnings will be more than enough to pay for what I need. Though the conditions will be far more modest than those we shared, I was quite used to living modestly before I met you.

So there it is. Night has fallen on Istanbul and it's my last evening in the hotel. I'm going to make the most of it and enjoy one last night in this vast bed. Every evening when I walk past the room you stayed in, I wish you good night. I'll keep doing so from my window when I've moved to Üsküdar.

I've written my new address on the back of the envelope. Write back soon. I hope you won't forget to list all the things you've put in the painting.

Take care of yourself.

Yours truly,

Alice

❖ ❖ ❖

Dear Alice,

Since you asked, here is the list . . .

The tram: Wood-veneer interior, slightly worn floorboards, a partition with a violet-tinted window-pane separating the driver from the passengers, the iron gear lever, two flickering ceiling lamps, the rest of the interior a shade of cream, paint chipping here and there.

The Galata Port: A roadway paved with crooked paving stones set with the tracks of two tramlines. Uneven pavements, stone parapets, a pair of wrought-iron crash barriers rusty in places and corroded where the metal is inserted into the pavement. Five fishermen are leaning against the railing. One of them is a boy who ought to be at school. A watermelon vendor standing behind his little cart with its red-and-white-striped canvas canopy. A newspaper vendor with a cloth bag slung over his shoulder, his cap on crooked, a plug of tobacco in his cheek (he'll spit it out soon). A souvenir peddler looking out across the Bosporus and wondering whether it wouldn't be better to just throw away his merchandise, drown himself, and call it a day. A pickpocket, or at least a dodgy character. Across the street, a disappointed businessman wearing a dark-blue suit, a fedora, and saddle shoes. Two women walking side by side, probably sisters. About ten feet behind them, a man who knows his wife is cheating on him. A bit farther along, a sailor is going down the steps to the water's edge.

And while we're on the water, there are two docks with a number of colorful little boats tied up, some of them are painted with indigo stripes, one is daffodil yellow. On the dock, five men, three women, and two children are waiting for a ferry.

On the street that winds up the hill, if you look carefully, you can see a series of shopfronts: a florist, a stationer, a tobacconist, a grocer, and a café. The street bends just beyond the café.

I'll spare you the color variations in the sky . . . You'll discover them for yourself. As for the Bosporus, we've both looked at it with sufficient frequency for you to imagine the play of light across the water's surface.

In the distance you can see the hill of Üsküdar, houses perched on its sides. I'll pay closer attention to them now that I know that you're living in one of them. There are also the minarets, not to mention hundreds of boats—dinghies, yawls, cutters—gliding across the water.

I admit that this overview is a bit scattered, but I think, in all humility, that I've managed to meet your challenge with success.

I'll send this letter to your new address and hope that it makes it to you. Üsküdar was one of the neighborhoods that I never had the opportunity to visit myself.

Your ever-devoted

Daldry.

P.S. Please don't feel obliged to pass on my greetings to Can, or his aunt for that matter. I also forgot to note that it rained Monday, Tuesday, and Thursday. The weather was mixed on Wednesday but very sunny on Friday.

Dear Daldry,

I can't believe it's already the end of March. I'm sorry I wasn't able to write last week. Between the days spent up in Cihangir and my evenings in the restaurant in Üsküdar, I often fall asleep as soon as I come home. You'd be proud to see how handy I've become—I can now carry three plates on each arm, and I haven't dropped one in nearly a week. Mama Can, as everybody calls Can's aunt, is very kind. If I continue to eat everything she puts in front of me, I'll come back to London as big as a house.

Every morning, Can picks me up at home for the walk to the ferry. It takes about fifteen minutes, but it's pleasant enough, unless the wind is coming from the north. Strangely, during the last few weeks it has been even colder than during the time you were here.

Crossing the Bosporus remains a great pleasure. How funny it is to work in Europe and return home to Asia! When Can and I get off the ferry, we take a bus, and when we're late, a *dolmu*.

Though it eats up what little I earn in tips, it's still cheaper than a taxi.

Once we arrive in Cihangir, we still have to walk up those steep streets that I'm sure you remember. I often pass the same cobbler as he's leaving his house in the morning. He wears a big box attached to his waist that looks like it must weigh as much as he does. We wave to each other and he heads down the hill as I continue my way up. There's a house a little farther up the hill where a woman is often standing in the doorway, seeing her children off to school. She watches them head down the hill with their schoolbags until they disappear around the corner. When I pass, she smiles at me, but I can see in her eyes that she worries until her babies return to the nest at the end of the day.

I've also become friends with a grocer, who offers me a piece of fruit from his stand every morning. He says I have to choose it myself, that my skin is too pale and that fruit is good for my health. I think he likes me and, to a certain extent, the feeling is mutual. At noon, when the perfume maker has lunch with his wife, Can and I go back to the grocer and buy something to eat. We often go to a beautiful little cemetery and sit on a stone bench under a fig tree, where we play a game, imagining details from the lives of the people buried around us. In the afternoon we go back to the workshop. I've been using a sort of makeshift organ that the perfumer helped me put together. I've been able to buy a lot of the equipment I need, and my research is coming along. Right now, I'm working on re-creating the illusion of dust. I realize how ridiculous that must sound, but dusty overtones are an important part of all of my memories, and Istanbul is full of the smells of earth, stone walls, gravel paths, salt, mud, and dry wood. The master has shown me a few more of his discoveries, and a real understanding seems to be growing between the two of us.

When evening comes, Can and I return along the same streets. We take the bus and then the vapur. Often it's cold, and we have to wait a long time before the boat comes, but I mix in with the other passengers, and every evening I feel a little bit more like I belong, like I'm one of them. I don't know why I enjoy the feeling so much, but I do. I'm living by the city's rhythms, and I've taken a liking to it. I've convinced Mama Can to let me work every night, but it's because I enjoy the work, not because I particularly need the money. I like weaving between the customers, hearing the cook shout because the food is ready and I don't come fast enough. I like the friendly smile of Mama Can, who claps her hands and scolds her husband for shouting. When the restaurant closes, Can's uncle yells one last time to call us into the kitchen, where we sit around a big wooden table. He puts down a tablecloth and serves us the kind of dinner I know you would love.

Those are the moments of my life that make me the happiest—happier than I've ever been.

I haven't forgotten that I owe it all to you, Daldry. You and you alone. I'd like to see you walk into Mama

Can's restaurant one evening, to introduce you to her family and her husband's cooking. It's so good you'd cry. I miss you and think of you often. In your next letter, give me more news. Your last letter said nothing about what you were doing, and that's really what I wanted to hear about.

Your friend,
Alice

◆ ◆ ◆

Dear Alice,

I ran into the postman this morning, and he gave me your letter—or rather threw it into my face, cursing. He has been in a bad mood lately and hasn't been speaking to me since I'd started worrying about not having heard from you. I kept blaming him for having lost your letter and eventually went down to the post office to make sure that they hadn't misplaced it. I swear it's not my fault, but I got into an argument with the man behind the counter because he refused to believe that one of his postmen might have made a mistake. To believe him, His Majesty's post has never lost a letter! I think there's something about the uniform that makes them so sensitive to criticism.

And now, thanks to you, I have to apologize to both of them. In the future, if your busy schedule means you don't have time to write, please at least take a moment to write to say so. Just a few words would be enough to calm my needless worrying. You have to understand that I consider myself responsible for the fact that you're in Istanbul alone, and I want to be sure you remain safe and sound.

I'm overjoyed to read that you eat lunch with Can every day and that your friendship continues to blossom, although I do find a cemetery a rather odd place for a meal. But if it makes you happy, I have nothing against it.

I'm also very curious to know more about the development of your project. If you're looking to recreate the odor of dust, there's no point in you staying on in Istanbul. There's dust aplenty in London, and to find it, you wouldn't even have to leave home.

You ask for news from my life. Like you, I'm hard at work. The Galata Bridge is starting to take shape on the canvas, and over the past few days I've been sketching the figures that I'll place upon it. I'm also working on the details of the houses in Üsküdar. I went to the library and found some old engravings of the Asian side of the Bosporus that have been very useful. On most days, I leave the flat at noon and have lunch at the end of the street. You know the place, so there's no point in me describing it. Perhaps you remember the widow who was sitting by herself at a table near ours the day we ate there together? Good news: she seems to be out of mourning and has met somebody new. Yesterday she came in with a man her age, rather shabby looking but pleasant enough, and they had lunch together. I hope it will last—perhaps they'll even fall in love. Why not, even at their age?

At the beginning of the afternoon, I usually go to your flat, tidy up a bit, and then paint until the evening. The light has been a revelation, and I've never worked so well in all my life.

On Saturdays I go for a walk in Hyde Park. With all of the rain we've been getting, I rarely see another soul, and I like it that way.

Speaking of running into people, I did happen upon one of your friends in the street earlier this week—a certain Carol, who spontaneously came over and introduced herself. I remembered who she was when she brought up the evening that I barged in on your party. I took advantage of the moment to apologize for my behavior. The knowledge that we had been traveling together and the hope that my presence might be a sign of your return had emboldened her to reintroduce herself in the first place. I told her that you were still in Istanbul, but we went and had tea together, and I took the liberty of bringing her up to date on your activities. I didn't have the time to tell her about everything, because she had to start her shift at the hospital where she's a nurse. Well, of course you know that—she's your friend—but I hate scratching things out, so you'll have to live with it. We're going to have dinner together next week so I can tell her the rest of our stories from Istanbul.

Don't worry, it isn't a bother, she's really quite charming.

Well, that's all there is to say . . . As you can see, my life is far less exotic than yours, but like you, I'm quite happy.

Daldry

P.S. In your last letter you mention Can picking you up at "home." Are you suggesting that Istanbul has become your home?

◆ ◆ ◆

Dear Anton,

I'm afraid I have to begin this letter with some sad news. Mr. Zemirli died at home last Sunday. His cook found his body, still sitting in his armchair, when she arrived on Monday morning.

Can and I went to the funeral. I didn't think there would be many people, but to my surprise there were about a hundred of us in the procession to the tiny cemetery where he was buried. It seems Mr. Zemirli was a sort of living encyclopedia to everyone in his neighborhood. The people crowded around his grave and remembered with both laughter and tears how he had more than managed to live a full and rewarding life, in spite of his limp. A man in the crowd kept looking at me during the ceremony. I don't know what came over Can, but he insisted that I meet him and we ended up going to a tearoom in Beyoğlu together. He turned out to be Zemirli's nephew, but stranger still, the owner of the musical instrument store where I bought that trumpet, you remember?

He seemed very affected by his uncle's death.

I'm delighted to hear that you ran into Carol. She's got a heart of gold and she's a wonderful nurse to boot. I hope the two of you had a nice time together.

Next Sunday, if the weather has improved, Can, Zemirli's nephew, and I are going to have a picnic on the Princes' Islands that I told you about. Mama Can makes me take Sundays off now, so who am I to disobey?

I'm glad to hear that your painting is coming along and that you've been enjoying working in my flat. I like imagining you there, paintbrush in hand. I hope that when you head out of the door every night you leave a little of your color and your madness behind to keep the place alive until I return. (Yours is usually a good sort of madness—take it as a compliment between friends.)

I often intend to write but feel too worn out to carry through with it. And here I am at the end of another letter that feels too short. I'd like to tell you a thousand other things, but I'm about to doze off.

Your faithful friend, who sends you affectionate thoughts from her window in Üsküdar every night before going to bed,

Alice

P.S. I've decided to learn Turkish, and I'm enjoying it a great deal. Can teaches me and I'm coming along quite quickly. He says I speak with almost no accent and is proud of my progress.

My darling Suzie,

Who, pray tell, is the Anton you had on your mind when you wrote your last letter to me? (A letter, I might add, that was no quicker in arriving than the previous ones . . .)

If I weren't such a stickler for never crossing out, I'd start again. You must think I'm in a dreadful mood. Which I am, to an extent. I'm not at all happy with the way the painting has been progressing (regressing?) over the past few days. I'm having a great deal of trouble painting the houses of Üsküdar, particularly the one where you live now. From the Galata Bridge, where we once stood, they seemed so tiny, but now that I know you live there, I want them to seem immense, or at least recognizable enough to see where you are.

You failed to mention your work in your last letter. I don't mention this as a concerned business partner, but as a curious friend. How are things going? Have you managed to recreate the illusion of dust, or would you like me to send a little sample from home?

In other news, my old Austin finally gave up the ghost. I know it's not nearly as sad as the loss of Mr. Zemirli, but it wasn't easy to leave her behind at the mechanic's. On the other hand, this has given me an excuse to waste a little more of my inheritance, and I intend to buy a new car next week. I hope, if you ever come home, that I'll have the pleasure of seeing you drive it.

Your stay seems to keep dragging on, so I took the liberty of paying your London rent directly to our landlord. Please don't make a fuss about it. It's completely normal for me to pay the rent as long as I'm the one using the place.

I hope that your outing to the Princes' Islands was as pleasant as you had anticipated. Speaking of Sunday outings, I've let Carol convince me to go to the movies this weekend. Very original idea on her part, actually, since I never go to the cinema by myself. I can't tell you what film we're going to see because she's keeping it a secret, but I'll tell you about it in my next letter.

I send my affectionate thoughts from your flat, which I'm about to leave for the evening to return to my place.

Until next time, Alice. I miss our dinners together in Istanbul, and your stories about Mama Can and her talented husband make me miss them all the more.

Daldry

P.S. I'm delighted to hear about your talent for Turkish. Nevertheless, if Can is your only source of information, I'd advise you to invest in a decent dictionary to double-check his lessons . . .

Dear Daldry,

I've just come home from the restaurant and am writing to you in the middle of the night. I doubt whether I'll get any sleep because I've had some rather disturbing news today.

Like every morning, Can came to walk me down the hill to the Bosporus. One of the konaks in the neighborhood caught on fire in the middle of the night, and the collapsed remains of the house had blocked off the street we usually take. The nearby streets were jammed with traffic, so we ended up making a broad detour.

I know I've already told you about how smells immediately call up old memories for me. As we were walking past a gate covered with climbing roses, I stopped in my tracks. The smell was oddly familiar, a mix of linden and wild roses. We went through the gate, and at the end of a passage we saw an old house. There was an elderly man pottering around in the garden. I recognized the smell of the roses, the gravel, the chalky old walls, and the old stone bench under the branches of a spreading linden tree. Suddenly, it all came back to me: I had known this courtyard when it was full of children, and I recognized the blue door at the top of a little flight of steps. A series of images came flooding back as though out of a dream.

The old man came over to us and asked what we were looking for. I asked him if the building had once been a school, and he confirmed that indeed it had been a small school a long time ago, but now he lived there alone. At the beginning of the century, his father was the schoolmaster and he was one of the teachers. The school closed after the revolution in 1923 and never reopened. He put on his glasses and gave me a closer look, one so intense that it made me uncomfortable at first. Then he said, "I recognize you. You're little Anouche!" At first I thought he wasn't right in the head, but I remembered we initially felt the same way when we met Mr. Zemirli, so I gave him the benefit of the doubt and told him that my name was Alice.

He claimed to remember me well and said he'd never forget the "lost look" that I'd always had. He invited us to have some tea. We had barely settled into our seats when he took my hand in his and told me how sorry he was about my parents.

I immediately wondered how he could possibly know about my parents dying during the war, and when I asked him to explain, I could see something was amiss. He said that my parents couldn't have escaped to England. He continued, saying that his father had known my father and that the violence of the young generation at the time had been a great tragedy. He said that they never knew what had happened to my mother, that I wasn't the only one who had been in danger, that the authorities would later close the school so that people would forget.

None of it made any sense, but he seemed so sincere and convinced of what he was saying that I didn't argue.

He said that I had been a studious, intelligent child, but that I refused to talk and that it worried my mother to no end. He talked about how much I looked like my mother, and how when he first saw me just now, he thought he was seeing her, before he realized it had been too long, that it was impossible. He remembered her bringing me to my first day of school, so happy that I was able to study at last. He said his father was the only schoolmaster who would accept me into his class. The other schools didn't want a child who wouldn't talk.

I started asking more questions. I asked how he could possibly think that my mother and my father had not died together, explaining that I myself had seen the house we all lived in destroyed by a bomb.

He looked very sorry for me, and then he started talking about my nanny, who, until recently, he used to run into when he did his shopping in Üsküdar. He said that he hadn't seen her in a while and thought perhaps she had died.

When I told him that I'd never had a nanny of any sort, he asked if I didn't remember Mrs. Yilmaz.

He told me how much Mrs. Yilmaz had loved me, how much I owed to Mrs. Yilmaz.

My inability to remember those lost years in Istanbul frustrates me no end, so you can imagine how much worse that frustration became when the old schoolteacher began telling me stories from my past and calling me "Anouche."

He showed us around his house, including the room that had once been the classroom where I studied. It's a little reading room now. He asked what I had become, whether I was married and whether I had any children. I told him about how I make perfumes, and he didn't seem surprised at all. He even said he remembered that, unlike other small children, who usually taste strange objects, I was more likely to smell them, and that I did so with remarkable care.

When our visit was over, he accompanied us to the gate, and as I passed the old linden tree and brushed against its leaves, I was certain once again that this was not the first time I had been in that place.

Can thinks that I probably went to school there, and that the old teacher just doesn't remember everything clearly, that perhaps he remembered me and then confused his memories with those of other children. He thinks other details may come back to me, and that I should trust destiny to reveal them. After all, if that konak hadn't burned down in the night, we would have never walked past the old school. Even though I know he was only trying to calm me down, he's probably not entirely wrong . . .

So, as you can understand, there are a lot of questions buzzing around in my head. Why did the old man call me Anouche? What violence was he talking about? Why does he think that my parents died separately when I know they died together? He seemed so sure of himself, so sad to see that I didn't understand.

I apologize for writing to you in such a state, but I can't get over it.

Tomorrow, I'll go back to Cihangir. After all, I know the essentials. I lived here for two years, and for one reason or another, my parents sent me to a local school in Üsküdar, on the other side of the Bosporus, perhaps in the company of a nanny named Mrs. Yilmaz.

I hope that all is well in London, that you keep making progress on your painting, and that you continue to be satisfied with your new studio. To make your work easier, you should know that the house where I live has four floors and is pale pink with white shutters.

Yours truly,

Alice

P.S. Excuse me for mixing you up with Anton—my mind was elsewhere when I wrote my last letter. Anton is an old friend I sometimes write to as well. Speaking of friends, did you enjoy your trip to the movies with Carol?

Dear Alice,

(Although, I must admit, Anouche is a very pretty name.)

I'm sure that the old teacher must have just confused you with another girl who went to his school.

You shouldn't torture yourself with the memories of a man who may not have all his wits about him.

The good news is that you found the school you attended during the two years you spent as a child in Istanbul. Even in difficult times, your parents saw to it that you got an education, and that's the important part.

I've given it a great deal of thought, and I believe there's a logical explanation for everything: during the war, and while they were in such a delicate situation (particularly considering the medical aid they were giving the people in Beyoğlu, which wasn't without its dangers), it seems likely that your parents preferred you go to school in a different neighborhood. And if they were both working at the university, it seems logical that they needed a nanny's help, which also explains why Mr. Zemirli didn't remember you. When he came to get his medicine, you must have been at school or in the care of Mrs. Yilmaz. With the mystery solved, you can return to your work, which I hope is advancing by leaps and bounds.

My own work is moving forward, not as quickly as I would like, but I think I'm doing fairly well. At least that's what I tell myself when I leave your flat every evening. I think otherwise when I return the next morning. What can I say? It's not easy being a painter—ours is a business of illusion and disillusion. One day you think you've mastered your subject, but the damned brushes often seem to have a mind of their own. They're not the only ones . . .

Your letters seem to indicate that you miss rainy old London less and less. I've taken to daydreaming about the excellent raki we drank together. Some evenings I imagine what it would be like to return to Istanbul and have dinner with you in Mama Can's restaurant. I'd like to come and visit, even just for a day, but unfortunately it's impossible as long as my work keeps me here.

Your ever-devoted Daldry.

P.S. Did you ever make it to that picnic on the Princes' Islands? Do they deserve their name? Did you meet a prince?

◆ ◆ ◆

My dearest Daldry,

You'll probably lecture me for taking so long to reply, but please don't take it personally. I've been working constantly for the past three weeks.

Things are coming along nicely, with both my Turkish and my perfume. The master perfumer in Cihangir and I are on the verge of a breakthrough. For the first time yesterday, we managed to create an interesting accord. The arrival of spring has helped a great deal. If only you could see how much Istanbul has changed over the past few months. Can took me out to the countryside last weekend, and I discovered some wonderful fragrances. The whole area surrounding the city is blanketed in roses, and I think I've probably seen a hundred different varieties. The peach and apricot trees are also blooming, and the redbuds that line the shores of the Bosporus are covered in little purple blossoms.

Can says it will soon be the season for mimosa, lavender, and all sorts of other fragrant flowers. Turkey really is a perfume maker's paradise. I'm tremendously lucky to be here. You asked about the Princes' Islands—they're very beautiful and lush with vegetation, but Üsküdar Hill isn't too bad these days either. At the end of my shift, Can and I often go for a late dinner in one of the many little cafés tucked away in the neighborhood's hidden gardens.

In a month the weather is supposed to heat up considerably, and we'll be able to go to the beach and go swimming. I can't help it: we're still in the middle of spring and I'm already impatient for summer to arrive.

I'll never know how to thank you for encouraging me to discover Istanbul. I love the hours I spend with the perfume maker in Cihangir, and my work in Mama Can's restaurant. She's so affectionate that she feels like family to me now. The warm evenings when I walk home from work are a pure delight.

I would like very much for you to come and visit, even for a short while, just to show you all of the beautiful things I've discovered since you left.

It's late now. The city is falling asleep, and I'm going to do the same.

I'll write you again as soon as possible.

Your friend,

Alice

P.S. Tell Carol that I miss her and that I'd be very happy if she found the time to write.

13

Alice posted her letter on her way to work the following evening. When she got to the restaurant, she could hear Can and his aunt having a loud argument that ended abruptly as soon as she came in. Alice noticed Mama Can frown at Can, warning him to keep quiet.

"What's going on?" she asked innocently, putting on her apron and tying the strings behind her back.

"Nothing," said Can. His face said otherwise.

"You were arguing. You both sounded angry."

"An aunt should be able to contradict her nephew without him rolling his eyes and showing her disrespect," said Mama Can. She sounded furious.

Can left without saying goodbye, slamming the door behind him as he went.

"Goodness. It must have been serious," said Alice, going over to the huge stove, where Mama Can's husband was already hard at work.

He turned to her with a spoon and had her taste his stew. She said it was delicious. He wiped his hands on his apron and went out of the back door to smoke a cigarette without saying a word. He seemed angry with Mama Can too.

"What on earth is going on?" asked Alice.

"The two of them are ganging up on me," complained Mama Can.

"If you tell me what happened, I might take your side. Two against two is a fairer match."

"That foolish nephew of mine is too talented a teacher. You've gone and learned our language, and now you think you can understand everything. He should mind his own business, and so should you. Get back to the dining room—there aren't any customers here in the kitchen. And don't slam the door!"

Alice obeyed, taking her notepad and a pile of freshly washed plates and heading back into the dining room. It was starting to fill up with customers.

As soon as the kitchen door was closed behind her, she could hear Mama Can shouting at her husband to put out his cigarette and get back to work.

The rest of the evening passed without any further confrontations, but every time Alice went past the kitchen, she noticed that Mama Can and her husband weren't speaking to each other.

Alice's shift never ended very late on Monday evenings, and the last customers usually left the restaurant around eleven. She finished tidying up the dining room, took off her apron, and said good night to Can's uncle (who muttered good night under his breath in return). Finally, she said good night to Mama Can, who gave her a strange look as she left for the evening.

Can was waiting for her outside, sitting on a low wall.

"Where did you go? And what on earth did you say to your aunt before I arrived? I've never seen her like that; she was in a dreadful mood. It was a miserable evening."

"We had an argument, that's all. Things will be better tomorrow."

"Am I allowed to know what you argued about? I had to suffer because of it."

"If I tell you, she'll be even more furious, and tomorrow's shift will be worse because of it."

"Why? Is it something to do with me?"

"I can't say. But it's late. I should take you home."

"You know, Can, I'm a grown woman. You don't have to walk me home every night. I know how to get to my apartment."

"I know that. But I'm paid to take care of you. I'm just doing my job like you do in the restaurant."

"What do you mean, you're paid to take care of me?"

"Mr. Daldry sends me money every week to take care of you."

Alice looked at Can in disbelief and then walked away without saying a word. Can caught up with her.

"I also do it out of friendship."

"Don't tell me it's out of friendship when you're being paid," she said, walking faster.

"One doesn't necessarily go without the other. Besides, Istanbul is a big city. The streets aren't as safe as you think they are."

"Üsküdar is practically a village. Everybody knows everybody. You always say so yourself. Now leave me alone. I know the way."

"Fine." Can sighed. "I'll write to Mr. Daldry and tell him I don't want his money anymore. Would that be better?"

"It would have been better if you had told me to begin with. I've written to tell him that I don't need his help, but I see now, once again, that it doesn't matter to him what others want. It makes me so angry."

"Why should somebody trying to help you make you angry?"

"Because I never asked him. I don't need his help."

"We all need somebody's help. Nobody can do anything worthwhile on their own."

"Well I can!"

"No, you can't. Would you be able to create your perfume without the master in Cihangir? Would you have even found him if I hadn't taken you to him? How would you have met the consul or Mr. Zemirli or the old schoolmaster?"

"Don't exaggerate. You had nothing to do with the schoolmaster."

"Who took you down the street that went past his house?"

Alice stopped walking and turned to face Can.

"Fine. Without your help, I would have never met the consul or Mr. Zemirli, I would have never worked in your aunt's restaurant, I wouldn't live in Üsküdar, and I probably would have left Istanbul long ago. I owe it all to you. Are you satisfied?"

"And you wouldn't have walked down that street and past that school."

"I apologized. Let's not spend the rest of the evening bickering over details."

"I missed the part where you apologized. You don't owe it all to me alone—you wouldn't have met any of those people, or found a job with my aunt, or lived in the room she rents you if Mr. Daldry hadn't hired me. So you might as well continue apologizing and thank him as well."

"I thank him in every letter I write, for your information. How do I know you're not just saying all this so that I don't tell him to stop sending money in my next letter?"

"If after everything I've done, you still want to go ahead and make me lose my job, that's your decision."

"I can't believe you!" said Alice.

"I can't believe you. You're more stubborn than my aunt," said Can.

"Fine. I can live with that. I've had enough arguing for one evening, anyway."

They looked at each other, not sure what to do with themselves now that their argument had dissipated.

"Let's have some tea and make peace," suggested Can.

Alice let Can take her to a café at the end of a narrow street. The outdoor terrace was still full of people, in spite of the late hour.

Can ordered them two rakis. Alice said she'd prefer the tea he had initially offered, but he wouldn't have any of it.

"Mr. Daldry wasn't afraid of drinking," said Can.

"You think it takes courage to be a drunk?"

"I don't know. I've never really thought about it."

"Well, you ought to. Drunkenness is a stupid way of forgetting about one's problems." She paused and thought for a moment. "But now that we're already drinking, you can tell me what the fight with your aunt was about. To make it up to me."

Can resisted, but Alice finally won him over.

"It was because of all the people I introduced you to. The consul, Mr. Zemirli, the schoolmaster, even though with him I swore that we only passed his house by chance."

"Why does she object to me meeting people?"

"She thinks we're getting mixed up in other people's lives. That I'm getting too involved in your business."

"Why should that bother her?"

"She believes that when you get too involved in other people's lives, even when you think you're doing them a favor, you will always bring them bad luck in the end."

"Well, I'll go tell Mama Can first thing tomorrow that you've brought me nothing but happiness."

"You can't say that! She'll know I talked to you, and she'll be furious. Besides, it's not entirely true. If I hadn't introduced you to Mr. Zemirli, you wouldn't have been sad when he died. And if I hadn't led you down that street, you wouldn't have felt so confused after meeting the old teacher. I've never seen you so distressed."

"Make up your mind, my friend. Was it your talent as a guide or chance?"

"Maybe a little of both. Chance made the konak burn, and I took you down that street. Chance and intention got mixed up."

Alice put down her empty glass, and Can refilled it immediately.

"This reminds me of the good old times with Mr. Daldry," he said.

"Could you just forget about Daldry for five minutes?"

"No, I don't think I could," said Can, after giving the question some thought.

"How did the argument with your aunt begin?"

"In the kitchen."

"Not where, how?"

"I can't tell you. She made me promise not to."

"Well, I release you from your promise. One woman can lift a man's promise to another, if the two women in question get along well. Didn't you know?"

"Did you make that up?"

"Just now."

"That's what I thought."

Alice begged. "Just tell me why you were talking about me."

"Why does it matter so much?"

"Put yourself in my shoes. Imagine if you walked in on Mr. Daldry and me in the middle of an argument about you. Wouldn't you want to know what it was all about?"

"I'd know what it was about. Mr. Daldry probably criticized me again, and you took my side and were scolding him. You don't have to be a mind reader to know that."

"You drive me crazy."

"Well, my aunt drives me crazy because of you, so I suppose we're even."

"Fine. Let's make a deal: I won't say anything about your pay in my next letter to Daldry, but you have to tell me how the argument with your aunt started."

"You're blackmailing me to betray Mama Can's trust!"

"Yes, but I have to sacrifice my independence and peace of mind by not saying anything to Mr. Daldry about him paying you to watch over me. We're even."

Can refilled Alice's glass. "Okay, but drink this first." His gaze was steady and penetrating.

Alice tossed back the drink and set the empty glass on the table. "I'm listening."

"I think I found Mrs. Yilmaz." Alice looked bewildered. He thought she hadn't understood. "Your old nanny. I know where she lives."

"How did you find her?"

"Well, I am the best guide in Istanbul. I've been asking around Üsküdar over the past month. I finally found somebody who knew her."

"When can we go and see her?" Alice couldn't hide her excitement.

"The time has to be right. And Mama Can can't know anything about it."

"What does it have to do with Mama Can? Why didn't she want you to tell me?"

"I told you. She thinks I'll only hurt you by taking you to meet Mrs. Yilmaz. My aunt has an opinion or a theory about everything. She thinks that the past should rest in the past, that it's never good to stir up old stories. She says that we shouldn't dig up what time has left buried."

"Why on earth does she think that?"

"I have no idea. Perhaps we'll find out. But you must promise that you'll be patient and wait for me to organize the visit without saying anything."

Alice gave her word, and then Can asked her to let him take her home. He had drunk an impressive volume of raki over the course of his confession, and it was imperative for them to be on their way while he could still walk.

The following evening, on her way from Cihangir to the restaurant, Alice stopped by her apartment to change clothes before her seven-o'clock shift.

The atmosphere in the restaurant seemed to have returned to normal. Mama Can's husband was busy in the kitchen, shouting whenever a plate was ready, and Mama Can watched over the dining room from her cash register, only leaving her perch to greet the regulars and point them toward the tables that she assigned according to her own personal opinion of their importance. Alice took their orders and hurried between the tables and the kitchen.

When the rush hour of the evening service hit around nine, Mama Can left her stool to lend Alice a hand. She was watching Alice, and Alice knew it. She did her best to act as if Can had told her nothing of the previous day's argument. When the last customer was gone, Mama Can locked the door, pulled up a chair, and contemplated Alice, who was setting the tables for the following day, as she did at the end of every evening. She had taken the tablecloth off the table next to where Mama Can was sitting when the rag she used for wiping down the tables was suddenly snatched out of her hand.

"Go make us some tea, my dear. And bring two glasses."

Alice welcomed the break. She went to kitchen and came back a few moments later with the tea and glasses. Mama Can told her husband to close the serving hatch between the kitchen and the dining room. Alice put down the tray and sat across from her.

"Are you happy here?" asked Mama Can as she poured the tea.

"Yes," said Alice, wondering what was coming next.

"You're brave. Just like me when I was your age, I was never afraid of working. It's a funny situation when you think about it, between our family and you, don't you think?"

"What do you mean?"

"During the day, my nephew works for you, and in the evening, you work for me."

"I'd never thought of it that way."

"You know, my husband doesn't say much. He says I don't leave him any time to get a word in edgewise, that I talk enough for both of us. But he likes you and respects you."

"I'm touched to hear that. I like you all very much too."

"And the room I'm renting you—you like it?"

"I love how quiet it is, yes. The view is lovely and I sleep well there."

"And Can?"

"I beg your pardon?"

"You don't understand my question?"

"Well, Can is the perfect guide. Probably the best guide in Istanbul. And we've spent so many days together that I think I can consider him a friend as well."

"My girl, do you realize how much time you spend together? It has been months, not days."

"What are you trying to say?"

"I'm just asking you to be careful with him. You know, love at first sight only exists in books. In real life, feelings grow slowly, the way one builds a house, stone by stone. Do you think I fainted with pleasure at the sight of my husband the first time I saw him? No. But after forty years of living together, I love him very much. I learned to appreciate all of his qualities. I got used to his weaknesses. When I get angry at him, like I did last night, I try to spend some time alone and I think."

"What do you think about?" asked Alice, somewhat surprised at this unexpected revelation.

"I imagine a set of scales. On one side I place all the things that I like about him, and on the other side I put everything that annoys me. And when I look at the scales, I realize that everything balances out, or even leans toward the positive side. That's because I'm lucky to have a husband I can count on. But Can is much more intelligent than his uncle, and unlike his uncle, he's also rather handsome."

"Mama Can, I never intended to seduce your nephew."

"I realize that, but I'm talking about him, not you. He would search all of Istanbul if you asked him to. Don't you see that?"

"I'm sorry. I never thought that—

"I know. You work so much that you don't have a minute to think about anything. Why do you think I forbid you from working on Sundays? So that you rest at least one day a week. So that your heart has a reason to keep on beating. But I can see that you're not attracted to

Can. You should leave him in peace. You know the way to Cihangir, and the weather is warm and pleasant now. You can go there on your own."

"I'll talk to him about it tomorrow."

"You don't need to discuss it. You just have to tell him you don't require his services any longer. If he really is the best guide in the city, he'll be able to find other customers."

Alice looked into Mama Can's eyes. "You don't want me to work here anymore?"

"I never said anything like that. What's got into your head? I like you very much, and so do the customers. I'm delighted to see you arrive every evening. I'd be bored without you. Keep up your work, keep the room where you sleep so well, concentrate on your days in Cihangir, and everything will be for the better."

"I understand, Mama Can. I'll think about it." Alice took off her apron, folded it, and put it on the table.

"Why were you angry with your husband last night?" she asked as she headed for the door.

"Because I'm like you, dear. I'm strong-willed and I ask too many questions. See you tomorrow. Go on. I'll close up behind you."

◆　◆　◆

Can was waiting for Alice outside.

"You don't look well. Are things still tense in the restaurant?" asked Can.

"No, everything is back to normal."

"Mama Can's bad moods never last long. Come on, I'll take you home."

They started off toward Alice's apartment.

"I have to talk to you about something, Can."

"I have news too. I think it's better if you hear about it now. The reason the old schoolteacher doesn't see Mrs. Yilmaz in the market anymore is that she left Istanbul. She went home to Izmit with her family. I even have her address."

"Is that far? When can we go and see her?"

"It's about an hour on the train. We could also take a boat. I haven't arranged anything yet. I wanted to make sure you were ready."

"Of course I am. Why wouldn't I be?"

"I don't know. Maybe my aunt is right when she says that it's better not to go digging in the past. What's the point if you're already happy? Maybe it's better to look ahead and think of the future."

"I'm not afraid of the past. Besides, we all need to know where we come from, don't we? I can't stop wondering why my parents didn't tell me about the beginning of my life. Wouldn't you want to know the same things if you were in my place?"

"Maybe they had a good reason to say nothing. Maybe they were trying to protect you."

"Trying to protect me from what?"

"From painful memories?"

"I was five years old. I don't have any memories from that time, and I don't think anything could be worse than the ignorance—the emptiness—I feel now. If I knew the truth, whatever it is, I might at least understand why I remember nothing."

"I suppose that the trip to Gibraltar in the cargo ship must have been difficult. Your parents were probably just glad you didn't remember."

"I suppose so too, but until I have confirmation one way or the other, it's all speculation. But more than that, I just want to hear some-body talk to me about them. I'd be happy to have any memory, even the dullest, most ordinary things—how my mother dressed, what she said in the morning when I left for school, what our life was like in that apartment, what we did on Sundays. It would be a way to reconnect with them, even if only for the length of a conversation. It's difficult to mourn somebody's death when you didn't have the chance to say goodbye. I miss them as much today as I did during the first days after I lost them."

"Instead of going to Cihangir tomorrow, I'll take you to Mrs. Yilmaz, but you can't speak a word of it to my aunt. Do you promise?" They had arrived at the foot of the steps to Alice's house.

Alice considered Can's imploring face for a moment. "Do you have somebody in your life?"

"I have a lot of people in my life, Miss Alice. Friends and a very big family too. Almost too big for my taste."

"I mean somebody special, somebody that you like."

"The pretty girls of Üsküdar pass through my heart every day. It costs nothing and offends nobody to love in silence. And you, do you love somebody?"

"I'm the one who asked first."

"What has my aunt been telling you? She would make up anything to stop me working for you and helping you with your search. She is so stubborn when she gets an idea in her head that she would say I was going to ask you to marry me. I reassure you, this is not my intention."

Alice took Can's hand in hers.

"I promise you, I didn't believe her for a second."

Can pulled his hand from hers. "Don't do that," he said in a broken voice.

"It was just a show of friendship."

"Perhaps, but friendship is never entirely innocent between a man and a woman."

"I don't agree. My best and closest friend is a man, and we've been friends since we were in our teens."

"You don't miss him?"

"Of course I miss him. I write to him every week."

"Does he write back?"

"No, but he has a good excuse. I don't actually send my letters."

Can smiled and left Alice on her doorstep, walking backward to keep looking at her as he went. "And you never asked yourself why you don't send them?"

◆ ◆ ◆

Dear Daldry,
I think I've come to the end of my journey, and yet, if I'm writing to you this evening, it's to tell you that I won't be coming home soon, or at least, not for a very long time. When you read the rest of this letter, you'll understand why.

Yesterday morning, I was reunited with Mrs. Yilmaz, the nanny who took care of me as a little girl. Can took me to see her. She lives in a house at the top of a little street that was just a dirt path until recently. And at the end of that little street, I found a long flight of steps . . .

◆ ◆ ◆

As they did every day, Alice and Can left Üsküdar early in the morning, but as Can had promised, they went to the Haydarpaşa railway station. Their train left at nine thirty. As she watched the landscape speed past the window, Alice wondered what her nanny looked like and whether the sight of her would stir up old memories. When they arrived in Izmit an hour later, they took a taxi that drove them to the top of a hill in the oldest part of the city.

Mrs. Yilmaz's dilapidated old house had been around for quite a bit longer than she had. The strange wooden structure leaned precariously to one side and seemed as though it might tip over and collapse at any moment. The wood siding was barely held in place by nails, whose heads had long ago rusted away, and the windows were so eroded by the salt and warped from the freezes and thaws of many winters that they rattled in their frames with even the slightest breeze. Alice and Can knocked on the door. A man whom Alice took for Mrs. Yilmaz's son answered and had them come into the sitting room, where Alice was struck by the odor of pine resin that came from the wood smoking in the fireplace, the sour-milk smell of musty books, a carpet that had the gentle, dry fragrance of earth, and a pair of old leather boots that still carried a scent of rain.

"She's up there," said the man, pointing upstairs. "I didn't tell her anything, just that somebody would be coming to visit."

As she climbed the creaky old stairs, Alice noticed the linen-closet perfume of lavender, the tang of the linseed oil that had been used to polish the banister, the starched, floury-smelling sheets, and the lonely smell of mothballs.

Mrs. Yilmaz was reading in bed. She slid her glasses to the tip of her nose to better see the couple that had come to visit.

She stared at Alice as she approached, holding her breath before exhaling a long, heavy sigh of relief. Her eyes filled with tears.

Alice, on the other hand, saw only a stranger, an old woman she had never seen before. Until Mrs. Yilmaz beckoned her over, took her in her arms, and clutched Alice to her breast, weeping . . .

. . . As she hugged me, I smelled the essence of my childhood, the odors of the past, of the kisses I received before going to bed. I heard the sounds of the curtains being opened in my childhood bedroom and my nanny's voice saying, "Anouche, get up, there's a beautiful boat in the harbor, come and see."

I remembered the smell of warm milk in the kitchen. I saw the feet of the cherrywood table that I loved to hide beneath. I heard the stairs creak under my father's footsteps, and I saw an Indian-ink drawing of two faces I had forgotten.

I have two mothers and two fathers, and now all four of them are gone.

It took Mrs. Yilmaz a while to dry her tears. She kept stroking my cheek and kissing my face, murmuring my name: "Anouche, Anouche, my little Anouche, my sunshine, you came back to see your old nanny." I started crying too. I couldn't help myself. I cried for all of my ignorance as I gradually learned the story of the people who brought me into the world and never saw me grow up. I found out that the parents I loved, who had raised me as their own, had adopted me to save my life. My name isn't Alice, but Anouche, and before becoming English I was Armenian. My real name isn't Pendelbury.

When I was five, I was a mute little girl who had learned to talk and then stopped. Nobody knew exactly why. My world was one of odors; in a sense, they were an alternate language. My father was a cobbler by trade. He had built up a business and owned a large workshop and two stores, one on either side of the Bosporus. Mrs. Yilmaz says he was considered the best shoemaker in Istanbul. People came to his shops from all parts of the city. My father ran the store in Pera and my mother ran the store in Kadiköy. Every morning Mrs. Yilmaz took me to the little school in Üsküdar. My parents worked hard, but on Sundays my father always took us out for a carriage ride.

At the beginning of 1914, a doctor suggested to my parents that there might be a cure for my silence, that certain medicinal plants might calm my violent nightmares, and that normal sleep patterns might help my ability to speak to return. One of my father's clients was a young English pharmacist who often helped families who could find no other solution. So every week, Mrs. Yilmaz and I went to Istiklal to see him.

It seems that whenever I saw the pharmacist's wife, I would call out her name.

Mr. Pendelbury's concoctions had a miraculous effect. After six months of treatment, I was sleeping normally and started speaking again with increasing fluency. Life was good. Then came the fateful day of April 25, 1915.

On that day, the elite of Istanbul's Armenian population—intellectuals, journalists, doctors, teachers, and shopkeepers—were all rounded up and arrested in a bloody pogrom. Most of the men were shot without trial, and those who were spared were deported to Adana and Aleppo.

At the end of the afternoon, word of the massacres reached my father's workshop. Our Turkish friends had come to warn us and hide us as quickly as they could. The Armenian community had been accused by some of conspiring with the Russians, one of Turkey's enemies at the time. None of it was true, but nationalist sentiments had got people fired up, and in spite of many Istanbul natives speaking out against it, the violence continued unfettered.

My father had tried to join us, but along the way, he ran into a mob that was hunting Armenians.

"Your father was a good man," Mrs. Yilmaz kept telling me. They caught him near the port. When they were done, they left him for dead. But he got up again. In spite of his wounds, he kept walking and found a way to make it across the water to Kadiköy, which the violence hadn't yet reached.

"We saw him come home in the middle of the night, covered in blood; his face was so dreadfully swollen that we hardly recognized him. He went to see you in your bedroom, where you were sleeping, and begged your mother to stop crying so that you wouldn't wake up. Then he took us to the sitting room and explained what was happening in the city—the murders, the burning houses, the rapes . . . All of the horror men are capable of when they lose their humanity. He said we had to protect the children at all costs. We were to leave the city at once, to hook up a carriage and head into the countryside, where the situation might be calmer. He begged me to hide you with my family, here in this house in Izmit where you had stayed before. Your mother couldn't stop crying and she asked him why he talked as though he wouldn't be coming along. I still remember how your father said, 'I'm going to sit down and rest awhile, I'm a bit tired.' He was such a proud man, the kind of man who made you feel like you had to keep your back straight in his presence. He sat down and closed his eyes. Your mother fell to her knees and embraced him. He put his hand on her cheek, smiled, and sighed. His head fell to the side and he never said anything again. He died with a smile on his face, looking at your mother, just as he had always wanted.'

"I still remember once when your parents quarreled, your father saying, 'You know, Mrs. Yilmaz, she's angry because we work too much, but when we're old, I'll buy her a beautiful villa in the country with lots of land all around, and she'll be the happiest woman on earth. And when I die in that big house, the fruit of our labor, when that day comes, the last thing I want to see is my wife looking back at me.' I remember him saying it very loudly so that your mother would hear. She let a few minutes pass, and when he put on his coat, she came to the door and told him, 'First of all, there is no way of knowing that you'll be the first one to die, and second of all, the day that I die, exhausted from your cursed ambitions, the last thing I'll see in the delirium of my death throes will be a pile of damned shoes.' She hugged him and sent him on his way, saying he was the hardest-working man in the city, and that she wouldn't have wanted anyone else for her husband.

"We moved his body to the bed, and your mother tucked him in as though he were only sleeping. She kissed him and whispered a few words in his ear before telling me to go wake you. We left as your father had told us to do. As I was hooking up the carriage, your mother packed a few things. One of the things she took was the drawing in the frame on my dresser between the windows."

I went over and picked up the drawing. I didn't recognize their faces, but the man and the woman smiling back at me were my parents.

"We drove the horses through the night, and as the sun was rising, we arrived in Izmit, where we were welcomed by my family. Your mother was inconsolable. Most days she sat underneath the big linden tree in the garden. On good days, she took you out into the fields to pick bouquets of roses and jasmine. Along the way, you told her all of the different things you could smell.

"We thought we were safe, that the murderous insanity had been contained, and that what had happened in Istanbul would be limited to the one bloody night that took your father. We were wrong. Hatred spread through the country, and in June my nephew came running up the hill, out of breath, to tell us they had started arresting Armenians in the lower neighborhoods of Izmit. They rounded them up like animals and herded them to the train station, where they were loaded into goods vans.

"I had a sister that lived in a big house on the Bosporus. That lucky girl was so beautiful that she managed to marry a rich and important man, the sort of man who is so powerful that other people never dare to come to his house unless they are invited. Thankfully, both she and her husband had hearts of gold. They would have never let anyone harm a hair on the head of a woman or her children. As a family, we decided you would take refuge with them, and that your mother and I would take you there. At ten in the evening— I remember it as though it were yesterday—we took your little black suitcase and ventured out into the darkened streets of Izmit. From the top of the steps at the end of our street, we could see the fires burning in the city below. They were the houses of the Armenians who lived near the port. We took to the alleys, trying to avoid patrols out hunting for new victims. We hid for a while in the ruins of an old church. Stupidly, we thought the worst had passed, so we went back outside. Your mother was holding you by the hand. And then, at the end of the street, we saw the patrol."

Mrs. Yilmaz went silent. She began crying, so I took her in my arms and tried to comfort her. She took her handkerchief, wiped her face, and kept telling her horrible story.

"You have to forgive me, Anouche. I know more than thirty years have passed, but I still can't talk about it without crying. It all happened so fast. Your mother knelt on the ground before you. She told you that you were her little wonder, her life, that you had to survive, no matter the cost. No matter what happened, she would watch over you, she would be in your heart, wherever you went. She said that she had to leave, but that she would never leave your heart. She pushed us into the shadow of a stable. She kissed us and begged me to protect you. Then she stepped out alone into the night to meet the patrol of barbarians. So that they would not come farther and see us, she went to them.

"They took her away. As they did, I led you down the hill on the old footpaths I had always known. My cousin was waiting for us in a boat. We set out across the water and traveled through the night. Well before dawn, we pulled up on the bank and walked again until we came to my sister's house."

I asked Mrs. Yilmaz what had happened to my mother.

"We never heard anything more from her. In Izmit alone, four thousand Armenians were deported, and across the Empire, during that horrible summer, they assassinated hundreds of thousands of people. Today, nobody mentions it; everybody keeps silent. Only a very few survived, and even fewer find the strength to talk about it. Nobody wants to listen—it takes too much courage and humility to ask for forgiveness. Some people talk about the 'displaced populations,' but it was much worse than that, believe me. I have heard from some people that they formed lines of men, women, and children many miles long, that they were forced to walk across the country to the south. Those who were not put in trains had to walk along the tracks without food or water, only to be shot and thrown in a hole when they couldn't walk anymore. The survivors were taken into the middle of the desert, where they were left to die of exhaustion, hunger, and thirst. "When I looked after you at my sister's house that summer, I wasn't aware of any of that, though I suspected the worst. When I saw your mother walk toward those men, I knew we would probably never see her again. I was very afraid for you. The next morning, you stopped talking again. A month later, when my sister and her husband had made sure that things were less violent in Istanbul, I took you to the pharmacist in Istiklal. When you saw his wife, you smiled again and ran to give her a hug. I told them about what had happened to your family.

"You have to understand, Anouche. It was such a difficult decision to make, but I did it to protect you . . .

"The pharmacist's wife had always had a soft spot for you, and you liked her very much too. You always spoke around her, even when you wouldn't speak anywhere else. Sometimes she would come and see me in the Taksim gardens, where I would take you to play. She had you smell the leaves, the plants, and the flowers, and she taught you their names. You came back to life around her. One evening, when I had gone to get the herbal remedies for your sleep, the pharmacist told me that they would soon be returning to their home country. He offered to take you with them. He promised that in England you would be safe and out of harm's way. He and his wife would give you the life they had always dreamed of giving a child, the child they were never able to have. They promised that with them you would no longer be an orphan, that you would want for nothing, that you would have a home filled with love and kindness.

"Letting you go broke my heart, but I was just your nanny. My sister couldn't keep you, and I didn't have the means to raise both of you. You were the fragile one. It was you, my darling, that I saved by sending you away."

When she reached the end of her story, I thought I had cried all the tears I had left to cry. But there were more. I asked her what she meant when she said I was 'the fragile one.'

She took my face between her hands and asked me to forgive her for having separated me from my brother.

Five years after I arrived in London with my new parents, the British Army occupied Izmit, as a part of the defeated Ottoman Empire. During the Turkish

Revolution in 1923, Mrs. Yilmaz's brother-in-law lost his privileges, his wealth, and his life. Her sister, like many others, fled the Ottoman Empire when it was reborn in the form of the Republic of Turkey. She immigrated to England and sold off her few remaining jewels to settle down in the Brighton area.

The fortune-teller was right about everything. I was born in Istanbul, not Holborn. One by one I met the people who led me to the man who would count the most in my life. Now I can find him, because I know for certain he exists. Somewhere I have a brother, and his name is Rafael.

Yours truly,

Alice

◆ ◆ ◆

Alice spent the rest of the day with Mrs. Yilmaz.

She helped her come downstairs, and after eating lunch under the pergola with Can and Mrs. Yilmaz's nephew, the two women went and sat beneath the linden tree.

Over the course of the afternoon, Alice's former nanny told her stories about the past, when Anouche's father was a cobbler in Istanbul and her mother was a happy woman with two beautiful children.

When they parted at the end of the day, Alice promised to come back and see her often.

She asked Can if they could go back to Istanbul by boat. When they arrived, she watched the luxurious houses that lined the waterfront slip past and felt overcome with emotion.

She went down the hill in the middle of the night to post her letter to Daldry. He received it a week later. Even years later, he would never tell Alice that he had cried when he read it.

14

Alice could think only about trying to find her brother. Mrs. Yilmaz said that Rafael had left on the day of his seventeenth birthday to try to make it on his own in Istanbul. He came to see her once a year and wrote her a postcard from time to time. He was a fisherman and spent most of his life at sea working on large tuna boats.

Alice spent every Sunday that summer walking up and down the port on the Bosporus.

Whenever a fishing boat docked, she would run over and ask the crew if any of them knew Rafael Kachadorian. The months of July, August, and September went by without her meeting anyone who had heard of him.

One Sunday, taking advantage of a particularly warm autumn evening, Can invited Alice to have dinner with him in the little restaurant that Daldry had so enjoyed. Tables had been set up along the wharf so that the customers could eat outside.

In the middle of their conversation, Can suddenly paused and took Alice's hand with great tenderness.

"There was something I was wrong about, and something I've always been right about," he said.

"Go on," said Alice, amused.

"I was wrong. Friendship between a man and a woman really can exist. And I consider you my friend, Alice Anouche Pendelbury."

"And what were you right about?"

"I really am the best guide in Istanbul." He chuckled.

"But I never doubted it," she said, laughing in turn. "Why are you telling me all this now?"

"Because the man two tables away from us has to be your brother."

Alice stopped laughing and turned, holding her breath. Just behind them, a man a bit younger than her was having dinner with a woman. She pushed back her chair and got up. The few steps she took seemed like they would never end, and when she came to his table, she excused herself for interrupting their conversation and asked if he was named Rafael.

The man froze when he saw the face of the woman with the foreign accent, lit by the pale light of the lanterns that swung in the evening breeze.

"I think I'm your sister," she said, her voice fragile. "I'm Anouche. I've been looking for you."

15

"I like your house," said Alice as she walked over to the window.

"It's small, but I can see the water from my bed. Besides, I'm not often here."

"I never believed that I had a particular destiny, or that little signs in my life were guiding me towards a path I ought to take. I didn't believe in fortune-tellers or in good luck . . . Even less that I might have a long-lost brother."

Rafael came to Alice's side. A cargo ship was slowly gliding through the strait.

"Do you think that the fortune-teller in Brighton might have been Yaya's sister?"

"Yaya?"

"That's what you called Mrs. Yilmaz when you were little and couldn't say her name. It stuck, and she has always been Yaya to me. She said that her sister never wrote or gave any sign that she was still alive after she went to England. She had run away, and I suppose Yaya was always a bit ashamed of that. It would be incredible if it really was her."

"It must have been her. How else could she have . . . ? And I did finally find you."

Alice gazed in wonder at her brother. She was still getting used to the idea that he actually existed.

"Why are you looking at me like that?"

"Because I thought I was all alone in the world, and now I find out that I have you."

Rafael nodded his head in understanding. It was clear he felt the same way. "And what are you going to do now?"

"I want to live here for good. I make perfumes, and if things go well, I might be able to leave Mama Can's restaurant one day and find a place to live that's a little bigger. And I want to find out more about my roots, make up for lost time, get to know you."

"I'm often out at sea, but I'd be happy if you stayed in Turkey."

"Have you ever felt like leaving? Living somewhere else?"

"To go where? Turkey is the most beautiful country in the world, and it's my home."

"And you can forgive it for what happened to our parents?"

"One has to forgive. Not everybody was at fault. Think of Yaya and her family, who saved us. They taught me tolerance. I think one person's courage can defeat the complacency of a thousand others. Look out the window. Look how beautiful Istanbul is."

Alice did so, as another question sprang to mind.

"You never felt like trying to find me?"

"When I was a child, I didn't know you existed. Yaya only told me about you when I was sixteen, and even then, it was only because her nephew had said something he wasn't supposed to, and I started asking questions. She told me I had once had an older sister, but that she didn't know if you were still alive. She talked about the choice she made because she couldn't raise both of us. Please don't be mad at her for keeping me and sending you away. The future of a young girl was very uncertain in those times, but a boy still stood for the promise of the old days that might return. She didn't send you away because she loved you less, but because it was all she could think to do."

"I know that," said Alice, looking at her brother. "Although she did tell me that she had a little preference for you and couldn't imagine letting you go too far away from her. But it doesn't make me angry. I understand."

"Yaya really told you that?"

"She did."

"That's not very nice for you, but I'd be lying if I said I wasn't touched to hear it."

Alice considered this for a while.

"At the end of the month, I'll have enough money to go back to London. I'll only stay a few days, the time it takes to pack up my things, say goodbye to my friends, and turn my flat over to my neighbor. He'll be delighted. He's a funny man, you know. He never imagined that the man I'd find at the end of my journey would be my brother, but he was convinced that there was a man waiting for me in Turkey."

"He had more faith in fortune-tellers than you."

"Honestly, I think he just wanted to take my flat and use it as his studio. But I have to admit that I owe him a great deal. I'll write to him to let him know I'll be coming back to London."

◆ ◆ ◆

Dear Alice-Anouche,

Your last few letters have been incredibly overwhelming, but the one I received from you this evening was the most touching of all.

So you've decided to stay on and make your life in Istanbul. God knows, I'll miss you, but the knowledge that you're happy gives me reason to be happy as well.

I wish I could have seen you again on your trip to London, but fate seems to have decided otherwise. I promised to go on holiday with a friend, and I'm afraid the plans are already set. She has already asked for the days off, and you know how difficult it is to change these things once they've been set up.

It's hard to believe that we're not going to manage to cross paths. You should have tried to stay longer! On the other hand, I understand that you have responsibilities of your own. Mama Can is already being generous enough to let you have the time off that you'll need even for a short visit.

I've taken all my things from your flat so that you'll feel at home. Everything is in perfect order. I took the liberty of repairing the window frame so that the cold wouldn't come in, because it would have never happened if we had waited for our pinchpenny landlord to get around to taking care of it himself. I suppose it matters little now, because when winter returns you'll be in a warmer place.

You keep thanking me for everything I've done for you, but it's important for you to understand that you allowed me to go on a beautiful trip that most men would only dream of taking. Our time in Istanbul will remain among my fondest memories, and no matter the distance that separates us, you will always stay in my heart as a faithful friend. I hope to come and visit you one day, and I hope that when I do, you'll have time to show me around and share your new life.

Dear Alice, my faithful travel companion, I hope that we'll keep writing to each other, even though I'm sure that we'll probably do so less regularly as time passes. I miss you, but I think I already wrote that. I send my warm regards.

Your ever-devoted,
Daldry.

P.S. I forgot to mention, it's a funny thing—just as the postman (we made up over a pint at the pub) brought me your last letter, I was putting the very last finishing touch on my painting. I thought about sending it to you, but I realized how silly it would be. You just have to look out the window to see an even better version of what I painted during your long absence.

◆ ◆ ◆

Alice walked down the street with a large suitcase in one hand and a smaller suitcase in the other. When she entered the restaurant, Mama Can, her husband, and the best guide in Istanbul all rose to their feet and led her to a table set for five.

Mama Can was particularly emotional. "Today the house is waiting on you," she said. "I hired a replacement for the time that you'll be gone, and for that time only! Sit, sit. You have to eat before your long trip. Your brother isn't coming?"

"His boat was supposed to come ashore this morning. I hope he'll get here in time. He promised to come to the airport."

"But I'm the one to drive," said Can, worried his place might be taken.

"Now that he has a car, you can't refuse him the pleasure of driving," said Mama Can, gazing proudly at her nephew.

"It's practically new. It only had two owners before me, and one of them was a very meticulous American. Since I have stopping working for you and Mr. Daldry, I have found new clients who pay me well. And as the best guide in Istanbul, I must drive people around. Last week, I even took a couple to the Rumeli Fort on the Black Sea. It took only two hours to get there."

Alice kept her eye on the window, hoping to see Rafael arrive, but when the meal was over he still hadn't shown up.

"You know," said Mama Can, trying to comfort her, "the sea is in charge. If the fishing is better than they expected, or worse, they may return tomorrow."

"I know." Alice sighed. "Besides, I'll see him again soon."

"We have to go or you'll miss your plane," said Can.

Mama Can kissed and hugged Alice goodbye and accompanied her to Can's new car. Her husband put Alice's suitcases in the trunk, and Can opened the passenger-side door.

"Can I drive?" she asked.

"Are you kidding?"

"I know how to drive. Daldry taught me."

"Not this car," said Can, pushing Alice in and closing the door behind her.

He got in, started the engine, and listened to the motor purr, beaming with pride.

Alice heard somebody calling "Anouche!" and she turned to see Rafael running over to them.

"I know, I know," he said, jumping in the back seat. "I'm late, but it's not my fault, one of our nets got tangled. I came as quickly as I could."

Can took his foot off the brake and the Ford started down the hill through the narrow streets of Üsküdar. An hour later, they arrived at Atatürk Airport. In front of the terminal, Can bid Alice farewell and then left her to be alone with her brother.

Alice went to the counter and checked in her larger suitcase, holding on to the smaller one. The ticketing agent said she should go through customs immediately. She was the last passenger to arrive and they were waiting for her.

Rafael walked with her to the door. "While I was at sea," he said, "I thought a lot about your story of the fortune-teller. I don't know if she was Yaya's sister or not, but if you have time, you should try to go back and see her, because she was wrong about one important thing."

"What are you talking about?" asked Alice.

"When you first saw her, she told you that the most important man in your life had just been walking behind you, didn't she?"

"Yes, that's what she said."

"Well, I'm sorry to tell you that she couldn't have been talking about me. I've never left Turkey, and I certainly wasn't in Brighton at Christmastime last year."

Alice thought about what her brother was telling her.

"Can you think of somebody else who could have been there behind you that evening?" asked Rafael.

"Perhaps," said Alice, clutching the tiny suitcase to her chest.

"You know you have to go through customs, right? What are you hiding in there?"

"A trumpet."

"A trumpet?"

"Yes, a trumpet. It might just be the answer to the question you just asked," she said with a smile. She kissed her brother goodbye and whispered in his ear, "Don't worry if it takes me longer to come back than I thought it would. I'll come back, I promise I will."

16

The taxi pulled up in front of the old house on Primrose Hill. Alice took her bags and climbed the stairs. The landing on the top floor was silent. She looked at Daldry's door and then went into her flat.

It smelled like the floor had been waxed. Everything was just as she had left it, except cleaner.

There was a vase of white tulips on the stool next to the bed.

She took off her coat and went to sit at the worktable. She ran her hand over the wood and peered up through the skylight at the clouds hanging over London.

She went back over to the bed and opened the case that held the trumpet and a carefully wrapped bottle of perfume, which she took out and set aside.

She hadn't eaten since earlier that morning, and there was still time to go to the grocer's at the end of the street.

It was raining now, and she didn't have an umbrella, but she noticed Daldry's raincoat hanging on the coat hook. She threw it over her shoulders and headed out of the door.

The grocer was delighted to see her again. It had been months since she'd last been in the shop, and he had started to wonder what had become of her. As she filled her shopping basket, Alice told him about her trip to Turkey and that she would soon be returning there.

When the grocer handed her the bill, she began to go through the pockets of the raincoat, forgetting it wasn't hers. She found a set of keys in one pocket and a scrap of paper in the other. She smiled when she recognized the ticket from the evening she and Daldry had gone to the carnival in Brighton. She paid and left with her basket full.

Back at home, Alice was putting away her shopping. She looked at the alarm clock and realized it was time to start getting ready. She was going to see Anton later in the evening. She closed the trumpet case and pondered what dress to wear.

As she was putting on her make-up in front of the little mirror that hung next to her door, Alice was overcome by a nagging doubt. A detail just didn't make sense . . .

"The ticket counter was already closed that evening," she said to herself out loud. She snapped shut the compact and checked the pockets of Daldry's raincoat, but only found the keys. She ran down the stairs and back to the grocer's.

"When I was here earlier," she said, bursting into the shop, gasping for breath, "I think I dropped a scrap of paper on the floor. Have you seen it?"

The grocer replied that he kept a very tidy shop. If something had fallen on the floor, it had probably been swept up and thrown in the wastebasket.

"The wastebasket?" she asked, desperate.

"I just emptied it in the bin out the back—"

Before he had the time to finish his sentence, Alice had already run through the back door and started rummaging around in the bin. In a panic, he headed after her, wringing his hands in despair at the sight of his pretty customer kneeling in a pile of rubbish.

"What exactly are you looking for?" he asked, wondering if he should try to stop her.

"A ticket."

"A lottery ticket, I hope."

"No, just the stub for the carnival on Brighton Pier."

"I suppose it must have a great sentimental value then."

"It might," said Alice, picking through the cabbage leaves and floor sweepings.

"You're not even certain?" said the grocer, beside himself. "Couldn't you make up your mind before emptying out all of my bins?"

Alice ignored him and kept rooting around. Suddenly, she saw it.

She picked up the ticket and unfolded it. At the sight of the date stamped on its end, she turned to the grocer and said, "I'm certain now. Immense sentimental value."

17

Daldry crept up the stairs, trying to make as little noise as possible. On his doormat he found a little glass vial and an envelope. The bottle was labeled ISTANBUL and the card in the envelope read "At least I kept my promise . . ."

Daldry removed the cork, closed his eyes, and breathed in the perfume. The top note was perfect—he felt transported beneath the redbud trees planted along the Bosporus. He walked up the steep streets of Cihangir and could hear Alice's voice calling over her shoulder because he wasn't fast enough. Then came a smooth, earthy accord combining the fragrances of flowers, dust, and cool water trickling out of old stone fountains. He could hear children shouting as they played in shady courtyards, the foghorns of the ferries, and the screech of the trams rolling up and down Istiklal Avenue.

"You did it, my dear," Daldry sighed as he unlocked his door and went into his flat.

He turned on the light and nearly jumped out of his skin when he saw Alice sitting in the armchair in the middle of his sitting room.

"What on earth are you doing here?" he asked, putting down his umbrella.

"What about you?"

"Well"—Daldry's voice became strangely evasive—"as strange as it seems, I'm just coming home. To my flat."

"You're not on holiday?"

"I don't really have a job, so you know for me, holidays . . ."

"Don't take it as idle flattery, but that is much better than anything I see from my window," said Alice, gesturing to the large painting on the easel across the room.

"Well, I'll take it as a compliment then, coming, as it does, from a native of Istanbul. I don't mean to change the subject, but how on earth did you get in here?"

"With the spare keys I found in your raincoat."

"You found it? Oh good . . . I love that raincoat. I've been looking—"

"It was hanging in my flat."

"I see. That makes sense."

Alice got up from the armchair and walked over to Daldry.

"I have a question for you. But before I ask, you have to promise not to lie, for once in your life."

"What are you implying?"

"Aren't you supposed to be off cavorting around with some lady friend?"

"Things got canceled," he grumbled.

"Did your traveling partner happen to be named Carol?"

"No, no. I only ran into Carol twice. The time that I came and interrupted your party, and again when you were sick in bed with a fever . . . And a third time at the pub on the corner, but she didn't recognize me, so that doesn't count."

"I thought the two of you went to the movies together," said Alice, taking a step closer.

"So, I do lie from time to time. But only when it's strictly necessary."

"It was necessary for you to pretend you'd started seeing my best friend?"

"I had my reasons."

"And that piano against the wall over there. I thought you said that it was the woman downstairs."

"That old thing? I wouldn't call that a piano. What was the question you wanted to ask? I promise to tell the truth."

"Were you on Brighton Pier the evening of December 23?"

"What makes you ask?"

"I also found this in your raincoat." She held out the ticket stub.

"It's not fair to ask questions when you already know the answer."

"How long has this been going on?" asked Alice.

Daldry took a deep breath. "Since the day you moved into this house, and I saw you coming up the stairs. Things have become more complicated since then . . ."

"If you felt that way, why did you do everything in your power to send me away? The trip to Istanbul was just about putting distance between us, wasn't it?"

"Well, let's say that if the fortune-teller had told you to go to the moon, I would have been even happier. But you ask why . . . Can you imagine what it means to a man like myself to realize he has fallen madly in love? For all of my life, I've never feared anybody the way I feared you. The love I felt for you made me fear I was starting to resemble my father. I would never, for anything in the world, impose that kind of pain on the woman I love." He paused. "I'd be especially appreciative if you could just forget everything I've just told you."

Alice took one step closer, put her finger on his lips, and whispered in his ear, "Be quiet, and kiss me."

The morning's first rays of sunlight shining through the skylight woke both of them.

Alice made some tea, but Daldry refused to get out of bed.

Alice set the tray on the bed. As Daldry buttered a piece of toast, she asked mischievously, "The things you said yesterday, which I've already forgotten because I promised I would . . . You weren't just trying to find a way to keep painting in my flat, were you?"

"If you doubted me for even an instant, I'd give up painting for the rest of my days."

"That would be a terrible waste," said Alice. "It was when you told me that you painted junctions that I really started to fall for you."

Epilogue

On December 24, 1951, Alice and Daldry returned to Brighton. The wind blew in from the north and made it particularly cold on the pier that afternoon. The stands in the carnival were open, with the exception of the fortune-teller's caravan. It had disappeared.

Alice and Daldry learned that the fortune-teller had died a few months earlier, and that, according to her wishes, her ashes had been scattered over the water at the end of the pier.

Leaning against the barrier and looking out over the waves, Daldry pulled Alice close to him and hugged her.

"We'll never know whether she was the sister of your Yaya," he said pensively.

"No, but it doesn't really matter anymore, does it?"

"I don't agree. It does matter. If she was your nanny's sister, she never really saw into your future at all, she just recognized you . . . It's not the same thing."

"I can't believe you really think that. She saw that I was born in Istanbul, and she predicted that we'd make a long journey. She knew that I'd meet six people—Can, the consul, Mr. Zemirli, the teacher in Kadiköy, Mrs. Yilmaz, and my brother, Rafael—before finding the seventh person, the man who would matter most in my life: you."

Daldry took out a cigarette but gave up the idea of trying to light it. The wind was blowing too hard. "The seventh person you say . . . If it lasts . . ."

Alice felt Daldry's arms pull her in closer.

"Don't you mean for it to last?" asked Alice.

"Of course I do, but do you? You don't even know all of my bad habits. Maybe with time, you won't put up with them anymore . . ."

"But I don't know all of your good habits yet either."

"I hadn't thought of that."

ACKNOWLEDGMENTS

Thank you to:

Pauline, Louis, and Georges, Raymond, Danièle, and Lorraine, Rafael, and Lucie.

Susanna Lea.

Emmanuelle Hardouin.

Nicole Lattès, Leonello Brandolini, Antoine Caro, Brigitte Lannaud, Élisabeth Villeneuve, Anne-Marie Lenfant, Arié Sberro, Sylvie Bardeau, Tine Gerber, Lydie Leroy, and the entire team at Éditions Robert Laffont.

Pauline Normand, Marie-Ève Provost.

Léonard Anthony, Sébastien Canot, Romain Ruetsch, Danielle Melconian, Katrin Hodapp, Laura Mamelok, Kerry Glencorse, Moïna Macé.

Brigitte and Sarah Forissier.

Véronique Peyraud-Damas and Renaud Leblanc in the archives department of the Air France Museum, Jim Davies at the British Airways Museum (BOAA).

And to Olivia Giacobetti, Pierre Brouwers, Laurence Jourdan, Ernest Mamboury, and Yves

Ternon, whose knowledge and work were essential to my research.

For the English translation, I'd like to thank Chris Murray, who translated the book, and Elizabeth DeNoma, who acquired it for AmazonCrossing and did the developmental edit, along with Kimberly Glyder, who designed the cover.

ABOUT THE AUTHOR

With more than forty million books sold, Marc Levy is the most read French author alive today. He's written nineteen novels to date, including *The Last of the Stanfields*, *P.S. from Paris*, *All Those Things We Never Said*, *The Children of Freedom*, and *Replay*.

Originally written for his son, his first novel, *If Only It Were True*, was later adapted for the big screen as *Just Like Heaven*, starring Reese Witherspoon and Mark Ruffalo. Since then, Levy has not only won the hearts of European readers, he's won over audiences around the globe. More than one and a half million of his books have been sold in China alone, and his novels have been published in forty-nine languages. He lives in New York City. Readers can learn more about Levy and follow his work at www.marclevy.info.

ABOUT THE TRANSLATOR

American-born musicologist and translator Chris Murray works in Paris and Brussels. Coauthor of *Le modèle et l'invention: Messiaen et la technique de l'emprunt* and coeditor of *Musical Life in Belgium During the Second World War*, he is also the translator of *The Gardener of Versailles* by Alain Baraton, *American Lady* by Sophie-Caroline de Margerie, and *All Those Things We Never Said* by Marc Levy.